SHE WAS OUT OF REACH

SHE WAS OUT OF REACH

ZACHARY GOLDMAN MYSTERIES
BOOK SEVENTEEN

P.D. WORKMAN

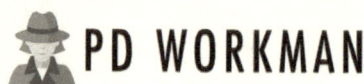

ISBN: 9781774687093 (KDP Paperback)
ISBN: 9781774687116 (KDP Hardcover)
ISBN: 9781774687123 (Large Print)
ISBN: 9781774687130 (Lulu Paperback)
ISBN: 9781774687109 (ePub)
ISBN: 9781774687147 (Accessible Audio)

ALSO BY P.D. WORKMAN

FIND MORE BOOKS AT PDWORKMAN.COM

MYSTERY/SUSPENSE:

Zachary Goldman Mysteries
Private Investigator
She Wore Mourning
His Hands Were Quiet
She Was Dying Anyway
He Was Walking Alone
They Thought He was Safe
He Was Not There
Her Work Was Everything
She Told a Lie
He Never Forgot
She Was At Risk
He Drowned in Memory
Their Walls Were Empty
They Came for Him
They Sought Vengeance
She Was Their Target
His Fear Was Real
She Was Out of Reach
He Was Deceived
She Once Vanished

To those who have been lost
and found families

1

Zachary had been surprised that Rose Bircher wanted to meet him in her lab rather than at home. Most women in her circumstances would have been at home, unable to focus on work. They would take a leave of absence until things could get straightened out.

But maybe that was an unjust judgment. He hadn't known many parents in her circumstances and supposed that a mother could want to bury herself in her work just as much as a father.

He only waited in the reception area for a couple of minutes. There was a lot of white. White walls, white tiled floors, a sign on the wall with the lab's name in silver letters mounted on a shiny white surface. It made him think of a school or hospital. Not a restful place. Somewhere important work was being done and people were all focused on their projects.

The door into the inner workspace opened and Zachary got his first glimpse at the woman who wanted to hire him.

Rose Bircher was casually dressed. No white lab jacket. She was a thirty-something woman, on the thin side, with straight brown hair and a pleasant face. She wore dark-rimmed glasses and an aqua polo shirt with the company logo. She looked at Zachary, giving him a quick once-over, then held out her hand.

"Mr. Goldman?"

"Just Zachary."

"Rose. Thanks for coming. Follow me." She turned away from him, back toward the door. "You want coffee?"

"Sure."

"Good." She led him first to a breakroom with a coffee machine, stacks of mugs, and a couple of vending machines. The smell of freshly brewed coffee filled the air. "We go through the stuff like water around here. And it's pretty good."

She poured them each a mug and handed one to Zachary. He followed her farther down the hall, through a bullpen with lots of cubicles and young people pounding away at keyboards, their eyes intent on their screens. Few looked up to see who was walking by as Zachary followed Rose to the meeting room.

Rose poked her head into one of the meeting rooms to make sure it was vacant and then motioned Zachary in. There was nothing special about the room. He'd seen a hundred like it before: a table, chairs, and a small side cabinet with supplies. A whiteboard on the wall. There was a projector and screen controlled by a remote and currently recessed out of view.

Rose sat down and motioned for Zachary to do the same.

"I really appreciate you coming."

Zachary nodded.

Studying her, he could see the signs of stress on Rose's face. Puffy skin under her eyes testified that she hadn't slept well, though a layer of concealer kept the dark shadows from being visible. Faint lines across her forehead. Her hand shook as she raised the coffee mug to her mouth.

"I was told that you have investigated missing children before."

Zachary nodded. He'd had a little experience in that area. Usually teenagers, though he had also rescued his ex-wife Bridget's twin babies.

"I have some experience in that area, though I don't do a lot of missing persons," he told her honestly. "It is your daughter who is missing?" He asked it tentatively. She was too young to be the mother of a teenager. But she was not frantic like he expected the parent of a missing baby to be. But Rose had already surprised him in several respects.

"Yes." she swallowed and stared past Zachary at the wall. "My daughter Claire. She is five."

"Did you report her missing to the police?"

He had learned not to take this for granted. Not because it was like on TV where kidnappers for ransom told the parents not to call the police or FBI *or else.* Many parents did not report their children missing to the police because they knew who had taken the child. Often a family member. And they just wanted the child found and returned with the least disruption possible. Without making family business public or making a parent or grandparent look bad in front of their friends. People preferred to keep personal business quiet, even when it involved a child being taken.

"Yes. I talked to the police. They think that it was Claire's father."

That explained why he hadn't seen anything about it on the TV or internet news. Parental abductions were routine, of little interest to the public unless there were some unique, attention-grabbing details.

"Are you married? Or were you?"

"No. I met him in school. We lived together for a while. But we weren't really compatible. It didn't work out."

"Does he have shared custody? Visitation?"

"No. He didn't want anything to do with Claire, and I respected that. He has never been involved in her life."

"And that hasn't changed lately? He hasn't come to you asking if he could see her? Talk to her? Maybe he offered to pay something for child support?"

"No. We have some mutual friends, so I've kept track of him from a distance for the last few years. Occasionally, we've ended up at a party together or something like that. He asked for a picture once."

"Recently?"

"How long ago is *recent?*" She held her palms up questioningly. "It was... maybe a couple of months ago."

Zachary pulled out his notepad. He made sure that the date was filled in at the top of the page and wrote down Claire's name and the fact that her birth father had asked for her photo a couple of months before. That could be significant. He *had* shown some interest in her recently. Depending on what kind of a picture it was, he might have been able to repurpose it for a passport photograph or other identification. Or maybe just a phone picture flashed at someone to prove that yes, he was Claire's dad, or he wouldn't have her picture on his phone, would he?

Rose watched him and didn't make any comment about his messy, nearly unreadable handwriting.

"Does that mean you're taking the case?"

"Let's get a few more details first. Why do the police think Claire's father has her? Have they talked to him? Where did she disappear from?"

"Such a high percentage of kidnappings are non-custodial parents or family members; that's just what they assume from the beginning unless you have eyewitnesses who saw her being taken. And no one did. We were at a kids' play place at the mall. I was... on my phone. You can't keep an eye on your kid the whole time; there are all kinds of tunnels, slides, climbers, and ball pits. Your kid just gets swallowed up by this place with all the other kids..."

Zachary nodded. He had seen places like that. A great adventure for kids. Playing tag or dare with their friends, running off excess energy, exploring.

"How did he get her out of there? Don't they have ID to make sure you can only take the kid you arrived with?"

"Yes. I don't know how anyone could get her out of there. Some of their security cameras were down. I always thought they had really good security: guards, monitors, sign-in logs, all that kind of thing. But someone got in there and got my daughter out without anyone noticing. I called her and looked for her. I got frantic. They thought I was just being a helicopter parent and freaking out because she was out of sight. But when they made announcements and had their staff members walk around looking for her, no one could find her."

Rose swallowed hard and sipped her coffee. Zachary wasn't sure why she felt it necessary to mask her emotions, to make it look like this hadn't affected her. Most mothers cried. They weren't afraid to show him just how upset they were.

"How long has she been missing?"

Rose looked at her watch. "Three days." She put her palms over her eyes, warming them. After three days with minimal sleep, she was undoubtedly feeling the strain. Scratchy, sticky, swollen eyes. A fatigue headache. Brain fog.

"Have the police talked to her father?"

"No. They tried to track him down to talk to him. But he's out of the country. They haven't been able to talk to him or to get other authorities to talk to him." Her tone was flat.

"Out of the country? Where?"

She stared down at the surface of her coffee. Her eyes glittered with unshed tears, but she didn't let them fall. She just stared as if mesmerized by the reflection of the light on the surface of her drink.

"Saudi Arabia."

2

Zachary's heart sank. He wasn't going to be able to do anything for Rose Bircher. *Saudi Arabia?* If Claire's father had taken her there, there wasn't much that Zachary—or anyone else—could do about it. That was one of the countries where non-custodial fathers liked to take kidnapped children—a country where he had all the rights, and Rose had virtually none. The authorities there would not cooperate with US authorities. They would not deal with the child's mother.

"I'm not sure there is anything I can do to help you," he told Rose gently.

She didn't look surprised, her expression unchanging.

"I was told that you were unconventional. And stubborn. That you could get results where the police couldn't."

"Well... sometimes that has been true. But I can't always find something helpful. The police are your best bet. I just... sometimes I can find something else that they missed or follow up on a hunch. But... Saudi Arabia is a long way away."

"I know it is. But the police will only follow their specific protocol. And if they think that the child is out of the country and in a place where they can't reach her... they just issue whatever paper they do to tell the government that they believe she is over there and object to them not helping with the kidnapping case... and that's it. Then they just put a flag on his passport so that if he ever comes back into the country, they can pull him aside and talk to him."

He wasn't going to bring her back. If he had taken his daughter to Saudi Arabia, he intended to keep her there. He wasn't going to bring her back to the US.

"What is his name? Claire's father?"

Rose looked at him for a moment before answering, considering his response. Zachary examined it himself. If he couldn't do anything for Rose and didn't intend to take the case, then why ask for his name?

"Amir Osman."

"Is he from there?"

"No. He was born in America. But I guess... with his family name he could get a visa or whatever you need to immigrate there." She rubbed her temples. "I don't know all the details of that kind of thing."

"So he had been planning this for a while. He asked for her picture. He had to apply for whatever paperwork he needed to take her there."

"I suppose."

"Do the police have confirmation as to whether she was traveling with him?"

"He had a child with him. But a different name. Not Claire Bircher. He was also traveling with a woman. The child is supposed to be hers, not his."

Zachary nodded. Just enough obfuscating to make it effective. If an Amber alert had been issued under the name Claire Bircher, no one would have connected her with a child of another name. Until it was too late.

And because Amir hadn't had anything to do with his biological daughter before that and had never said he even wanted a visit with her, there was no reason for her mother to mention him when Claire went missing from the mall. It wasn't a case of a non-custodial parent not returning her on time after a visit. There had been no reason to suspect that her biological father had any interest in her until it was too late. And getting a child back from a country like Saudi Arabia… Zachary had heard stories.

"I'm not sure what you're hoping I can do for you," he told Rose. "The police have done everything they can, and I assume you've talked to experts in this kind of case. I don't have a lot of familiarity with international kidnapping and certainly have no experience flying to another country to try to get her back."

Rose took off her glasses and rubbed the bridge of her nose.

"There hasn't been much of an investigation into this case," she said slowly. "I mean, on the surface, they've done everything they should. They locked down the mall and made sure that no one could get her out but, obviously, she was gone by the time that happened, because there was no sign of her. They set up roadblocks. They did a search with K9s. They talked about an Amber Alert, but it didn't go out until quite a bit later because they didn't have a description of the kidnapper or the vehicle. But once all that preliminary stuff was done and they found out that I am… estranged from Claire's biological father, they decided that it was him. They put out all those travel alerts and searched to see if he had left the country during the window from the last time I saw Claire until they stopped him from traveling outside the United States."

"And that was when they found he had already fled with his daughter."

"With his girlfriend's daughter. They don't have any evidence that it was Claire."

Zachary was starting to get a feeling for what Rose was getting at. "Do they have any footage of Amir with Claire?"

"No. They have a few fuzzy airport surveillance pictures of him… but there's no way to tell if the girl with him is Claire or someone else. The girl in the picture is dark-haired."

At Zachary's look, she pulled out her phone and, after finding a picture, turned the screen around to face him. A little girl with long, blond hair and an impish smile.

"He might have dyed her hair."

Rose nodded. "Of course. And that is what the police are assuming. They all assume that the girl Amir had with him when he left the country was Claire."

"No full facial views"

"No. I thought all the airports had those check-in terminals that take a picture of you. But I guess they don't. Or they don't take pictures of kids who are too small to reach it, just their parents."

Zachary nodded slowly. There were holes in airport security procedures, despite what the officials would have people believe. People still traveled under forged documents. And the holes for children were even bigger than those for adults. Children weren't terrorists. They were vulnerable, but they were not a danger. It was a different mindset.

Zachary scratched a few more notes into his notepad and turned his eyes back to Rose.

"So there have been no confirmed sightings of Claire since you last saw her at the play place."

"Yeah. Exactly."

So, was she taken by a stranger? Or had she been taken by her birth father, passed off as another child, and flown out of the country? Without putting eyes on her, they couldn't be sure. The police might be right. They probably were. The ex-spouse or the child's non-custodial parent was the number one suspect in any child abduction case. It was far more likely to have been committed by a parent or other family member than by a stranger.

But Amir had not been part of Claire's life. He would only know where to find them if he had been following them.

"How many times have you seen Amir in the last six months?"

Rose shook her head. "Not at all. Well, maybe once, I guess. When he asked about a picture."

"You said that you sometimes run into him at events. You have mutual friends? Or are you in the same profession?" Zachary looked around him. "What exactly do you do here?"

"Like I said, I met him in college. We were both in computer science together. He went into industrial applications and I went into research, so we didn't exactly follow the same path. But we were both techies. And… yeah… some mutual friends."

"Have you talked to any of those friends about him? About Claire being missing?"

She shook her head. "No. Do you think I should?"

"If you could give me names and contact numbers, it might be better if I reach out to them. An unbiased third party rather than the mother accusing her ex of doing something."

"Okay." Rose didn't argue about it or say Zachary wouldn't find out anything talking to them. But if she'd been told by whoever referred her to Zachary that he was unconventional and dogged and might be able to find something out, then Rose would be more open to giving him whatever he needed without question. She looked at her phone. "Do you want me to read them out to you?"

"Why don't you just share the contacts with me from your phone? Then I won't get any digits reversed."

She nodded her agreement and spent a few minutes reviewing her contacts list and texting some of them to Zachary.

"Maybe Amir would have talked to one of these people about Claire," Zachary said. "If we can even get confirmation that he has been talking about her in the last few months, that would be a start. And if he has been saying that he wants to be a part of her life…"

Rose shook her head. "If he wanted to be a part of her life, then why wouldn't he come to me and ask me about seeing her?"

"That would be the logical approach," Zachary agreed. "But people make choices that aren't logical. Maybe he figured you would say no, and he didn't want to tip his hand. Easier to get away with it if he never let on that he wants to be in her life."

"I guess," Rose agreed. "If he'd been trying to get visitation or custody and then she disappeared from the mall or anywhere else, then he is the first one I would have thought of. It wouldn't have been hours before the police put a stop on Amir leaving the country."

Zachary nodded his agreement. "Who was the first person?"

"What?"

"You said he would have been the first person you thought of. As being her abductor. Who *was* the first person you thought of?"

"Oh… well, I just thought of someone who had been hanging around the play place. Some perv who went to watch the kids and was watching for a little girl to be by herself. A stranger, like on TV. I know parental abductions are more common, but I never thought of Amir as being her parent. I'm the only parent she's ever had in her life."

"What about your parents? Is there anyone else who helps to take care of her?"

"They're in New York. They only see her now and then when they come for a visit. And they don't babysit."

"Do you have a caregiver? Who looks after her while you're at work?"

"She's in school now. I have a woman who does after-school care until I can get there. But it's only an hour or so. A woman in the neighborhood who looks after a bunch of kids."

"A day home."

"Like that, yes. But just for after school."

"Can you give me her information?"

Rose shrugged and conceded.

"Did you see anyone at the play place you were suspicious of? Uncomfortable around?"

"Well, like any other mother, I kept a pretty close eye on any men who were there without a wife or girlfriend. The play place isn't supposed to let people without kids of their own in. You know, it's supposed to be a safe place where pedophiles can't hang around watching kids. It's just kids and their parents."

"I don't imagine it's too hard to get around that. Tell them that your wife and kid are already there. Point someone out and say you're with them. Or go with your sister or best friend and her kid."

Rose sighed and nodded. "It's great if everyone is honest and follows the rules, but the people who really want to get around the rules will."

"Like gun registration," Zachary suggested. "The people who follow the rules are the ones who are not planning to break the laws. Those who are planning to use their guns for illegal purposes are the ones who *don't* register them."

"Right."

"Was there anyone at the play place that day that stuck out to you?" Zachary waited a few seconds to see if she would answer before prompting her further. "Anyone you felt was watching Claire? Or watching you?"

She hesitated, then shook her head. Zachary raised his brows. "Who did you just think of?"

"No one. I didn't think anyone was watching Claire."

"Someone watching you?"

There was another instant of hesitation before Rose shook her head. "No."

"Did the police get any surveillance video from the play place?"

"Some. But they said that only a few of the cameras were recording." She pressed her lips together and shook her head. "I always thought they were much more secure than they really are. There are lots of cameras around and signs saying that you are on camera. I don't know if they were even all real cameras. But only a couple were maintained."

"Did they show you any of the surveillance videos? Show you any pictures of men who had been hanging around that might have been suspicious? What did you tell them when they first arrived?"

"They didn't show me anything. I guess they must not have found anyone suspicious."

"I'll see if I can get copies of them. You never know. The police might have missed something." He'd been able to spot tiny details on videos before. Details the police had missed or not thought important.

"What did you tell the police when they first arrived? That Claire had disappeared? That she was gone? That she had been taken? What did you think had happened?"

"I said… that someone must have taken her."

"You'd never had any episodes with Claire before? When you lost track of her for a few minutes, thought something had happened, and then found her again?"

"No... maybe when I lost sight of her for a minute, but I always found her again. She stayed close by. She'd be on the other side of the clothes rack at the department store. Or looking at a toy or snack she wanted to buy. Something like that."

"And at the park? School? The play place? What did she like to do? Did she ever play hide-and-seek? Play a prank on you?"

"No. She was a pretty easy kid. Lots of energy, but she was a good girl. Mostly, she followed the rules. She was never far away."

"So when you couldn't find her, she didn't come back to you, didn't come when you called, you believed that someone had abducted her."

Rose nodded. "Yes."

"A stranger. You never thought that someone you knew might have come and... taken her out for ice cream or taken her because they didn't think you were a good parent. Or Amir because he wanted her to be a part of his life and didn't think you would allow it."

Rose shook her head slowly. "None of those things ever occurred to me."

Zachary looked at the notes he had written down while they talked. The girl was missing. The police thought the case was solved, but the girl was out of their reach.

But there was no proof that Claire was with Amir. He understood why Rose felt so unsettled about the case. Not angry because Amir had come and stolen Claire away, but full of questions and not sure the police were right about what had happened to her little girl.

"Okay." Zachary dug a card out of his pocket and laid it before her. "Those are my rates. I'll need a small retainer to get started. I will see what I can dig up."

She let out her breath in a long sigh. "Thank you. I needed somebody in my court. I really don't think Amir took her to Saudi Arabia."

3

Zachary was sitting on the couch, hunched over his computer in a clear demonstration of how he should *not* sit while working, when he heard the garage door activate and Kenzie's car drive in. A few moments later, she came in the door adjoining the kitchen and looked through the doorway at him.

"I'm not slouching," Zachary told her with a laugh. He sat up straight and then rolled his shoulders to try to loosen the tension in his back.

"You're going to be a hunched-over old man by the time you're fifty," she told him.

"I know, I know. I need to sit with proper posture, shoulders back, head up, all of that." He looked back at his computer, but the screen was too low for him to work from that position.

"What you should do is use the ergonomic furniture in my office and a separate monitor," Kenzie pointed out. "One of us should put that chair and desk to use."

She was just as bad, sitting on the bed with her laptop or tablet when she wanted to relax. They both knew better, but they liked to be comfortable. And Zachary liked to be in the middle of the house, where he could see everything as it unfolded, rather than down the hall at the end, removed from the doors and the living room and kitchen. In Kenzie's home office, he felt isolated and alone. On the couch, where he could look out the window and see the activity of the neighborhood, he rarely felt alone, even when he was.

Kenzie removed her coat, boots, and winter gear and picked up her purse to carry it into the bedroom. "How was your day?"

"Pretty good. Got a new client."

She paused, not going directly to the bedroom. "Yeah? Tell me about it."

"A woman with a missing child. The police think that the girl's biological father abducted her and took her to Saudi Arabia."

Kenzie's brows rose. "Are you planning on international travel? It's not the best time of year for it."

"It would get me away from this!" Zachary looked over his shoulder out the big living room window to the street. Ice and snow. Dark sky. Temperatures that curtailed his outdoor walks.

"That it would."

"I'm not going to Saudi Arabia. I'm going to investigate here and see what I can find. I might phone, email, or video conference with Saudi Arabia, but I'm not going there."

Kenzie nodded, her dark spiral curls bouncing around her face. "Good. I would rather you weren't traipsing all over the globe without me."

"You wouldn't come with me?" Zachary teased.

Kenzie was just a bit of a workaholic. He didn't imagine he would be able to get her away from the medical examiner's office for more than a few days. The week or two that he would need to investigate things in Saudi Arabia? Highly unlikely.

"Well…" Kenzie's gaze went to the window. "It would be warmer."

Zachary nodded his agreement. "It would."

"I'm going to shower," she announced, stretching. "Don't leave without me," she said with a teasing smile.

"Anything you want me to put on?" he asked, referring to dinner. Sometimes she was okay with Zachary starting something while she was in the shower and sometimes she didn't want him to touch anything in her kitchen.

"You can put together a salad if you like."

"Okay." Zachary stood up so that he wouldn't look back at his computer screen and get distracted. Kenzie would return in twenty minutes and find that he hadn't even moved from his spot to start making the salad.

He had learned that "you can... if you like" didn't mean he could do or not do the thing she suggested depending on how he felt at the moment. It was a polite request for him to do what she asked. He wanted to stay with her and have a strong relationship with her; therefore, he always "liked" to do whatever she suggested. Unless he really couldn't for one reason or another. Of course, if that were the case, he shouldn't have offered to start working on supper for her.

Zachary walked to the kitchen while Kenzie headed toward the bedroom and her en suite bathroom. She must have been doing an autopsy that afternoon. That was when she was most likely to have sore muscles and want a shower as soon as she walked in the door to rinse off the sweat and the smell of decomp that only she could detect.

When Kenzie returned to the kitchen, hair still damp and all her makeup washed off, but her bright red lipstick reapplied, she seemed to be in a good mood.

"How was your day?" Zachary asked, trying to stay focused on setting the table while he listened to her answer.

"Pretty good. Things are quiet for now."

Until the Christmas and New Year rush. That was when the rubber really hit the road at the medical examiner's office—a bad time of year for a lot of people. Zachary checked the table for cutlery, forcing himself to think of something other than the approaching Christmas season. He was one of those people who had a difficult time at Christmas. He was hoping that this would be the year that he could get through it without a major depressive cycle and enjoy the holidays with Kenzie. He was on a good med protocol and was determined that this year he would be home for Christmas, not in the hospital. Kenzie deserved a nice, quiet Christmas at home with Zachary and with her parents. And if they could get down to see them, Lorne and Pat, Zachary's chosen family, as well.

But determination was not enough. Zachary could not will himself into not being too depressed as Christmas Eve approached. The meds were a key factor. And then... he would see what circumstances life threw his way and how his physical and mental health held up. He was doing as Dr. Boyle had suggested, taking time each day to visualize having a nice, peaceful, warm and happy Christmas Eve and Christmas Day with Kenzie. Hoping that by seeing it, he could integrate it into his recalcitrant brain and make it a reality.

"Zachary?"

"Hmm?" He looked at Kenzie and smiled, pretending he hadn't gotten distracted from their conversation.

"How did you get your new client?"

Hopefully, she hadn't asked the question more than once already. Anyone could miss a question once. It was when she repeated it two or three times and he was still lost in his own head that it became a problem.

"She had a referral but didn't say who gave her my name. She just said, 'she had heard' that I have done missing persons cases before and that I am... persistent."

"A bulldog."

Zachary shrugged. "She wanted someone to look at it from another perspective and see if... the police are right in their conclusions."

"She doesn't think that it was the father that took the little girl? Are they divorced?"

"They haven't been together since before the girl was born. Never married. He's never shown any interest in raising the girl or being part of her life."

"Oh." Kenzie nodded, considering this. "Then it does seem a little strange that he would take the girl away without warning."

"Yeah, it is a bit off. That doesn't mean it didn't happen exactly the way the police think it did. It still could have. But I'm the second set of eyes on the case. Questioning all their assumptions and conclusions."

Kenzie was working some magic at the stove, the rich, savory smells of some kind of soup or stew starting to fill the kitchen. Neither of them had a natural talent for cooking, but they were improving. Not just warming up frozen dinners and setting out bagged salads and bottled dressings on the table. Not every night, anyway.

Zachary had not made the homemade salad dressing in a jelly jar that he had set out on the table. That had been Kenzie's doing. It was Zachary's job to adjust to dressings that were different from the grocery store dressings he had grown up eating in foster care and not to complain about new tastes and textures.

He had also cut up the vegetables for the green salad without cutting off any digits. He could be proud of himself for that.

"But she didn't tell you who had recommended you?" Kenzie asked. "Why not?"

"She didn't say and I didn't ask. I thought maybe... it might have been someone who didn't *want* their name mentioned."

Kenzie looked at him, frowning. "Why would someone refer her to you but not want you to know they had?"

"Maybe Gordon. Or maybe Joss. Or one of the cops who worked one of the human trafficking cases."

Gordon wouldn't want his name mentioned because he wasn't supposed to have any more contact with Zachary. Kenzie had made it very clear that she did not appreciate Zachary's ex-wife's new partner contacting him anymore. Zachary always ended up going off the rails after any contact with Bridget, even through Gordon. But Zachary had done a couple of investigations for Gordon in the past, had protected Gordon's and Bridget's twins when they had been in danger, and rescued them when they had been abducted.

Joss was a different matter. She was Zachary's oldest sister. He wanted to be involved in her life as much as she would allow. But Jocelyn was prickly, and whenever Zachary's cases had anything to do with human trafficking or the cartels that Joss had been involved with for so many years, she always discouraged him in the strongest possible language. If she had referred a kidnapping case to Zachary, she would not want him to know the referral had come from her. She wouldn't want to be seen as "soft" or encouraging him to have anything to do with the type of organizations that kidnapped children.

None of the law enforcement officers he had contact with on previous cases would want it to be known they'd had anything to do with a private investigator. Cops and PIs did not mix—not at the cops' behest, anyway.

"Hmm. I suppose you're right. But I still think she should have said who sent her to you. It's common courtesy. You should be able to make a judgment about the case based on who sent it to you."

Which was another reason the referrer might not have wanted his name mentioned. If it were someone who had burned Zachary in the past, he wouldn't want Zachary to know he was the one behind the new case.

Zachary should just take each case on its own merits.

4

The next morning, Zachary had breakfast with Kenzie and saw her off to work. Then he finally had a chance to get started on his new case.

He dove into his email, which was not the most productive way to start his day. Heather, the other of his older sisters, had been helping him with the private investigations business. She had taken it upon herself to keep track of his emails and to sort and collate them as they came in, adding the jobs that needed to be done to his task list and filing or putting the rest of them into folders marked "personal" or "to be read" where they were out of sight until he was ready to deal with them. She had raised two kids with ADHD and learned a lot of strategies for helping them keep themselves on track, so she had some really good ideas to help Zachary keep his distractibility under control and put his assets to good use.

She had first taken over his email the previous year when he had been in the hospital, and she seemed to have a better idea of how to manage everything that came in on a day-to-day business than he did by now.

After glancing over the few emails she hadn't had a chance to sort yet and finding nothing urgent, Zachary opened the project and task manager they shared. It was amazing how much Heather helped him to stay organized when they didn't even live in the same town. Zachary created a new project for the Rose Bircher kidnapping case, and it was immediately populated with a checklist of the administrative tasks they each needed to do to get a new file set up. He followed the checklist, setting up a folder on the cloud storage to store any notes or documents he created, dropping Rose's contact information and the other contact cards he had collected from her into the folder, filling in a little form that Heather had set up with a summary of the case, checkboxes to indicate that he had given Rose his rate sheet and collected a retainer, and a few other miscellaneous items.

As he had known she would, Heather called while Zachary was setting everything up. She was notified whenever Zachary created a new project, and they would talk it through if it were something other than a skip trace, insurance file, or one of the other routine matters that were the daily bread and butter of the investigations business. Things like the kidnapping only came along now and then and, while they could be lucrative, Zachary and Heather needed other work to keep the coffers full between such cases.

Zachary tapped the answer button on his phone, tapped the speaker button, and kept typing the intake form. "Hi, Feathers."

"Hey, Zachy. New file?"

"Yeah." He knew she could see on her computer what he had done so far, everything being updated in real time. "Kidnapping of a little girl. Four days ago now. Police think the non-custodial parent took her out of the country. But there isn't any proof either way, so we're going to do some digging."

He was probably being generous with the "we." He would do most of the investigative work. But Heather would do her part.

"Father is Amir Osman? That's who they think took her?"

"Right. Could you run background on him? Start a profile. Family, education, work history, residential, credit check, ties to any middle eastern countries. He apparently has a girlfriend and she has a child, so anything you come across for them could be helpful too. According to the TSA, he took his girlfriend's daughter to Saudi Arabia. The police think it was actually Claire."

"They can't tell?"

"No."

"I'll see what I can pull together."

Zachary could see the tasks she was creating for herself popping up on the project manager. When they finished talking, he would switch the filter so that he would only see his tasks and not be distracted by hers.

"What else do you need me to do?" Heather asked.

"Uh… background on the client, too. I want to know if what she's told me is reliable. Credit check there, too. She said she hasn't had any involvement with Amir since Claire was born. Let me know if that turns out not to be true. If they've actually been battling over visitation or custody for Claire, then that will change things. If she's active on social media, watch for anyone who might have been stalking her. See how much she posts about where she and Claire are going to be or places they visit regularly. Would someone watching her social media have known to find them at this play place?"

"In case it was a stranger kidnapping."

"In case it was a close family member or friend who sees her social media feeds. Strangers aren't always strangers."

"I can do that. Anything else?"

"Not related to this case."

"Okay. You got something else for me?"

Zachary hesitated. It was something that had been on his mind for months, but he hadn't yet shared it with anyone.

"Zach?"

"Well… it's not related to work at all, actually."

"Mm-hmm?"

"I was wondering… what you thought about getting together for dinner. About *all of us* getting together for dinner sometime?"

"All of us?" Heather repeated. "You and Kenzie and me and Grant?"

"No… I meant all the siblings."

Heather was silent.

Zachary wasn't sure what he had expected. He and his siblings had been separated when Zachary was ten and had grown up in different homes. The younger children had mostly been together, but the older children, including Zachary, had been by themselves after that. In the last couple of years, Zachary had been reunited with each of them. But always separately. They had never gotten everyone together in one place.

Maybe that should have told him the others were not interested in a big reunion. They were okay with meeting one or two at a time, but were reluctant to get everyone together in a room at one time.

"That sounds like a nice idea," Heather said eventually, but her voice sounded strained. "Have you talked to any of the others about it?"

"No. This is the first time I've mentioned it to anyone. I just thought… well, we know where everyone is now. Don't you think everyone would agree?"

"Hard to say. Joss isn't big on any family stuff. You tend to get overwhelmed, even if it's just me and Tyrrell. If T feels pressured… he's never been good about stress. He's in a good place emotionally right now, and I don't think any of us want to take the chance of him falling off the wagon."

Zachary made a noise of agreement, though there was a lump in his throat. Heather's points were all good.

"And Vince and Mindy?"

"They've been a unit by themselves… I don't think they feel connected to the rest of us. They were too little to remember anyone but T. Mindy's always been kind of cool toward me when I've called. And she has to check everything with Vince. If he doesn't agree, you know she won't either."

"But you haven't ever asked them."

"I've never gotten further than talking on the phone and saying we should get together sometime. I haven't bothered to try to set something up. Never felt like I had the green light."

"Would *you* want to get together with everyone?"

In her summary of all the reasons it might not work out, Heather had left herself off the list completely.

Heather cleared her throat. "Well… if everyone wanted to get together, I would agree. But I don't know if it would work. We're all… so different."

And traumatized. They had each reacted to a childhood of abuse and being separated from each other in different ways. The younger children had been able to be raised in one foster home and had eventually been adopted by their foster parents. Zachary had moved from one foster family to another every few months, or else bounced into institutional care when he couldn't manage living with a family.

Heather had mostly been raised by one family, but had been through a lot of trauma there too, and had eventually been out on the street. Joss had been trafficked and addicted for years, living a life that Zachary would not have wished on his worst enemy. She was in a better place now, sober and helping to rescue street kids from the life, but she was not friendly or easy to get along with. Any interaction had to be initiated by Zachary, and she was very prickly about his overtures.

"So you don't think it is a good idea."

"I didn't say that. I just think it would be hard, and I don't know if everyone will agree or be really happy doing it. You know? Maybe… Goldmans are better in small doses."

Zachary laughed at that.

He had to admit that even though it was his own idea, the idea of getting everyone together made him anxious. He wanted them to be all together again, as a sign that they were healing and over-coming their past. A sign of solidarity and family closeness.

"And what about the rest of them?" Heather asked.

Zachary didn't have to ask what she meant by that. He knew that she didn't mean their parents. While their father and mother were both still alive, as far as Zachary knew, he would never try to put parents and children in the same room again. He had met his father recently and had no desire to have a relationship with him. Not like Tyrrell did.

While Zachary had begged for years for the social workers to reunite his family, he knew as a grown man that he never wanted to see his mother again. He was never going to be able to be the child she had wanted him to be, and she was never going to love him the way that he had wanted her to. She had told Zachary at age ten that he was incorrigible and she wanted nothing more to do with him, and she never had. He had wanted for years to fix that rift and earn her love and approval, not understanding that she was just as messed up as he was. It wasn't his fault that she had dissolved the family, even though that was what he had always believed.

Maybe that was why Zachary wanted to get the family back together again in a big reunion. He believed the dissolution of the family had been his fault and it was his job to bring them back together.

"The others" Heather referred to were the other siblings they had discovered. The other children that their dad had fathered after the family had broken up. There were quite a few of them. And probably even more that they didn't know about because they hadn't sent their DNA to any of the ancestry companies. And their mother could have had other children, too. But Heather didn't mean *all* of them, only the ones Tyrrell had found through DNA analysis.

"I wasn't thinking of them. I just meant… the siblings we grew up with. Our family."

"Well, that's good. I think our little group will be hard enough."

"Yeah. Well," Zachary decided it was time to move on from the conversation. "It's something to think about, anyway."

He decided not to ask Heather to help him to pull together a family reunion. Not yet. As close as they had grown working together over the past couple of years, he couldn't ask her to do something that was obviously so difficult for her. He didn't want her to pull away from him.

It would have to be up to him.

5

Zachary let his eyes travel over the play equipment that filled "All Played Out," the activity center from which Claire Bircher had disappeared. There had been nothing around like that when he had been growing up. It would have been an ADHD boy's dream. So many places to run, hide, climb, and slide. Ball pits and foam pits to jump into and burrow in. Energetic pop music blared over the speakers, and the smell of pizza and fries from the concession scented the air, sweetened with popcorn and candy floss. Of course, many parents resisted the pull of junk food by bringing apples and carrot sticks for their kids to eat when they took breaks from their noisy play, but it was a losing battle.

Most of the sweaty kids looked happy, unless they were being dragged out after long hours of play by their parents, exhausted and tearful. But there were a few who must have felt like Zachary did now, overwhelmed by the color, the noise, and the activity. While he would have loved it as a kid, that was when he could have immersed himself in his play and focused on having fun. As an easily distracted adult trying to focus on a case, it was a different story. He felt like his head was about to explode.

"I would like to talk to the manager," he said to the heavyset security guard as clearly as he could. "Somewhere… quiet where we can talk."

The guard gave him a grin, showing off his even white teeth in what looked more like a shark's predatory smile than someone who intended to help him.

"You cannot enter unless you are accompanied by a child. That's the rule."

"I don't want to go into the play area. I want to talk to someone who is in charge."

"They won't change the rules for you, buddy. You want to get your jollies, you're going to have to go somewhere else."

Zachary presented one of his business cards, which had a large yellow shield that looked like a police crest, even though the card clearly stated, "Private Investigator."

"I'm investigating the disappearance of Claire Bircher a few days ago. From this facility." He tried to draw himself up taller, though he had no hope of making himself look as tall as the guard. "Were you on duty when that happened?" he demanded, pulling the notebook out of his pocket and holding his pen at the ready.

The guard frowned and looked from side to side as if he suspected that one of his friends might be playing a prank on him.

"What is this?" he asked. "I didn't have anything to do with that. That was my day off, man; I wasn't even here."

"Are you sure? Do you have someone who can verify that? An alibi?"

"I don't need an alibi. The cops that were here that day know that I wasn't on. They questioned everyone who was on when it happened. I was nowhere near here. It's the honest truth."

"What would you say if I told you that your card had been swiped that afternoon? What would you have to say about that?"

"That's not possible. I wasn't here. Why would I come in to work on a day when I wasn't scheduled?"

"Because you wanted to take that little girl, and you wanted to be able to say that you weren't here. Just swipe yourself in and out, nice and clean, and take that little girl. And no one would have been the wiser *except that your card was logged.*"

"You're crazy. There's no way that my card was used that day." He looked around for an answer that didn't pop up. "Unless someone cloned my card. That could happen, you know. It isn't hard."

This was something that hadn't occurred to Zachary. He had no reason to suspect the security guard and was only trying to scare him into cooperating. But it was a good thought. How *had* the kidnapper gotten in and out? Whether it was Amir or someone else, he had to have a way to get into the play place. With an employee swipe card, he could have the run of the place. There would be no need to bring a kid to get in or convince a guard that he was with someone already inside.

Since Zachary already had his pen and notebook out, he made a note to investigate the possibility further.

That made all the employees suspects, whether they had been on shift or not. There must be a swipe card log somewhere on the computer system. They could weed out whether anyone was there who shouldn't be. And everyone who had been on site when Claire had disappeared. He had heard that phones and credit cards could be cloned just by someone walking close by. The same must apply to the simple proximity cards used to unlock the supposedly secure doors.

"So you have someone who can verify that you were not here when your card was swiped?" he asked the guard.

The man was paler than he had been when he'd been giving Zachary a hard time. Starting to rethink his entire career in the security sector, maybe. Was it worth getting fingered for a kidnapping? After all the other things a guard in a place like this must have to deal with. Parents who thought they deserved special rules, vomiting children and pooping babies, spilled drinks and thrown fast food, management who didn't think that their employees had lives outside of work. Was it worth being a suspect in a child abduction, too?

"I'll get the boss," the guard told him. "Can't hear a darn thing out here. Wait right here."

Zachary waited. Another guard standing at a nearby security

gate kept an eye on him. If the original guard didn't show up with the manager, Zachary would harass one of the others. Sooner or later, he would get his way and would get in to see someone with more authority. Though whether they would be able to tell him anything of value was debatable. They couldn't produce closed-circuit footage that hadn't been recorded. They had provided whatever they had to the police already, and there was no reason to think that Zachary could find anything the police hadn't.

Zachary was pleasantly surprised when the security guard he had talked to came back into view, accompanied by a tall, skinny kid who didn't look older than nineteen.

"You're the manager?" Zachary asked, aware that his tone had taken on a note of disbelief. But it was noisy. They wouldn't be able to hear his intonation. A conversation in a place like this consisted mostly of lip reading.

The young man nodded. "I'm older than I look," he said, pushing back a paper hat that suggested the guard had pulled him away from working the concession stand.

"Well, you'd have to be!" Zachary shook his head. "What are you, twelve?"

"I'm over twenty!" he retorted, which probably meant he'd only just passed his twentieth birthday.

"Is there somewhere quiet we can go to talk?" Zachary asked, pointing to his throat, which was getting sore from yelling over the music.

"Yeah, yeah." The boy nodded at the guard to return to his post, and he gestured impatiently for Zachary to follow him. They entered the employee-only hallway through a hinged wall section painted to look exactly the same as the rest of the wall. The noise of the play area was muffled, but could still be heard at a low roar.

The manager swiped through a couple of security doors and, eventually, they reached his destination, a closet-size security booth with several camera feeds. A guard even more paunchy than the first sat watching the screens while chewing on a fried chicken drumstick. It was mercifully quiet.

The boy manager pointed to the chairs at the small table behind the guard, and he and Zachary sat down.

"Now, what's this all about? We already answered all the cops' questions the day that little girl disappeared. They haven't found her?"

"No. They haven't. It is clear at this point that she was abducted. She didn't just wander off."

The boy ran his fingers through his hair. "It wasn't anything to do with anyone here. And we have good security practices in place. Corporate has developed all the policies and procedures and we follow their guidelines rigorously."

"And, Tim, is it?" Zachary asked, looking at the young man's name badge. "Does that include only having two live cameras to keep track of a hundred kids and everyone around them? You have all kinds of cameras mounted out there, and only two that work?"

Tim nodded reluctantly. "I know it looks like there are more than there are. Most of the cameras out there are just deterrents. Dummies. They're just shells. They look like the real thing and even have a red light, but there's no guts. They don't record anything. They don't feed anywhere." He tapped his fingertips on the table. "Some of the ones that are supposed to work are down. We should have a view of the entire floor. We've put in service requests, but Corporate hasn't fixed them yet."

"Even after you had a kid abducted?"

He shrugged. "That's at least got some movement on it. They're supposed to be here Monday to fix them. That's pretty good, considering some have been down for a year or more."

"How many people know that your security surveillance is so lax?"

"Uh… I don't know. It isn't really that bad. We have live eyes out there on the floor, too. That's far more important than a camera feed. People who can analyze human behavior and be right there to intervene if necessary."

Zachary agreed that was important. "But none of your live eyes knew what happened to Claire Bircher or when they had last seen her."

"Yeah. That was too bad. We get so many kids through here… you can't expect them to be able to track the kids' movements. It's just not possible."

"Which is why it is important to have them on camera. You said that the whole floor is supposed to be visible on camera."

"Yeah. If all the cameras are working."

"What about inside the play equipment? All those forts and tunnels and ball pits."

"What about it?"

"No cameras can see in there. What if you've got older kids bullying or molesting younger kids? Or employees who have an eye for the little ones? There are so many places that are out of sight."

Zachary looked at the screens the security guard was watching. The little "rooms" between the slides and hamster tunnels were not solidly covered; the walls were just tubes and netting so, if a person were standing close by, they would be able to see if there were a child inside them. But they were fairly well screened and, in some cases, two or three cells deep. It wouldn't be hard to get a kid alone and take advantage of their vulnerability. Zachary tried to ignore the squirmy feeling in his stomach.

"We have Play Assistants everywhere," Tim explained. Standing up, he approached the security monitors and pointed a few times. "Here, here, here… they can go anywhere the kids can, and they help them to climb or to slide if they are afraid, help them find their friends, get back out to their moms, whatever. They keep an eye out for any bullying and are the only adults allowed there. It's a safe place. Ask any of the moms out there."

"How about Claire Bircher's mom? Is that what she said to you the day that Claire disappeared? Thank you for looking after her so well? For all these great security measures you have in place?"

Tim's mouth twisted into a sneer. "Of course not. She was pretty upset. But that's the first time anything like that has ever happened."

"And have you figured out what did happen? How someone got in and took Claire out quietly without anyone noticing?"

Tim sat back down across from Zachary. "Not yet." He shook

his head. "We're still working on it. We're supposed to have some sessions this weekend to brainstorm security holes and figure out what happened. I know it's like closing the barn door after the horse is gone—that's how the saying goes, isn't it?—but we don't want it to happen again."

"I'm glad you're doing something." Zachary sighed. "I would like to get a copy of the footage you gave the police. The more people we can get looking at it, the better the chances are that we'll be able to find something."

Tim frowned, his brows furrowing. "I thought *you* were the police." His eyes widened. "Are you FBI?"

When asked directly, Zachary couldn't lie about who or what he was. There were penalties for impersonating a cop or federal agent. "No, this is a private investigation."

"Private?"

"We were hired by Mrs. Bircher to investigate what happened here. I hope I'll have your full cooperation. We want to be able to tell Mrs. Bircher that there is no fault on behalf of All Played Out. I'm sure Corporate wouldn't want to hear that she was filing civil charges for negligence that took place here…"

Tim's face went pinched and white. He shook his head. "There was no negligence. We have done everything we were supposed to."

"I'm sure you *tried*," Zachary allowed, clearly implying that Tim and the other employees had fallen down on the job, and their negligence had resulted in Claire's abduction. Zachary sighed and raised his hands, palms up. "And maybe the video will exonerate you."

"The police said that there wasn't anything on it. No abduction. No one hanging around looking suspicious. They don't know what happened." He lowered his voice and shot a glance toward the guard's back. "If it was me, I'd be looking at the mother." He nodded and sat back, looking proud of himself. "She comes in here with a friend and *pretends* that she's lost her daughter. And maybe the girl was never even here. Maybe the mother did something to her, and she came here to establish an alibi and make it look like there was an abduction. Throw the cops off the trail. How many times have you seen these moms making appeals on TV to help them find the person who stole their kid, just to find out that they killed 'em and buried 'em in the basement or drowned them in the lake?"

It happened. Zachary knew that. He hadn't gotten a bad vibe from Rose, but a person couldn't always tell. That was why people got away with it. If Zachary and the cops could always tell who was lying, there would be no innocent people in prison, and those responsible would always be arrested and convicted.

"You think Mrs. Bircher came in here without Claire?" he asked, keeping his voice as flat and neutral as possible.

"I'm not saying that's what happened, but you gotta consider it, don't you? It could all be a cover-up."

"How hard would it be for her to do that? Don't you ID and check everyone in? And no one gets in without a kid, right?"

"Sure. But we don't have any proof of what kids belong to what people. If I get a group at the gate, three moms and six kids, I don't grill them on which kids belong to which women. I don't demand everyone's birth certificates and interview the kids to make sure they really are who they say they are. We don't fingerprint or do mugshots or facial recognition or anything like that. We let in the three moms and their six kids, and the adults sign the logs with their names and the names of the kids. They sign their waivers, and they're off to the races. The kids can play for as long as they like and, when the group leaves, one mom checks everyone off the log."

"So one of the moms checks off herself and her kids and leaves Claire and Mrs. Bircher on the log, even though Claire was never actually there."

He nodded and folded his arms, waiting for Zachary to acknowledge the cleverness of his scenario. He'd obviously had some time to think about it and construct a scenario where a parent could game the system and fool All Played Out and the police into believing that a child who had never actually been there had disappeared.

"But that would require someone else to be complicit in the plot," Zachary pointed out. "The other mother who puts Claire on the log and then doesn't check her off, knowing she was never there in the first place."

"Well, yeah."

"Why would someone do that?"

"I don't know. Because they're friends and she wants to protect her friend."

"Was Mrs. Bircher here with a group that day?"

"I don't know. She could have been."

"I'll need a copy of your log sheet, too, along with the closed-circuit recordings."

Tim looked at him, trying to figure out how to tell him no. Then he finally shrugged. If Zachary could prove that Rose had just been faking her daughter's presence, that was good for him and his company. It would prove that they had not done anything wrong.

"Okay. I'll get another copy for you."

"And which of the guards who were on when Claire disappeared are on today? I'd like to talk to them."

"There are only a couple. I'll see if they are ready for a coffee break."

6

Zachary took a leisurely drive around the neighborhood, getting a feel for the area Rose and Claire Bircher had lived in. It was one of the wealthier areas of town. Whatever research Rose did in the computer lab apparently paid well. It was a nice place for a single parent to live, especially considering the fact that she was not getting any financial support from Amir.

He drove slowly past the elementary school Claire attended. Not slow enough that anyone would notice and think he was some stalker or pedophile. It was a couple of blocks away from Rose's house. Not far, but probably too far for a five-year-old to walk by herself. But she hadn't walked home from there. If Claire had a stalker, she hadn't picked him up walking home from school. It would have been a good place for him to snatch her, except for all the other school kids who would have been walking at the same time. Predators tended to target kids who walked alone. Those in pairs or groups were more difficult targets. And criminals like to go with what is easy.

From school, Claire had gone to her after-school care. Rose had advised him that Mrs. Moore, the woman who looked after the kids after school walked to the elementary school doors every day before school let out, and picked up her charges there. Then they walked back to her house together. Again, a difficult target for a predator. Trying to put himself into a stalker's head, Zachary drove the route they would have walked from the school to the house and didn't see any points that offered a particular tactical advantage for a snatch. It was all visible, all out in the open, walking where other school kids would be walking. Nice and safe.

At the house, he got out of the car, locked up, and checked that the car alarm had armed. Even though he would be close by, he wanted to know if anyone tried to mess with his vehicle. Better safe than sorry. He clicked the door lock on his key fob one more time for good measure and eyeballed the locks to ensure that they had lowered into the locked position. He checked up and down the street twice, then walked up to the house. He watched the street while waiting for Mrs. Moore to open the door.

Eventually, he heard her heavy footfalls within the house and turned back toward the door before she opened it.

Mrs. Moore was a large woman, her hair pulled back into a French braid, face ruddy, puffing a bit as if she'd had to run for the door. But she was not unpleasant to look at. She seemed like a friendly, comfortable woman that the children would trust and like to be around. Sort of a stern grandmother with a cookie jar that was never empty.

She studied Zachary briefly, wiping her brow with the back of her hand and pushing a few stray strands of hair back from her face. "You're Mr. Goldman?"

"Zachary. Yes."

She evaluated him for a minute before deciding to allow him in. She stepped back from the door and motioned him to enter. She offered him a seat in the living room and sat in her favorite easy chair.

"It's such a terrible thing that happened," she said mournfully. "I just couldn't believe it. One of *my* kids! I told my husband when I saw it on the TV, 'That's one of my kids!' It seems so unreal."

"It was awful," Zachary agreed. "I'm sure it must have been quite the shock for you."

"It was indeed," she agreed. "And the other kids have been so sad since they heard about it, too. You would think that at that age they wouldn't really think much about it. But they understand what happened, and they have all been affected, poor dears. Even the older kids. In fact it might be worse for them even though they were not as close to her. They understand more…"

Zachary hoped that they didn't understand too much about what happened to little girls who got kidnapped. The scenario of a barren mother longing for a baby and stealing a child because she wanted someone to love that played out on TV was not at all common. Predators wanted to hurt or kill. In some cases, they wanted money, either from ransom or trafficking. But there were few happy endings. Especially since it had been several days since Claire had been taken, and there had been no call to say that she was still alive and the kidnapper wanted a ransom paid. No one wanted to just hang on to the evidence for days on end. Especially when that evidence was in the form of a child who needed to be fed, clothed, and constantly supervised or bound.

But he tried not to show any of these thoughts in his expression. He just kept a pleasant smile in place as if he weren't thinking about what might have happened to Claire if she wasn't with her father.

Even if she was with her father…

Zachary had spent the small hours of the morning reading or watching videos on the internet, educating himself about non-custodial parent kidnappings and other family kidnappings. The statistics were not encouraging. People thought that if a child were in the hands of her parent, she was safe, even if the court had not granted that person custodial rights. But the facts did not bear that out. Overwhelmingly, people who kidnapped were violent, whether they were related to the victim or not. The kidnappers had poor impulse control and did not think things through logically. They tended to be motivated by pride or revenge rather than love for the kidnapped child, and most did not have the skills needed to properly parent a child.

The consequences were dire for the kidnapped child.

"I know that Claire didn't disappear from here or from school,"

Zachary said, getting down to it, "so you might be wondering why I am here. But I wanted to look into the circumstances surrounding her disappearance. If she was taken from the play place, then she might have been specifically targeted. The person who targeted her might have been watching her for some time, looking for a good time and place to take her."

Mrs. Moore's eyes were sharp. She nodded a couple of times. "And if he was watching her, maybe I saw him around here."

Zachary agreed. "Yes. Did you see anyone suspicious over the last few weeks? Or has anyone ever approached Claire while she has been with you or before you picked her up? Or she might have said something about a new friend or person in her life."

"We are always very careful. I pick up all the kids together, and they must stay together while we walk home. I keep a very close eye on them."

"I have no doubt. You can't be too careful in today's world. These parents have entrusted you with their children's care."

"And they are so precious. I couldn't let anything happen to them."

"Has there been anyone new in the neighborhood or at the school when you pick them up? Even if they haven't given you any cause for concern. Has there been anyone around who wasn't a parent or teacher that you knew?"

"No. I can't think of anyone. I talk to people. You know, be friendly, reach out to people who are new to the community, faces I don't know. Ask them how they are. Ask them about their kids. Get to know who they are and why they are there. I think it is important."

"That's a good policy to have. It's good to build community and keep track of people in your sphere. A lot of preventing crime is being aware of what is going on around you and letting people know that they have been seen."

"People who walk down the street with their noses in their phones—involved in a conversation or messaging or whatever else they might be doing—make good targets for the criminal element. We need to be aware of what is going on in our environment."

"The best advice I could give you," Zachary agreed. "And you haven't seen anyone new lately. No one that you have struck up a conversation with because they were hanging around the school or your kids."

"No." She grimaced, dissatisfied. "I wish I could think of someone, put you on the right track."

"Well, the police already have a suspect, so they may not even need our help. But sometimes the police are wrong. So you and I need to help Rose to find Claire. To find out who took her and get her home."

"That poor girl. I can't imagine how frightened she might be." Her expression went through various contortions as she tried to control her grief and fear.

Zachary was too far from her to reach out and comfort her physically. He sat forward instead, leaning closer to her, bowing his head in acknowledgment of the difficult time she was going through. Mrs. Moore might not be one of Claire's parents as far as the law was concerned, but she was obviously attached to "her kids."

7

M rs. Moore wiped at the corners of her eyes. "If she is even alive. I keep thinking about all the terrible things that might be happening to her. Do you think she's alive?"

"All indicators are that she is," Zachary tried to make it sound positive. "There is a suspect and speculation that he took her out of the country. The police are not looking for a body. They think she is alive and well and being cared for."

"That's good." She sniffled. "I'm sorry for being such a mess over this. You probably think that I'm putting it on. I only saw her for an hour or two each day. But I liked her very much. I love all my kids, but some are just... more special."

"Tell me about her."

Claire wasn't yet a real person in Zachary's mind. She was the target, a possession to be recovered. Precious, of course, and he'd always had a tender place in his heart for little children. But he didn't know Claire yet.

"Oh..." Mrs. Moore sat back, folding her hands and gazing up at the ceiling. "She just started this year, so I've only had her for a few months. She is very smart and very kind. Her mother is a kind of a scientist, you know, and I think Claire must have inherited her intelligence. She is very curious about everything and eager to share what she knows. And she knows all kinds of things that you wouldn't expect a little five-year-old girl to know. Her mother obviously talks to her about all kinds of things. Some parents are very good at encouraging curiosity in the world around them."

"I guess scientists have a lot of curiosity, so they encourage it in their children."

"Yes. She is clearly not a child who has just been plunked down in front of the TV when Mom gets home from work and needs some time to herself. But she's not too bookish, either. She likes to be outside, play with the other children, and is always very concerned if someone is being bullied or gets hurt."

Zachary was beginning to wonder if Mrs. Moore might be looking at the little girl through rose-tinted glasses. Remembering all her best attributes.

"Sometimes smart, curious kids get into trouble," he suggested.

Mrs. Moore gave him a tolerant smile. "Well… yes, of course. Curious kids cause messes. They break things. They step out of bounds and question every rule. A child without that curiosity will usually listen to what you tell them, accept that adults know more and that there are good reasons for all the rules."

"But a child like Claire, not so much?"

"Always questioning everything. It could be frustrating. But I understood she was a good girl. The mistakes—when things got wrecked or broken or she put herself in danger—were annoying, but not malicious. She would be just as distressed as I was when things went wrong. Or even more so. She didn't think she should make mistakes. Very hard on herself."

"Firstborn child."

"I suppose so, yes. They are often driven. Lots of expectations on them. They carry the world on their shoulders." She cocked her head, looking at Zachary. "You were not a firstborn."

Heat blossomed in Zachary's cheeks and ears. "You would be right about that."

"But you still carry too much on your shoulders. You have… a lot of responsibility and sadness."

He was embarrassed by her insight. She was way too intuitive. It was no wonder she connected so well with her kids. He'd known foster mothers like that. So finely attuned to the feelings of a new foster child, even one with little to say, they could instantly identify what a child needed to hear, which other child to pair him with, and what areas he needed the most help in.

But even those exceptionally intuitive foster mothers would eventually break under the pressure of a child who couldn't seem to behave no matter how hard he tried. The very sensitive could only deal with an unmanageable child for so long.

"We're not here to talk about me," he said uncomfortably.

Mrs. Moore gave a slight smile. "I'll bet you were a handful as a kid."

"Oh, I was. Too much for anyone to handle," he admitted. She might think he was joking, but it was the unfortunate truth that he'd never found a home for more than a few months at a time. Even the one foster parent he had stayed in contact with all these years later, Mr. Peterson, had only been able to give him a home for a few weeks. He hadn't been the one to give up on Zachary, but he hadn't been able to dissuade Mrs. Peterson when she decided Zachary had to go.

Mrs. Moore shook her head. "Well, I only had Claire for an hour or two every school day, but she was a joy, despite any messes she might have made or trouble she might have gotten into."

"Did she ever say anything to you about a new friend? Or about her biological father?"

"No, not that I recall. I don't think her father had ever been part of her life. She never mentioned visiting him or anything about him. I assumed that Claire was raising her as a single mother. No husband or father in evidence." Her eyes widened a little. "Is that what happened? Her father took her?"

"We don't know. It is a possibility. But not something that I am willing to bet on at the moment."

She nodded slowly, understanding. "The police must be looking into him."

"Of course. And if it was him, they will get it sorted out. But I want to stay open to all possibilities. Did she mention any new friends to you? Someone who gave her a treat, had a dog, or told her to keep a secret?"

"No. If she'd said anything like that, I would have been concerned. You always have to be on the alert. Candy and puppies are well-known tools of child predators."

"Did you have any concerns about Mrs. Bircher? Rest assured that if you do, nothing is going to get back to her from me."

"I thought she was a good mom. Maybe she treated Claire like she was older than she was. That's a common problem with a child as intelligent and verbal as Claire. You start treating them like a small adult instead of a child. But they were well-suited to each other. They were close and had a strong bond. You could tell that they loved each other and were good friends."

"But…" Zachary prompted, even though she hadn't given him any reason to think there was a "but" coming.

"Well…" Mrs. Moore frowned, brows drawing down. "She was sometimes late without giving me any warning. Sometimes an hour or more. I think that being the type of person she was, it was easy for her to get lost in her work and forget that she had other responsibilities. She lost track of the time."

"Sure, that makes sense." Zachary knew what it was like to get so hyperfocused on a project that everything else around him ceased to exist. This was fine for a private investigator living and working by himself, but not so good when he was supposed to be spending time with Kenzie or if he'd had a child to look after.

"I warned her more than once that she needed to get here on time. Asked her to set alarms on her phone. To call me if she found she was running late. And a couple of times, she did. But the rest of the time… I think she probably shut her alarms off without even looking at them, if she had set them in the first place. She would show up here, hair a mess, looking for Claire and not under-standing why I was so upset."

"And how did Claire feel about that?"

Mrs. Moore laughed. "She took her mother's side. She wasn't one of these kids who worried that Mommy was never coming to pick her up. She didn't fuss when she was the last one left here. She would lecture me. 'Mommy has very important work to do,' or 'She just doesn't know what time it is.' It was cute. I was glad she wasn't the whiny, clingy type when Rose was running late. That makes it more stressful and difficult. Claire would just sit down with a book and wait."

And Rose, finding her child there calmly waiting for her, didn't understand why Mrs. Moore would be upset at the lateness of the hour.

8

Zachary looked at the time on his phone, weighing how long he had before Kenzie would get home from the medical examiner's office. He probably had at least an hour before she rolled in. Maybe more if she had a heavy workload.

Things had been better since Dr. Cook's arrival. He was substituting for Dr. Wiltshire until his badly broken hand healed and was rehabbed well enough for him to do autopsies again. Dr. Cook split the workload with Kenzie so that she wasn't doing everything. They had caught up on the backlog that had piled up while she had been the only doctor working there so she was working more reasonable hours again.

But she was still often late. Kenzie enjoyed her work and sometimes took on too much, not realizing how late she was working. She had never been a nine-to-five worker. Not as long as he had known her.

He sat down at his computer and checked his email inbox before giving Heather a call. She answered on the second ring.

"Hey, Zachy."

"Hi. I was just wondering how things were going with getting some background on Amir. I know you haven't had very long."

"Just preliminary stuff. Things are pretty normal up until a couple of years ago, when it looks like he pulled back socially. Then sudden silence on his social networks, a move to a different residence, and a new job. The company he is supposed to work for doesn't appear to exist."

"Really." Zachary considered. It certainly wouldn't be the first time a guy had put a fictional employer on his online resume to make it look like he had a good job when he was really out of work. "What's the new residence look like? Is it real or a box number?"

"It's real. If it's his real residence, he's moved up. But with the fake job, I wonder if the address is a fake too. That he didn't actually live there, just used it as his address so people would think he was doing well. He could get all his bills and everything electronically, and not ever actually have anything directed to the physical address."

"Might do a land titles search to see if he owns the property. But he could be a tenant. We might have to do a physical check, talk to the neighbors. See if he actually lives there. And he stopped posting to socials?"

"Yeah. That's kind of weird, isn't it? He was pretty active up until this big life change."

"I wonder whether the company is a front for something else. Criminal or law enforcement."

"Hmm." Heather thought about this. "And they don't want him to post anything on his social accounts about what he is doing."

"He might have opened new socials with a fake name to keep it completely separate from his real identity. Or he might just not be posting anymore if his employer prohibits it."

"Do you really think that's what it is? Not that he's unemployed or lying about where he really works because he's embarrassed? You think he could really be involved in something criminal?"

"Or doing something for law enforcement. It's a possibility. He could be embarrassed about just working as a dishwasher at the Burger Barn, but two years is a long time to keep quiet about it. Especially if he was active before. And…"

"Mm-hmm?" He could hear her typing as they talked. Maybe getting more creative with her searches.

"He flew to Saudi Arabia. If he's living in poverty, that would be out of the question. Unless someone else paid for it. Which again leads to the question of why would someone pay for him to go there? Because he's on a job? Supervising an operation? He's not washing dishes for Burger Barn Saudi Arabia."

Heather chuckled. "Probably not. I don't think those guys get travel allowances or transfers to the other side of the world."

"No. So you said everything was normal before that. Tell me about that."

"Sure." Heather was on firmer ground here, and her voice strengthened. "Amir was born to naturalized US citizens. They were Saudi born. Amir went to school here. Then on to college, where he was in computer sciences."

"And where he met Rose Bircher."

"Ah. That detail didn't show up in my research. He was very intelligent, top of his class. I'm not sure exactly what he went into. Solving networking problems for big companies."

She listed a few contracts he had worked on, and Zachary recognized the company names.

"Computer networks?" he asked.

"I'll send you the job titles and descriptions of the projects, but it is all Greek to me. Somebody throwing around multi-syllable words to impress the reader."

"Industrial espionage, do you think?"

"I don't know." Heather pondered. "I guess he could be a spy or hacker. I'd say he has the skills, from the courses and certificates on his profile. If they're true."

"And then he suddenly decides to take a trip to Saudi Arabia."

"With his family. His girlfriend and her daughter."

"Maybe," Zachary allowed. "Or another child who is not his girlfriend's daughter."

"Then what happened to her daughter?"

"Maybe she didn't have one. Or maybe she died. Maybe the

girlfriend was mourning the loss and Amir knew where to get a replacement."

Heather hummed, thinking about it. Zachary enjoyed the brainstorming, pitching ideas back and forth to see what they could come up with. Maybe the idea of Amir replacing the girlfriend's dead daughter was too far a reach.

"The girlfriend has no internet presence," Heather said eventually. "No social media. No mentions on any website or newspaper. Not mentioned in any obituaries. No college or alumni records that I can find."

"A ghost. Credit rating?"

"I have possible matches, not having any birth date or social…"

"Any listing at Amir's address? Former or current?"

"Oh, good idea… no. Nothing there. Is it possible this woman has never had a credit card?"

"Not under that name. But maybe under something else. What is her name?"

"Orna Temple."

"That doesn't sound Saudi."

"No, I don't think so. I could only find one picture of her, and she's fair. Not that there aren't white Saudis, of course. But she isn't your stereotypical Saudi woman."

"Where did you get her name and picture? Amir?"

"Yes, one picture and mention on his socials."

"How do you know it is his girlfriend? And if the mention is more than two years old, how do you know it is the same woman he is with right now?"

"Well, it's all surmise, but they look very cozy in the picture. Not just a casual friend. Amir, Orna, and a little girl, maybe three or four years old. The cutest little thing you ever saw."

Zachary's mind flashed to Claire and the pictures that Rose had given to him. Two little girls of about the same age connected with Amir. Had he substituted one for the other?

"Can you send me that picture?"

"Sure. Of course. I've already downloaded it. You said that Amir might have used Orna's passport for Claire."

"Yeah."

The police had undoubtedly turned up the same information. And they also might have had access to her passport, which Zachary didn't. They knew who he had been traveling with and, in their opinion, he was a non-custodial parent taking his child out of the country.

But as far as Zachary knew, they hadn't been able to get in touch with him. Places like Saudi Arabia were notorious havens for absconding fathers. Getting Claire back, if Amir had taken her there, would be difficult if not impossible. Rose hadn't heard anything back from the investigators, which probably meant they were still dealing with the red tape, trying to figure out how to advance the case. Or they had already given up.

"Do you have Amir's parent's names? They live here?"

"Yes. Are you going to go see them?"

"I might. It might be the only way to get in contact with him."

9

"I'll get you everything tonight," Heather promised. "I need to take a break for supper now. And so do you."

"I'll eat when Kenzie gets home. Promise."

He was starting to feel vaguely hungry. After years of meds that suppressed his appetite or made him nauseated, he was surprised whenever he actually felt hungry. And most of the time, he ignored the uncomfortable feeling and it went away. But he was supposed to be keeping his weight up, which wasn't easy if he didn't eat.

"One more thing," Heather said as he was about to end the call.

"Oh, sorry. What?"

"About that other thing." He was in the dark until she clarified. "The family dinner."

"Oh. Yeah. Don't worry about that. I'll do something else. Just see people separately."

"No, that isn't what I was going to say. I think you're right. I think it's time we put our past aside and get together again. It's been decades. Why are we letting *them* hold us back from reuniting?"

Them might mean their mother and father. Or it might mean the various social workers they had dealt with who had kept them apart through their childhoods. But childhood was long over, and

50

there wasn't any reason they couldn't get together if they wanted to. There were no longer any other adults to tell them what they were or weren't allowed to do.

"Yeah. I think we should," Zachary said tentatively. "But it might be too soon. I can wait… let people heal… get to know each other separately before we all have to be in the same room together."

"No. I think you're right. I think it's time now. Don't chicken out on me."

"I'm not afraid. I just don't want to push. I don't want it to be a negative experience. I don't want people saying, 'I'm never going to do *that* again.' "

Heather laughed. "I think we should tell the others we're doing it. We're going to get everyone together for a pre-Christmas dinner. It's not going to happen if we don't take charge."

"Won't everybody just get their backs up? Or Joss anyway. We want her to come, but if we tell her what she has to do or that she has to see us all together, she'll just tell us to go to hell."

"Let me deal with Joss. I know she'll push back, but she loves the family, no matter how she might act. It will still mean something to have everybody get together. It will be hard for her, just like it will be hard for you… and me. But that doesn't mean we call it off. She'll come if we work on her."

Zachary was buoyed up. Maybe it would be possible. Maybe it wouldn't take them another thirty years to get up the courage to all get together.

"If you think so. You want me to start to talk to people, then? Do you think we should set a date? Or poll for a date?"

"Let's just start by saying that we are planning to do it. I'll talk to Joss. You can talk to Tyrrell. Tyrrell can talk to Vince and Mindy. Okay? But tell them we're doing it. It's going to happen."

"Okay." Zachary nodded. He swallowed, straining at the lump in his throat. "Sounds good. Thanks, Feathers."

10

Kenzie arrived home just as Zachary was ending his call with Heather. He put his phone in his pocket and smiled at her, though he was still feeling a little emotional from the call and Heather's reassurance that they would get the siblings together for dinner.

Kenzie looked at him, eyebrows raised. "You're not ready?"

Zachary looked into the kitchen. He should have started dinner for her. But she hadn't told him she was on her way home or wanted anything particular.

"Uh, I can put something on now. What did you want?"

She gestured at him with an open palm. "I want you cleaned up and ready for family dinner."

His brain bounced from one possibility to another, confused. He had just been talking to Heather about the family dinner, but that wasn't yet finalized. They didn't have a date, let alone agreement from the others to be there. He wasn't ready for dinner with Kenzie, but it wasn't like they usually did anything formal.

They sometimes had family dinner with the Petersons, but that was usually on a Sunday, and he was pretty sure it wasn't Sunday. Kenzie tried not to work on Sunday. She would go in for a while Saturday morning and then take the rest of the weekend off, unless something really bad or political happened that needed her immediate attention. And now that Dr. Cook was there, he could handle any emergencies.

Zachary slapped his forehead as his brain fastened on to the next possibility. Family dinner with Kenzie's parents. They had asked for the chance to have more regular meals with Kenzie and Zachary. Actually, they had asked for equal time with the Petersons, but Kenzie said there was no way she would be able to pin both of her parents down for dinner more than once every few months. It wouldn't be every second week like their visits to Lorne and Pat.

"Is that today? I completely forgot."

And she had reminded him that morning at breakfast. He had promised to be dressed and ready to go when she got home. Zachary's guts knotted.

"I'm so sorry, Kenzie. I'll do a quick change now. I'll be ready in five minutes. I'm sorry, it was on the calendar and everything. You even reminded me this morning. I have been so wrapped up in this case…"

Her face was carefully composed. Neutral, rather than showing her anger at Zachary's falling down once more on his obligations after multiple promises had been made. "Well, you'll have to catch us up on it. I'm sure that will make interesting dinner conversation," she said lightly.

Zachary swallowed and hurried toward the main bathroom to strip down, spray his pits, and run the electric razor over his stubble. That done, he dashed to the bedroom to throw on a button-up shirt and pants with a crease. Back to the bathroom to grab his phone, wallet, and keys out of the pockets of the clothes he had discarded there, and to the back door, where Kenzie stood absolutely still waiting for him.

"If you want to go ahead, I'll be right out," he assured her, grabbing his winter coat and threading his arms through the sleeves.

She pivoted and went back into the garage to wait in her car. Zachary blew out his breath, trying to calm his speeding heart and the feeling of dread and doom that he always got when he screwed up badly with Kenzie. He almost preferred the way that his ex-wife

Bridget used to tear a strip off him when he stepped out of line and did something really stupid. At least then, it was out in the open, and he knew exactly how she felt and what she expected of him. Verbal abuse was familiar and expected. Kenzie's tight-lipped, uninflected responses made him more sure that the worst was yet to come. One day, she would break up with him over something like this, and it would all be over.

He hesitated between dress shoes and boots in the wintry weather and decided he'd better stick with dress shoes, choosing formality over practicality. Then, one more pause before he went into the garage. Should he take an anti-anxiety pill before he left? It would calm him down and help him be more relaxed during dinner.

But it would also make him tired and distant, and he wanted to be fully engaged and to catch any nonverbal signals from Kenzie.

He didn't take anything before he left. He could always take something later in the evening. Excuse himself from the dinner and swallow one in the restroom. He always had them on him. He patted his pockets to be sure, then followed Kenzie out to her car.

It was too cold for the little red convertible. Kenzie had commented several times that it was time to put it up for the winter and rely on his car instead, but she couldn't seem to bring herself to. She loved her "baby" and didn't want to spend the next few months just driving Zachary's car or getting a short-term lease for herself.

Zachary slid into the passenger seat and pulled his seatbelt across, clicking it into place. Kenzie's was already on. Without a word of acknowledgment, she started the car, reversed out of the garage, and they were on their way.

The drive to the restaurant was uncomfortable. Zachary tried not to be distracted by anything else, to give Kenzie his full attention, but she was driving and didn't want him staring at her. He kept an eye on the time, and they reached the restaurant at the appointed time.

Kenzie's lips were pressed together. He knew that for her, being "on time" meant getting there early, preferably before her dinner companions were all assembled. That was the way it was done in the Kirsch family. Even though Zachary had always thought that being fashionably late was the thing for the rich and powerful.

They had apparently arrived there just behind Walter and Lisa, who were still in the reception area of the richly appointed restaurant. Lisa's dinner jacket had a faux fur collar, and Walter wore a tie that probably cost more than everything Zachary was wearing. Kenzie had not changed at the house, but Zachary saw as he helped her out of her coat that she was wearing a smart blouse, jacket, and pleated pants with too-high heels that made her several inches taller than Zachary. He couldn't remember if she had been wearing the blouse and pants when she had left for work that morning. She certainly had not been wearing the heels. A great observer of human behavior he was. So much for being a private investigator who took note of every detail around him.

"Mother," Kenzie greeted, touching her mother's shoulders and giving her air kisses. Walter wasn't having any of that and gave her a tight hug before releasing her. Walter shook Zachary's hand. Zachary always expected a crushing grip from him, the alpha male challenging the younger, smaller man's claim on his daughter. But Walter spent all day shaking hands. A battle for who had the tighter grip would just leave him with bruised knuckles that would hinder the next day's handshaking. So instead, his handshake was firm, brisk, and turned into a supportive two-handed shake when he clapped his other hand over Zachary's arm.

"Zachary, how are you doing?"

"Fine, thank you, sir," Zachary replied immediately, the words springing to his lips without any thought. He had been well-trained in social greetings by numerous foster moms, institutions, and Bridget. "And how are you?"

"No need to 'sir' me, Zachary. I've told you that before. Would you like me to call you Mr. Goldman?"

"No," Zachary laughed, "please don't!"

Walter slapped him on the back, chuckling, and driving

Zachary into Lisa, who insisted on an actual kiss on the cheek, not just an air kiss. Zachary restrained himself from wiping his cheek after, though he worried about lipstick. They all turned to the restaurant hostess, who greeted Walter and Lisa by name and offered to escort them to their table.

Once seating arrangements were made, Zachary breathed out heavily a few times, trying to calm himself down. It was just Kenzie's parents. He'd had a meal with them before and had enjoyed their expertly directed dinner conversation. They had not put him on the spot or made him feel awkward about his work or his mental health issues. They didn't look down their noses and imply that they didn't believe he was good enough for Kenzie. But they were rich and powerful, and that was enough to intimidate Zachary, no matter how courteous they were.

Drinks were ordered. Still unsure whether he would need to take an anxiety pill before the night was up, Zachary stuck with Coke while Kenzie and Lisa had wine and Walter a Scotch.

"So, tell me what you have been up to lately," Walter invited as they pored over their menus.

Zachary glanced aside at Kenzie, looking for any warning that she wasn't comfortable with him answering or wanted to send the conversation in a different direction. She simply smiled at him and looked back down at her menu.

"Well, I've just started on a new missing person case," he answered hesitantly. "A missing child."

"Oh, dear," it was Lisa who responded first. "How tragic. What happened?"

"Today was my first day on the investigation, so I don't have all the answers yet. But she was out at a mall play center with her mother and disappeared."

"Just vanished?"

Zachary nodded. "They haven't been able to find any security footage that shows her leaving. Don't have any witnesses or a description of the person who left with her. She was just there, playing, supervised by her mother, protected by security gates and guards, and then she disappeared."

"That's terrible," Walter shook his head. "Her poor parents must be frantic. Do they think that she just wandered off? Or that she was taken? Was there a ransom demand? I guess if this just happened, you don't have any of those answers yet."

"It happened a few days ago. There was no ransom demand. No contact from anyone."

"And no body," Kenzie said, letting them know that the little girl hadn't turned up on her table. "They think it was a parental abduction, don't they?"

"That's the police theory at the moment. They think that the father took her and left the country with her."

"Oh, it's one of those parental things," Lisa nodded. "Always so heartbreaking. One parent stealing the child from the other. And you never know whose story to believe."

"Well, in this case, the father has never had anything to do with her since the day she was born. Didn't even ask for visitation or send a birthday card. So the chances he showed up where they were and stole the child…" He trailed off, shaking his head. "I think the truth may be something quite different. But I don't know yet what."

"Can't they just call the authorities in the country she was taken to?" Walter asked. "That would seem to be the obvious course of action. Speak with their embassy, maybe. Get people working on it from that end."

"That doesn't always work," Lisa disagreed. "Haven't you heard any of the stories? It's just dreadful. Sometimes, the children are overseas for years or never see their mothers again. Not all countries are open to dealing with these cases, or have any law under which the non-custodial parent could be charged. I hope it isn't in the Middle East."

Zachary sighed. "It is."

Though Zachary looked at his menu like everyone else, he had no idea what he was going to order when the waitress came over. His ability to read with any comprehension was severely limited by his learning disabilities, the cursive writing, and the names of dishes written in French or another foreign language. He couldn't even pick a dish by comparing the prices and choosing something that was mid-range. There were no prices on the menu at all. Zachary always felt at a distinct disadvantage in fancy restaurants.

He tried to catch Kenzie's eye, hoping she would give him a clue. "The chicken marsala is always wonderful here," or "You must try the veal," or something along those lines. But she looked at the menu and her parents and not at him. One trick he had learned from Bridget was to ask what the special was, and then after due consideration to nod and say he would take that. But the special was often one of the highest priced options on the menu, and he didn't want Walter and Lisa to think he was greedy.

Kenzie ordered something that sounded like fish, which wasn't helpful since Zachary didn't particularly enjoy anything fishy. Everyone looked at Zachary. He motioned to Lisa, "I'm still deciding. Why don't you come back to me?"

Lisa ordered a chicken dish, which sounded nice but was accompanied by a green salad. Zachary would eat salad if he had to, but preferred not to. Walter ordered a steak with potatoes, and that sounded like a winner. He nodded and handed his menu back to the waitress. "I'll have that too, but maybe the six-ounce?" He didn't have a big appetite even when he was hungry and didn't want to embarrass himself by only having a few bites of a huge steak. The waitress nodded, asked him how he wanted his steak and potato prepared, and started moving away.

"They have garlic bread," Kenzie murmured.

"Oh!" Zachary hadn't even thought of that. "Yes, I'd love a side of garlic bread, too."

"Why don't we order garlic bread for the table?" Kenzie suggested, "I'm sure everyone would enjoy it."

And that would give Zachary the chance to eat more than just one slice. His mouth watered just thinking about it, and he gave Kenzie a smile of appreciation.

11

Zachary thought that things had gone pretty well at the family dinner. Kenzie and her parents seemed relaxed, without the underlying tensions they had been experiencing recently. Maybe they were past the trouble over Rhys and his treatment and what Kenzie perceived as her parents interfering with his life behind her back. Zachary was alert for any undercurrents, ready to smooth things over or change the subject. But things went well without his having to say anything.

Not that it was his place to mediate between Kenzie and her parents. She knew them better than he did and, if he had a different opinion on their behavior than she did, she was the one who was most likely to be right.

The food was delicious, of course. He wouldn't expect anything less at a restaurant the Kirsches had picked out. Despite their wealth and influence, Kenzie's parents seemed to be down-to-earth people, and he didn't need to worry about them picking out some weird vegetarian fusion new-agey restaurant.

But when they walked back to the car in the heated underground parking, Kenzie was silent. Zachary reached for her arm to put his hand through and walk arm-in-arm with her as they often did when out on dates, but Kenzie jerked her arm away and did not allow him to walk close to her, much less touch her.

Zachary's stomach, pleasantly full, became uncomfortably heavy and tight. She was still angry. He had hoped it was still over forgetting about the dinner, and not something new he had done at the dinner. He had frequently embarrassed Bridget at fancy dinners by using the wrong fork or saying something she considered gauche or inappropriate. He hadn't been allowed to talk about his work when he had gone places with her, severely limiting his conversational repertoire.

But when Zachary got together with Kenzie and her parents, it was her work they couldn't discuss. Not in any detail, anyway. Corpses and dissections were not appropriate discussions for the dinner table or in polite company.

Even Zachary knew that.

He decided it was best not to try to settle things with Kenzie before they got home. He didn't want to distract her from her driving. She would tell him what was on her mind once they returned to the house.

They drove in absolute silence. Zachary's stomach roiled and he was afraid he would lose his supper when they got home. It wouldn't be nearly as pleasant coming up as it had been going down.

Kenzie didn't say anything when she pulled into the garage and she got out of the car and went into the house. Zachary followed a few steps behind, giving her as much space as possible. He did not want to step on her heels or crowd her. She shot him a look when she stepped in the door, clearly communicating she was still angry at him and the pains he was taking to avoid aggravating her further were not having the desired effect.

"I'm sorry," he tried.

She turned away from him, then changed her mind and turned back to face him. "I don't know what else I can do. We talked about the dinner. It's on your calendar. I reminded you at breakfast. You knew this was a big deal and I wanted you to be ready when I got home. But it's obvious that it is totally unimportant to you." She held up her hand to stop him from responding. "I know that you have disabilities. I know that being distracted from things you don't care about is perfectly normal and not something you can control by willpower. But what am I supposed to do about something that is important to me? We show up there in a rush, almost late, with you all rumpled and half-shaven. Your mind is somewhere else for most of the dinner. This was important to me, Zachary, and you blew it."

He swallowed a few times, trying to stay in control of his emotions. He tried to think of what he could have done differently. How he could have kept the dinner date in mind even when he was working on something else.

"I'm sorry," he said again. "I know I screwed up. I'll try..." he trailed off, still trying to come up with a solution. But he'd never found a solution to his ADHD forgetfulness and distraction.

"Maybe on a day like today, when you know there is something important going on, you could take your meds," Kenzie suggested. "Or you could set more alarms and reminders. Put a big sign on the fridge or a sticky on your computer screen. I don't know. You could at least *try*."

Zachary nodded, unable to find the words. He only took his ADHD meds when he had a particular task he needed to focus on. It hadn't occurred to him that remembering he was going out to dinner with Kenzie and her parents was something he needed to focus on for the whole day. He rubbed his forehead. Maybe the next time Kenzie had an important event, he would take his ADHD prescription in the morning when she reminded him about it. Then he would be able to remember to prepare for it before Kenzie got home.

Except that if he took the prescription in the morning, it would start to wear off right around the time when he needed to remember and get ready for the dinner. He would be rebounding, his symptoms twice as bad as usual. Rather than staying focused on the task at hand, his mind would jump from one thing to another like a rabid squirrel, and his emotions would be very close to the surface.

He remembered the meltdowns he had experienced when he had first started on meds as a child. The prescription he had now was better—extended release with a more gentle taper off—but he could still feel the letdown and rebound as his symptoms rushed back twice as strong as usual. What time did he need to take the prescription for it to last throughout the afternoon and evening, but still taper off by the time Kenzie wanted to go to bed? Noon?

He drilled a knuckle into his forehead, trying to release the tension headache that was gathering there. The combination of the headache, his anxiety, and the rich meal was too much. After quickly toeing off his shoes, he murmured another apology to Kenzie and hurried to the bathroom, where his discarded daytime clothes were still strewn across the floor.

Zachary took the time to wash up and change back into his comfortable clothes after being sick. He looked at the poor shaving job he had done before the dinner and considered tidying it up, but decided that might just be adding insult to injury with Kenzie and disgustedly left it as it was.

He took one of the anti-anxiety pills. It was not shaping up to be a relaxing night. If he wanted to get any sleep at all, he needed to unwind the knot in his gut. After a few deep breaths, he exited the bathroom and looked for Kenzie.

She was in the bedroom, having changed into her warm, comfy jammies. She was rubbing cream on her feet.

"Sorry, I guess something didn't agree with me," he apologized.

"Oh, now the food was bad too? I don't think so, Zachary."

He had been trying to keep from admitting that it was the anxiety and stress of their argument that had made him sick, but he'd made it worse instead. That was par for the course. He sat on the edge of the bed.

"I wish there was something I could do or say that would help," he told her miserably.

"Well, there's not."

At least there wasn't some response she was expecting from him that would wipe it all off the slate. She admitted that there wasn't anything he could do.

"I could have called you this afternoon to remind you," Kenzie said. "And called you before I left work to make sure that you were ready. But I shouldn't have to do that. It shouldn't be my responsibility to make sure that you remember."

"No. I'll try to do some of the things you suggested. More alarms and reminders. But you know that sometimes…"

"You're hyperfocused on something else and don't know the rest of the world exists. I know. What were you working on today? The kidnapping case?"

"Yeah."

"Well, that's good. I'm glad you're working on it. I hate to think of a little girl out there with someone she doesn't know, even if it is her father. She needs as many people on her side as possible. But hopefully… if it's her father, he'll take good care of her, right?"

Of course Kenzie knew that not all parents were loving and good providers. She'd heard Zachary's stories, reports in the news, and seen children on her table at the morgue who had died from abuse. She knew the terrible things that happened in the world, but if the hope that it was *only* a parental abduction made her feel better, he didn't need to try to disabuse her of the notion.

He nodded and made an encouraging sound, not actually saying that she was right.

"I'm just going to stretch out with a book," Kenzie said. "I need time to relax and unwind, and I'm not very good company right now. If you want to watch TV or do whatever to entertain yourself…"

"Okay." He reached out to touch her knee but hesitated, his hand an inch away from it, not sure how she would react.

Kenzie took his hand in hers and gave it a squeeze, then rested their joined hands on her leg briefly. "We'll be fine," she assured him. "Sometimes couples fight."

He nodded, appreciating the reassurance. He was sure she knew, with the time they had been together and the many couple's therapy sessions, that his mind would immediately fasten onto the idea of the catastrophic failure of their relationship. Whenever she got upset about something, he thought he was halfway out the door. Being moved out of foster homes after big blow-ups and the devastating end to his marriage with Bridget had conditioned him to think the worst. Not to mention the decision of his mother to dissolve the family after the fire that fateful Christmas Eve years before. As far as Zachary was concerned, any relationship could go up in flames at any moment.

Kenzie released his hand. "All right, shoo. Give me some space."

Zachary stood up. "Yes, ma'am."

12

Left to his own devices rather than spending the rest of the evening with Kenzie like he normally did, Zachary went back to work. As Kenzie had said, there was a little girl out there somewhere with a stranger and he needed to find out who and where and work on getting her home. He couldn't just relax in front of the TV and surf channels while Claire was missing.

He hadn't yet had a chance to review the information provided by the manager at All Played Out, so he dug the USB stick out from his bag and plugged it into the computer.

It took a while to go through the various video feeds, watching the time indicator at the bottom during the time Rose had said they were at the play place.

He looked at each of the children, who he could separate from the crowd at any point in time. Kids arrived, running into the climbing structures like feral animals released back into the wild. Others left the playground to talk to parents, begging for treats or game tokens, taking bathroom breaks, and responding to calls that it was time to go.

There was no audio track on the recording, but he could remember the noise level. Anyone who wanted to be heard had to shout over the background play and music. When children didn't want to leave yet and had to be dragged out by parents or staff members, Zachary could only imagine the volume of their shrieks and screams. The noise level had been consistently high when he had been there. How could anyone have heard one little girl being grabbed and taken away?

Of course, she could just as easily have been lured out with a toy or treat. Or by a story that her mother was hurt. There were a lot of ways to get a child away from where she was playing, even if she was intelligent and had been well-trained about stranger danger.

Zachary studied the people in the crowd. Was there anyone there without a kid? Someone hanging around paying too much attention to a kid not his own? He looked for the flash of Claire's white-blond hair or for Rose's thin figure, brown hair, and glasses. Eventually, he was rewarded with the sight of Rose walking Claire into the play area and releasing her to play. Like the other children he had watched, Claire excitedly raced to the play equipment. She stopped for an instant to look around at the many different play areas, then picked a rock wall and started to climb. It was just a short wall, not one that required a harness and belaying rope, and in a few seconds, she had scaled it and dived into the cube above it.

There was a maze of passageways, twisting tubes, and slides, and it wasn't long before, despite his best efforts, Zachary had lost track of her. He rewound and tried to follow her progress. But even with the ability to slow down the video, freeze frame, and rewind as necessary, she was out of his sight most of the time.

What had Rose said about it? "Your kid just gets swallowed up by this place." That had certainly been true. He had pictured something far tamer in his mind. The types of playgrounds he had played on as a child or where he had watched Tyrrell's children, Alisha and Mason, play. Sitting on a bench at the edge of the playground, he had been able to see them most of the time and, if they were out of his sight, it was only for a few seconds. All Played Out was a paradise for kids looking for adventure, but a nightmare for parents trying to watch their kids.

He scrubbed the video, looking for the point at which Rose

realized that her daughter was missing. Rose was very intent on her phone, looking up rarely and gazing toward the play equipment, then she dropped her head and continued with her reading, or social media, or whatever research she was doing.

Zachary had thought that she was probably at the play place for an hour or so. He knew it had been several hours before the police had been called, but it must have taken a long time for them to be sure Claire wasn't there, hiding in a ball pit or other hidey-hole.

But it was several hours before he saw Rose leave her table and walk around looking for Claire. It would take a long time for Zachary to go through all that footage at a slow speed, looking for any glimpse of Claire or the man who had supposedly taken her.

He watched Rose's movements getting more frantic as she moved from one play structure to another, looking for the little girl. There was a lump in his throat as he watched, knowing she wouldn't find Claire and would go home alone, devastated and baffled as to what had happened to her child.

Staff members collected around Rose and then spread out to look for the child. After some time looking for Claire, an announcement was made, and children streamed to their parents as they shut down the play so they could make a concerted search for the missing girl. Much easier with all kids matched up with the adults who brought them there.

More employees assembled in the play area, taking instructions on what part of the equipment to check. It was all done very efficiently. It did not take as long as Zachary had imagined for them to thoroughly search the tunnels and ball pits for the girl.

And then the police had been called and began their investigation.

Zachary rubbed his dry, gritty eyes and put the videos aside for a few minutes while he looked at the check-in/check-out log that parents had been required to fill in as they arrived and departed. Rose's handwriting differed from the other names on the page. If she had come in with a friend, they had not signed each other in. And Zachary hadn't seen her enter with anyone else on the tape. They at least had proof that Claire had, in fact, been at the play place and that Rose had not just been attending there in an elaborate attempt to cover up the fact that something bad had already happened to Claire.

He looked at the log carefully, looking for any patterns or anything that seemed unusual. No unaccompanied adults were allowed in, so there was no adult name without at least one child's name beside it. There were no names that were obviously fictitious. No Mickey Mouse or John Smith. And no Amir Osman. What had his girlfriend's name been? Zachary checked his notes and looked for Orna Temple or any similar name on the login sheet.

Tim, the helpful manager at All Played Out, had also provided Zachary with a printout of all the card swipes on the various security doors and gates the afternoon that Claire had gone missing. Long lines of data in tiny type indicated the gate, what time it was accessed, and which prox card had been swiped. Zachary had another printout of which employees had been assigned which cards, and the duty roster for the day showing which employees should—or should not—have been present.

He started going through each list, looking for patterns, painstakingly cross-referencing between them. Matching the card a gate was accessed with to the employee name, and the employee name to the duty roster for every single entry.

The greatest activity was on the entrance and exit card readers. Which of course made sense. That was the only way for the parents and children to get in and out of the play place. They couldn't leave without being checked through any more than they could arrive without being swiped in. Everything seemed perfectly logical and carefully thought out.

But employees had ways of circumventing even the most carefully-thought-out security procedures. Zachary stopped and re-examined one of the door logs. For most of the day, there had been swipes at regular intervals. And then there were several hours in the afternoon when no swipes had been recorded.

Why not?

It had, in fact, been around the time that Claire had disappeared.

Zachary glanced at the window, confirming to himself that it was the dark of night. There would be no one at All Played Out to answer his questions now. And although he had Tim's cell phone number, he didn't think calling in the middle of the night would be taken too well. Especially when he might need the records at All Played Out in order to answer Zachary's questions.

He stared at the identifying numbers and letters of the card sensors, trying to discern what he could from the serial number itself. They didn't appear to be random.

13

enzie came out of the bedroom and into the kitchen where Zachary was working. He rubbed his eyes and looked at her. He had thought that she was already in bed asleep. Maybe she'd had a nightmare or had unwound enough that she wanted him near her now. Maybe needed to cuddle with him to get back to sleep. He opened his mouth to greet her, but she beat him to it.

"Did you ever come to bed?"

Zachary sat there with his mouth open for a second, mind racing. "Uh, I was going to in a few..." His eyes slid over to the system clock on his computer to see just how late it was. He hadn't meant to let so much time pass, but he'd been immersed in the video and logs analysis. As she'd already acknowledged, when he got hyperfocused on a thing, the rest of the world ceased to exist. Kenzie included.

He cleared his throat, playing for time, as he blinked and tried to focus on the status bar.

"Oh..."

"You've been up all night?" Kenzie demanded.

"Uh... I guess I have. I didn't realize it was that late."

"You know you need to sleep. You'll get… *sick* if you don't sleep."

"Yeah." He rubbed the bridge of his nose. Everything was aching. He should have been paying attention to his body signals and realized he'd worked right through the night. "I was so focused on this…" He motioned lamely to the computer screen.

Kenzie shook her head slowly. "Why don't you put the coffee on while I shower? Though I don't think you'd better have any if you are going to try to get in a couple of hours of sleep. You can tell me about it at breakfast, and then I'll go to work and you can hit the sack for a while."

She knew that there were many nights he didn't get more than two or three hours of sleep anyway. He could go to bed now and still be up again by the time most office workers were settling into their day jobs.

She was doing a remarkable job of staying calm and dealing with this new wrinkle after his mistake the day before. Maybe he should take both incidents as a warning that he was getting too deep into the case.

But that was when he solved the puzzles. It wasn't until he lost himself in a project like this that he would find the things the police had missed. Those tiny details that had escaped everyone else's notice, until Zachary brought his hyperfocus to bear.

"I'll put the coffee on," Zachary agreed, standing up and heading for the kitchen so that he wouldn't look back down at his work and lose himself again by the time she got out of the shower.

Kenzie nodded, ran her fingers through her tousled curls, and retreated to the en suite bathroom to shower.

Zachary went directly to the coffee machine, loaded the grounds, and started it brewing. He waited, watching it until it was finished dripping. One cup to help keep his thoughts clear, and then he started getting breakfast on the table.

It wasn't anything complex. Toast and marmalade or jam for Kenzie. A yogurt or granola bar for himself. But it was easy to miss a step if he allowed himself to be distracted by something else. He tried to focus only on his movements and getting everything done efficiently, pushing the kidnapping case out of his mind for the moment. Kenzie had said he could tell her about it while they had breakfast, and he was eager to let her know what he had figured out. It wasn't a huge leap, but at least he was moving things forward a little.

He unwrapped the granola bar while Kenzie was still getting ready so that she didn't have to see the involuntary grimace he made at the crinkling of the wrapper, which also made his toes curl and the hairs on his neck stand up like when he heard the sound of fingernails on the blackboard. Misophonia was one negative effect of his current medication cocktail. Annoying, but not enough of an issue for him to allow them to make any changes to a protocol that was working well otherwise.

Kenzie finished her ablutions and returned to the kitchen, looking relaxed, refreshed, and professional. Sometimes, he wondered how he had managed to land someone like Kenzie, so beautiful, polished, and smart. He felt like such a wreck so much of the time that he didn't have a clue why she let him hang around.

She must see *something* in him.

Kenzie's eyes went to the table, and she nodded, letting Zachary know that he could relax and hadn't forgotten anything obvious. She eyed his coffee cup when he sat down.

"I thought you weren't going to have any coffee."

That had been her suggestion, not his, so he just shrugged. "You know it doesn't keep me awake. It helps to keep me focused."

"I don't know if focused is what you need right now. It looks like you've had enough hyperfocus for a while."

He hadn't checked the mirror to see how bloodshot his eyes were after staring at the computer half the night. They were probably as red as tomatoes. He should have put drops in his eyes before breakfast.

"I'll put a cold compress on for a few minutes once you've gone to work. Before I fall asleep."

"That would probably be a good idea."

He always felt better when she said something like that than "Make sure that you do," which always made him feel rebellious and resentful. He didn't need anyone telling him what to do. It was an attitude he had probably adopted as a teenager. Being a grown man with years of experience, he should realize by now that he could use all the help he could get and that in the time they had been together, Kenzie had been right more often than she had been wrong.

He loved her and tried to respect her wishes and listen to her suggestions; he just couldn't help that little twinge of rebellion when she told him what to do instead of encouraging him to make good choices for himself.

"So…" Kenzie took a bite of her toast and chewed it for a moment. "You made progress, then? You said you were going to tell me what you found."

Zachary nodded. He put his phone on the table, screen on and oriented toward her so she could read it—a long list of serial numbers.

"My first breakthrough was sorting these out so that they made sense."

Kenzie looked down the list of numbers and shook her head. "You put these in some kind of order?"

"Do they look random?"

Kenzie frowned, examining them. "Not random, no. There are repeated sections."

Zachary nodded. He used his finger to scroll down to the same set of numbers organized in a way that made sense to him. Kenzie nodded, looking them over again.

"Okay. I can see the combinations better now. What do these numbers identify?"

"Security doors or gates. Ones that you need a swipe card to get through."

"Oh, I see. First digit is always I or E. Then you have N, S, E, or W—compass points?"

Zachary nodded, impressed that she had gotten it so quickly.

"And then the remainder look like they were just assigned in sequence. Like apartment doors when you go down a hallway."

"Yeah."

"So what are I and E? They must mean something."

He grinned. "They do."

She pushed the phone back toward him, motioning him to get on with it. "So tell me. What are they?"

"Interior and Exterior."

"Ahh. That makes sense! So how does this help you solve your case?"

"Because someone took that little girl out of there without having to sign the log-in/log-out sheet and without being noticed by anyone."

"And the numbering of the doors is significant?"

"Mostly because this one..." he dug the slip of paper out of his pocket and put it on the table in front of her, "is an E door."

"Exterior. And you think she was taken out of this door. Because...? You suspect the person whose swipe card was used? Or there was something on the video?"

"Because no one used a swipe card."

"I'm going to need more coffee." Kenzie took another swallow. She looked at him challengingly. "No one used a swipe card? How do you know that, and what does it mean?"

"This door was seeing plenty of activity, at least once every twenty to thirty minutes, all day long. Almost. There were no cards logged between two and five, the window for the abduction."

"Why not?"

"Well, I took a little field trip over there to have a look and test my theory."

"You went over there when?"

"Uh... last night," Zachary admitted, with dawning awareness that maybe he should have saved this discussion for dinner so that she would think he had gone over there during the day. In the daylight, when sane people ventured out to investigate crime scenes.

But he was a PI. He had done plenty of nighttime surveillance. Driving to the mall and looking around with his flashlight was much more pleasant than sitting in front of some target's house for hours, hoping to catch a glimpse of them doing something wrong.

"You went to this place in the middle of the night, while I was sleeping, to test a theory."

"I armed the burglar alarm," Zachary assured her, "and I wasn't gone for more than an hour."

He didn't want her to think he had abandoned her or didn't have her safety in mind. It hadn't seemed like he was taking a significant risk. Not that he was the best judge of risky behavior. He always jumped first and thought second. Impulsivity would be his undoing. Luckily, not this time.

"Is this place even open at night?" Kenzie shook her head at the ridiculousness. Of course, a child's play place wasn't open in the middle of the night. Maybe if they wanted to turn it into an adult playground at night, with some neon lighting or black light, maybe adults in camo gear playing first-person shooter games live…

"No. But I didn't need it to be open to test my theory. I just wanted to verify that E meant exterior door and see if there were any signs that this door on the south side of the building—" he tapped the scrap of paper on the table— "was left open for some time during the day."

"How could you tell if it had been left open for some time during the day?" Kenzie asked skeptically. "Did you *interview* the door lock?"

Zachary grinned. He took a bite of his granola bar, which he had forgotten up until that point, and chewed it slowly, savoring the anticipation on Kenzie's face. She hadn't even looked at the clock to see if she was on time for work.

"Because I found upside-down buckets, a pile of cigarette butts, and a broken cinder block outside that door."

"Showing that someone propped the door open with a cinder block and sat out there smoking during their shift."

Zachary approved. "Exactly. And not just once in a while, and not just one person. There were a lot of cigarette butts. Different brands. People are regularly propping that door open in the afternoon for an unauthorized smoke break because they don't want to get caught by management swiping their cards there when they are supposed to be doing something else."

"And they are leaving it open for hours, not just sneaking out for ten minutes and then shutting it again?"

"Yes. Because you have to swipe to open it. So even if you are only going out for thirty seconds, you are still logged as leaving the building. One person opens it, and then leaves it propped for everyone else, so none of them get logged swiping out. Then, at the end of the day, they let it shut again."

"So for that three-hour period, there are no swipes."

"Exactly. And since everyone is taking advantage of it, just leaving the door open, there isn't always someone there to see if, say, someone walks out of there with a kid one day. Or if they did, the employee would have to explain what he was doing outside and why he wasn't logged out."

"So do you think it is an inside job? Someone who works there or has worked there?"

"I don't know. It could be. No telling for sure. If I was trying to find a way to get into and out of a building like that without detection, the first thing I would do is walk around the building and look for weak points. Open or unlocked windows, doors, weak locks, and a pile of cigarettes to signal that the door is frequently open for workers to take their smoke breaks. And then I would sit out there, watching, and see what the pattern was. Probably for a few days or a week."

"That would mean that it was random. A stranger kidnapping."

"Maybe, maybe not. It sounds like Rose took Claire there fairly often. Did she mention it to people? Was she seen there? Followed? Was it someone who hung around and decided they liked the looks of Claire?"

"So it could be either. Random or targeted."

"Unfortunately. We can't eliminate anyone unless they have an alibi that absolutely places them somewhere else during the kidnapping."

"Well, I still think it is progress. Any time you get closer to the truth, you're closer to solving the case."

"That's right." Zachary had been telling himself something similar every time he reminded himself that he was nowhere near cracking the case. It was progress. Not a solution, not yet. But he was getting closer. He was starting to gather details that were important. Finding out how the kidnapping took place helped him put himself into the criminal's mind, and putting himself into the criminal's mind meant he had a chance of figuring out who it was and why they had done it.

"Do you think it was the father?" Kenzie asked, putting the last piece of toast into her mouth.

Zachary shook his head slowly. "It's too early to tell. That's what the police think. It is a pretty big coincidence that right after she is abducted, he leaves the country with a little girl."

"Yeah. That's pretty damning. If I was the police, I would want to question him."

"But unfortunately, they can't. He's in a country that is not known for cooperating in child custody matters."

"Does the mother think that he took her?"

"If she did, she probably wouldn't have hired me. She would just be involved with trying to contact him through one means or another. Maybe she would get on a plane and go out there herself."

"If she has the money for something like that."

"She seems to be fairly well off. If not, she could borrow. Take it out of her mortgage, get a loan from the bank, from her parents. Crowdfund. There are a lot of people who would be eager to help rescue a poor little girl from a misogynistic country."

"So she doesn't think it was the father."

"The thought never even entered her mind until the police brought it up. He'd never shown any interest in even seeing Claire since she was born. Never asked for visitation. But he did ask for a picture of her."

"And did the mother give it to him?"

Zachary had another sip of coffee. "Yeah. She gave it to him."

14

Amir Osman might have gone underground a couple of years ago, but it had not been hard to find his parents' names and address. Zachary knew a little about them from Heather's background research on Amir. They had immigrated to the US from Saudi Arabia before Amir's birth. They were comfortably well-off and lived in a nice neighborhood. They had a couple of daughters who were younger than Amir. They were Muslim, as was most of the population of Saudi Arabia, and appeared to be active in their mosque. There was not a very big Arab population in Vermont, so Zachary wasn't sure why they had decided to settle there. Or what kind of prejudice they might face by being the only Middle Eastern faces in their neighborhood and schools. That being the case, they might be wary of a stranger showing up on their doorstep.

But he had to assume that if they were targeted by hate groups, their attackers would want to remain anonymous and would only commit their vandalism under cover of darkness, and any threats would be sent through the mail or over the internet, not face-to-face on their front step.

The house was bigger than Kenzie's, an attractive bungalow surrounded by a large yard. Covered with snow now, but probably a rich green lawn in the summertime, landscaped with flowering trees, bushes, and pretty gardens. It was located in a nice neighborhood and reminded him a little of Lorne's and Pat's house, always well-maintained and flourishing under Pat's green thumb.

Zachary locked his car, armed the alarm, and double-checked them twice more before taking the sidewalk up to the house and ringing the doorbell. It was a few minutes before the door opened, and he faced a Middle Eastern woman of about sixty. He had been prepared for traditional dress, with robes and a headscarf and possibly a veil, but she was dressed like any other woman of her age in the neighborhood. Slacks and a pretty print blouse, makeup, jewelry, and sensible shoes. She raised her plucked eyebrows questioningly.

"Mrs. Osman? I wonder if I can talk to you and your husband about a private matter. Is he at home?"

He knew that her husband was retired, but didn't know if he spent his days at home or had a consulting business, volunteer work, or a hobby like fishing that took him out of the home for significant amounts of time.

"What private matter?" she asked. She still had an accent, pronounced even in those few words.

"It has to do with your son, Amir."

She considered this for a moment, and then opened the door wider to admit him. "Come in."

Zachary entered. He didn't see many cultural items in the living room he walked into. Furniture, bookcase, family pictures on the wall. Like any other living room in the neighborhood. There was an adjoining dining room with a large, heavy table, and a doorway beyond that led into the kitchen. It was clean and neat and smelled faintly of incense.

He sat in the chair he was directed to. Mrs. Osman called for her husband. "Hassan? We have company."

Mr. Osman joined them. He wore a white collared shirt and pants with an elastic waist. Typical retirement dress. He didn't wear the red headdress that Zachary often saw in pictures of Saudi men. His hair was neatly trimmed, and he was clean-shaven.

Zachary stood back up to shake hands with him, and then they sat down, husband and wife exchanging glances.

"My name is Zachary Goldman," Zachary introduced himself. "I'm a private investigator. I'm looking into the disappearance of Amir's daughter."

Mrs. Osman looked alarmed. "Maeve? What happened? We haven't heard anything about this!"

"No, not Maeve. Claire."

"Claire?" They looked at each other, both looking confused. "Who is Claire? You must have the wrong person."

"Claire is Amir's daughter with Rose Bircher."

"Rose? I remember Rose from when they went to school. She was here once or twice. But Amir didn't have a daughter with her."

"Actually, he did. I know she wasn't part of his life, so it isn't surprising that you didn't know anything about her. But she is now missing, and... I'm surprised the authorities didn't reach out to you. They are trying to reach Amir in Saudi Arabia."

"That doesn't make any sense. Why would they want to reach him there? He obviously can't have anything to do with a girl disappearing here in Vermont, no matter who she is."

"She disappeared the same day that he left for Saudi Arabia. Which is a little suspicious, you must admit."

Mrs. Osman shook her head. "Suspicious how? He couldn't have had anything to do with her disappearance. He has his own family to look after."

"Maeve?" Zachary asked. She had to be Orna Temple's daughter.

"Yes, Maeve and Orna. He went to Saudi with them."

"Why?"

Hassan Osman leaned forward in his seat. "What business is that of yours? We have no idea who you are, Mr. Goldman. Why would we give you any information? We don't owe you any explanation."

"I can show you my identification if you like."

Hassan scoffed. "What good would that do? We still don't know you from Adam, and identification can be forged. We've never seen you before. You aren't a friend of Amir's. You could be Orna's ex-husband, for all we know. Why would we give you any information?"

"What do you know about Orna's ex?"

Hassan looked Zachary over and glanced aside at his wife. "He doesn't look like Orna described. He was… a bigger man."

She nodded, agreeing. "But he could send someone else in his place to ask questions and try to confuse things. This story of a missing girl doesn't make any sense."

Zachary considered how to best approach it. "I'm sorry to just spring this on you. I can understand how confusing it must be. You knew Rose when she and Amir were going to school."

"Yes. Of course."

"Rose became pregnant with Claire, but she and Amir didn't stay together and he wasn't part of Claire's life. He didn't pay child support or have visitation or anything like that. They saw each other occasionally at events, but not romantically. They never got back together or talked about being a family or sharing custody of Claire."

"How do you know she is Amir's?"

"I don't have any proof. I'm just going by what Rose told me. And you know her, so you can judge from what you know of her whether she is telling the truth or not."

"She was always very straightforward," Hassan admitted. "I don't think she ever lied or tried to mislead us."

"If you want to, you can call her and check my story with her. She didn't send me here specifically, but she hired me to investigate Claire's disappearance."

"How could this little girl disappear? What happened to her?"

"She was in a play place at the mall, and someone took her away from there. It was the same day that Amir went to Saudi Arabia. With a girl Claire's age."

"Maeve. They took Maeve to Saudi," Mrs. Osman insisted. "We don't know anything about this Claire."

"She is five years old, with blond hair."

"Maeve is five. But she has dark hair. It is a coincidence. She isn't even Amir's biological child. He didn't know Orna when he was going to school."

"Maeve is Orna's daughter with her ex? What's his name?"

"Michael."

"Michael Temple? Or is that Orna's maiden name?"

"Michael Temple," Hassan confirmed.

A bigger man, they had said. To Zachary's ears, it sounded more significant than just someone taller than he was, which was true of most men. Someone who used his bigger size and strength as a weapon.

The police believed that Amir had left the country with Claire and gone to Saudi Arabia because they wouldn't extradite him and return Claire to her mother. But what if he had gone to Saudi Arabia for another reason?

"Was Michael abusive? Is that why they went to Saudi?"

"They didn't do anything wrong. Orna has custody of Maeve. She is allowed to take her wherever she likes," Mrs. Osman insisted.

"Her ex doesn't have any rights? Visitation? Shared custody? Did Michael give her permission to take Maeve there?"

He already knew the answer, of course. A controlling ex would not have permitted Orna to take his daughter around the world, where they would both be out of his reach.

"I don't know anything about the details," she admitted. "But Maeve is her daughter. She has the right to take her wherever she wants to. And it has nothing to do with this other girl disappearing."

Zachary couldn't reconcile it in his mind. Was it just a coincidence? It seemed highly unlikely that Amir would take his girlfriend's daughter to Saudi Arabia the same day that his biological daughter was kidnapped. But sometimes, the inexplicable did happen.

"Why don't you tell me about Michael?" he suggested.

More exchanged glances. These were private people who were not accustomed to sharing their daughter-in-law's private troubles with a stranger. But they also didn't want their son to be mixed up in the kidnapping of another little girl or for Zachary to believe that there had been something wrong or illegal with his taking Orna and Maeve to Saudi Arabia. If Zachary understood the circumstances, they were sure he would believe Amir had done the right thing.

"He is a terrible person," Mrs. Osman said eventually. "He hurt Orna. He even hurt Maeve. She had to get away from him. But it didn't matter what she did, he kept coming back. Finding them, stalking them."

Zachary thought about what Heather had found, or had not been able to find. Withdrawal from social networks. A fake employer. Fake address. Orna's lack of an internet presence or anything that would show up in an online search. Maybe Amir was not doing something illegal or questionable, but simply trying to avoid a stalker.

"Did they go to the police?"

"Over and over again. She had a restraining order against him. But that isn't any protection. Even if the police catch him violating it, he goes to jail for a day or two and then he is back again. There aren't any real consequences unless he kills her. And then they would still have to prove it. You see these guys in the news, on TV movies, how they kill their wives and hide her body, and no one can prove that they did anything. They walk around free for years afterward."

"What did he want from her? Did he want her back?"

"I don't think these people have any logical plan in mind," Hassan said gravely. "They just follow an impulse, a compulsion. They can't stop themselves. And it just keeps escalating and escalating until something terrible happens."

Zachary shifted uncomfortably. He knew what it was like to want someone so much. To be unable to resist the compulsions to check on her, to follow her, even just to drive by the house to see if the lights were on. It took a lot of work, medication, and therapy to break him out of that track. A person had to really want it and be willing to put a lot of work into overcoming such a strong compulsion.

"Did he harm her?"

"I told you he hurt both of them."

"Before she left. Yes. But what about afterward? When she was gone out of the house and he followed her. Stalked her. Did he hurt her then, too?"

"I don't know." Both of them shook their heads. Mrs. Osman was the one who answered. "They did not tell us all the details. It was horrible, and they did not want to discuss it in front of Maeve. Can you imagine everything that little girl had been through? She was such a serious, solemn child. You knew just looking at her that she had seen things that no grown-up should have to see."

Zachary made a noise to encourage her to go on.

"Orna didn't like to talk about it and Amir didn't want to disrespect her. I don't know all of what happened. They didn't really say much about it until they decided to go to Saudi. Then they came to talk to us, to find out how they could emigrate."

"So you helped them with the paperwork?"

"No," Hassan waved his hand back and forth to negate this. "We gave them the names of people to get in touch with. Contacts who could help them. That is all. They did all the paperwork and other arrangements on their own."

Because they had wanted to? Or because Mr. and Mrs. Osman had refused to help with the kidnapping of the little girl?

"You didn't see the passports?"

Mrs. Osman blinked. "Why would we see the passports?"

"I can't see why you would. But I am curious."

"No. We didn't see any of the work that they did. They handled that themselves. They just told us they had all the approvals they needed and would be going soon."

"This was planned for months," Hassan told Zachary. "They didn't just pick up and go on the spur of the moment because they had stolen someone else's daughter! That does not make any sense."

Zachary couldn't work it out, either. If it had all been a big show for Amir to get his daughter out of the country, then what had happened to Maeve? Was she being babysat by a friend until Orna could come back and retrieve her? And then what? How would she get Maeve to Saudi Arabia when, as far as the officials were concerned, she was already there? Or would they even check that? Was it possible to take both girls out of the country on the same passport without anyone questioning how she had gotten back to the US in between? And wouldn't they know that the officials would put a flag on their passports after the kidnapping?

Zachary scratched the back of his neck, thinking about it.

"And Amir never said anything to you about Claire. Never told you that he might have had a child or that Rose had a baby."

"No. He never said anything," Mrs. Osman insisted. "If he had, we would have wanted to see her. We would have told him that he had to take care of his own. Children are a gift from God. If he brought a child into the world, he should take care of her. Have a place in her life." The woman grimaced and shook her head. "My heart is broken at the thought that Amir has another daughter and something has happened to her. It is unthinkable."

15

Zachary sat in front of his computer, chewing on a pen, thinking about what he had learned from Amir's parents. Of course they had told him that Amir was a good boy and not at fault for what he had chosen to do. He had expected them to say that he had nothing to do with any kidnapping. But he had not anticipated the information about Orna and Maeve being stalked and harassed by her ex, which explained many of the holes in their profiles of Amir and Orna. It explained why he had gone quiet a couple of years earlier and why they had chosen to emigrate to Saudi Arabia, something Zachary had never seen anyone do before.

He wasn't sure yet what it meant to his investigation.

Had anything changed? Amir had a legitimate reason to be in Saudi Arabia and, as far as his parents knew, it had been Maeve he had taken with him. He had a reason to take her with him, but he didn't have a reason to take Claire. Not unless he thought that Rose wasn't taking good care of her.

If he was so concerned about Maeve and about her being able to stay with her mother where she belonged, and he had never been involved in Claire's life, then what reason would he have to take her away from Rose unless he thought she was being abused or neglected? He had a daughter. He didn't need a second one to complete his family. He hadn't thought her enough of a part of his family to introduce her to his parents or even tell them of her existence. The only things that pointed to him being the possible kidnapper were the timing of his departure and the fact that he was the girl's biological father.

Zachary tapped his pen on the desk. Was there any possibility that Rose was a negligent or abusive mother? The fact that she had hired Zachary to investigate her daughter's disappearance did not negate the possibility. She could still be upset about the loss of her daughter and want to know who had done it and to get her back, even if she were abusive. Zachary had known plenty of abusive parents who seemed to love and be very attached to their children despite their propensity for violence. They would wail and weep over their children being apprehended, roar and rage over the injustice of it, swear that they would change and that it had only happened once.

He would have to see if he could find out from someone whether she had ever been investigated by DCF. Maybe stop by to visit a few neighbors to see what they thought of her. Sometimes, neighbors saw or heard things, even if they didn't feel confident enough about abuse to make a report.

Zachary's phone rang. He looked at the screen before answering it and was surprised to see *Department of State* splashed across the caller ID. A wrong number?

"Goldman Investigations," he greeted.

"Is this Mr. Zachary Goldman?" a careful, refined voice inquired, diction precise.

"Yes, this is Zachary."

Apparently not a wrong number.

"I am told that you are making inquiries into the abduction of Claire Bircher."

Even more surprising. Since when did the Department of State know anything about his investigations? And even if they did, why would they be calling to inquire so politely, rather than having a low-level lackey call him up to tell him to stay out of the way and not get involved in their case?

"Well, my client list and cases are confidential," he said slowly. "But I would certainly be interested in how you heard that."

"Let us say we have a mutual friend."

Rose? Surely, she would have told Zachary if she'd had contact with someone at the Department of State who was willing to talk to him. He had the impression that she had been locked out of the investigation. No bureaucrat wanted to deal with a hysterical parent. Matters of state proceeded slowly. They could take years to be resolved, and parents thought that they should have their kids back in a few days. The cases that Zachary had read about—the real-life cases, not TV dramas—had all taken years to be resolved, with a lot of pushing from the parents and others who had an interest in the child.

"And this mutual friend told you to call me?"

"He suggested that it might be beneficial for us to speak."

He. Not Rose, then.

"Well, I would be happy to discuss it... if our friend thinks that it would help *me* out."

He wasn't interested if the Department of State representative just wanted to pump him for the details that his investigation had turned up. He was looking for someone who could give him some information on the international end of things.

"We both want the same thing, don't we?"

"I don't know yet. Are you interested in finding Claire?" Zachary asked bluntly.

"Of course. It is a tragedy to see a child taken away from a loving parent. We are all for getting her back and reuniting her with her mother."

Zachary had too many questions to even know where to start.

"We should get together, then. Do you want to meet somewhere?"

"Well," there was a muffled laugh from his caller. "Since I am in Washington and you are in Vermont, I'm not sure there will be a convenient place for both of us. How about a videoconference?"

"Sure, I could do that. Or we can just do this over the phone if you like. I thought that you would want to meet in person."

"In the age of technology, we find it much more efficient to deal with phone and video hookups than to travel across the country or make other people come to us."

Zachary nodded. "Let me just get my thoughts in order… how sure are you that Amir Osman is the kidnapper?"

"His sudden departure for Saudi Arabia is quite telling."

"But did you know that he took his girlfriend and her daughter there to escape a stalker?"

There were several long seconds of silence from the Department of State.

"I didn't catch your name," Zachary told him.

"Oh, that was rude of me. Of course. My name is Derek Schultz. With The Office of Children's Issues, of course."

"Mr. Schultz. So you weren't aware that Amir's girlfriend has a restraining order against her ex, but that has not prevented him from stalking her, confronting her, and abusing her and the girl?"

"That was not mentioned to us, no."

"You only looked into Amir?"

"The police looked into him. The biological father is always the suspect in a case like this. They were estranged. He left the country suddenly, with a girl matching her description, fleeing to a non-Hague Convention country. So, yes… he looked suspicious. The police should have done the background work on other reasons that he might have had to leave the country."

"I talked to his parents today. Apparently, Amir and Orna have been working on the paperwork for this trip for months. They did want to get away from a parent. But from Michael Temple, not from Rose Bircher."

"That is an interesting development."

"So… what have you been able to do on your end? Have you been able to contact Amir?"

"No. We don't have a phone number or address for him. We have been doing what we can with the US Embassy in Saudi, but it is not an easy matter. Since they are not signatories to the Hague

Convention, it is much more difficult to get a child back from Saudi Arabia than from many other countries, where there is a set authority and procedure in place. The Saudis are… less likely to help an American citizen whose child has been taken there. Especially by the father, who has more rights in that country than the mother."

"So you haven't been able to talk to him? To get his side of the story or find out if he even has her?"

"No. As I said…"

"I hear you. These things take time. But we don't know how much time this little girl has. If she was *not* taken by Amir, then she could still be here in Vermont or being trafficked to another state or country, and her life could be in imminent danger. It could be some violent psychopath."

Zachary gave an involuntary shudder. He was intentionally trying to use triggering words to prod the snail's pace Department of State forward. But he hadn't meant to trigger himself. His mind went back to his own dark place, held in a cabin away from civilization by a violent psychopath who had candidly told Zachary all the cruel and depraved things that he planned to do to Zachary both before and after he killed him. Zachary had been under the control of a drug cocktail that had kept him awake and alert, but unable to defend himself beyond a few grunts of protest, which had entertained his torturer.

"Mr. Goldman."

Zachary cleared his throat, wishing the nightmares were as easy to clear away. "Zachary," he corrected hoarsely.

"Zachary. I thought we had lost the connection for a moment."

"Yeah, the phone was acting up. I couldn't hear you either. I think… we really need to know whether Amir has Claire. If he only has Maeve, that's a different matter. If he doesn't have Claire, then someone else does."

"Of course he is going to say that it is Maeve."

"Yeah, you'll need to get someone from the Embassy over there to see her face-to-face and confirm that it is the right girl. I don't have a current picture of Maeve. The only one I have is a couple of years old, and children change a lot during that length of time."

"I will see if I can get something more recent. The photo on her passport…"

"Might be her, and might be Claire. Amir asked for a picture of Claire. I don't know… I worry that it might have been to falsify the passport. He might have wanted to muddy the waters even if he didn't take Claire. To make it so that if Michael Temple tried to use facial recognition technology to track her, he would hit a dead end."

"We can get another photo of her," Schultz agreed immediately. "There will be other sources. School photos, grandparents, classmates, social media."

"You won't find anything on social media. I'm not sure of the other sources. They have been trying to live under the radar to avoid Michael Temple for a couple of years. Orna might not have allowed her to be photographed during that time, for fear that it would help Michael to find them."

"I see. Do you have a suggestion, then?"

"Not a good one. Age progress the two-year-old photograph, but it will still only be a guess. Find out from the grandparents if she has any identifying features—moles, birthmarks, some other unusual physical characteristic."

There was a pause, and Zachary pictured Schultz writing these ideas down on a notepad.

"Good. Would you send me the photograph you have?"

"Sure."

He gave Zachary his email address.

"And could you send me the picture from the passport?" Zachary suggested. "I can show it to Rose and see whether it is the picture that she gave Amir or whether it really is Maeve."

"Good idea," Schultz agreed.

"And you'll pressure the Embassy to track Amir down? The police are not looking for Claire here because they think she is in Saudi Arabia. If she isn't… there may be something they can do, other leads they can follow."

"Yes. I will follow up with our people there."

"Get back to me... and to the police."

16

With someone else looking after the Saudi angle, Zachary felt more comfortable investigating the possible domestic suspects. He had the feeling that the police had been blinded by their investigative bias, as Rose had feared, and he needed to look at some of the other options before the clock ran out for Claire. Children who were the victims of stranger abduction didn't typically last longer than three days, the point at which Zachary had come into the investigation. It had now been almost a week, and the chances she was still alive and well were slim if she had been taken by someone who didn't have an emotional connection to her.

Rose had given Zachary the names of a few friends, especially those she'd had during college. Those who had gone to school with the two of them might have some insight into Amir or how he felt about having a daughter with Rose. He might have told her that he never intended to pursue any custody arrangements, but that might just have been to put her at ease so as to catch her off guard. They might also have an idea of who other than Amir might have targeted her

He would also find out whether the neighbors had seen

anything or had any suspicions. Neighbors sometimes saw a lot more than they appeared to. Zachary could tell some stories…

Checking the time, Zachary decided to make some phone calls. It was toward the end of the average office workday and people would be tired and bored, ready to go home, happy for any distraction to take them away from their work until it was time to clock out.

He looked over the list he had compiled and picked out Jenna Patriot. He had no reason to pick one person over another, so he just picked one at random, going by his gut. Maybe it was because he had some association with the name; maybe it was how Rose had described her, her voice or body language. He didn't know, but he would just keep calling people until he had some forward movement on the case.

His guess about people wanting to be distracted at the end of the day seemed to hold, as Jenna answered the phone before it rang a second time.

"Jenna here."

"Jenna, my name is Zachary Goldman. I don't know whether Rose said anything to you, but I am looking into the disappearance of her daughter…"

There was a sharp intake of breath.

"Are you kidding? Oh my goodness. Poor Rose. She must be absolutely frantic. I can't imagine what she must be feeling right now. What happened? Does she know who it was?"

"The police are following up on some leads, but I wanted to take a different approach. There's no point in me following the path they've already taken."

"Sure, that makes sense."

"You're an old friend of Rose's? You've known each other for a few years."

"Yes. Of course. We met at school. I guess you know that already. We were all in computer science. There is still a much larger proportion of male students than females in that field, so Rose and I and some of the others were pretty tight. It was us against the men, you know."

"Was there a lot of discrimination? Was it adversarial?"

"No, I wouldn't say that. People were pretty good... but as women, we were very aware of the ratio of men to women. Of course, even while we were competing with the men, we were also competing with each other for the men." She laughed. "There were lots to choose from. But some of them were so nerdy... There were only a few who were really good prospects. And we had to convince them that *we* weren't too nerdy. They wanted the beauty queens, not the geek club."

Zachary had never been to college, so much of what he imagined college to be like came from movies. And like with anything else, he was sure that their portrayals of college life were highly fictionalized and exaggerated.

"I don't imagine you had much time for... social pursuits."

"Some people carried heavier loads than others. Or were more interested in their studies than others. There was plenty of socializing if that was what you wanted to do. But of course, if you spent too much time on boys—or girls—your grades would suffer. Most of us in computer science were serious about doing the work. But we still took breaks, if you know what I mean."

Rose had taken enough breaks to end up pregnant. Though, of course, that technically only required one.

"Was Rose taken with Amir from the beginning? Were they a couple throughout college?"

"Oh, no. I wouldn't say that. They were friends, but didn't get that... friendly until the last year of the program, maybe. We spent time together as a group but didn't pair off too much. Amir was a nice guy, but his parents were strict. Even though he was an adult, he was kind of religious and tried to honor his parents' wishes. They didn't want him to get serious about anyone unless he was going to marry her, and I think they would have preferred a good Muslim girl. Which Rose was not!"

"Do you mean not Muslim or not a good girl?"

Jenna giggled. "Well, neither one, as far as Amir's family thought. He never came out and said they didn't like Rose, but he always tried to... manage things. If he took her to have dinner with his family, he would tell her what she should and shouldn't do, topics to avoid, and stuff like that. Trying to mold her into the closest thing to a good Muslim girl that he could. Even though she was Christian, she should behave a certain way and respect their faith."

"He was controlling?"

"Well… not in a bad way, I wouldn't say. But he did his best to manage expectations. He wasn't rough with her or anything like that. I can't see him ever being violent. But I don't think she was quite the kind of person he wanted to marry. He didn't know that yet. But…" In his mind's eye, Zachary could see her expressive shrug. "Well, he tried to squash her into that mold, and she just didn't fit."

"When did they break up? And how did that go?"

"Near the end of our graduating year. I think it was probably when Amir found out that she was pregnant. Neither of them ever explained what had happened to break them up, who had initiated it and why, but it wasn't long after that Rose started showing. I think Amir probably realized at that point that he didn't really want to be with her for the rest of his life. That they had too many differences to raise a child together."

"Did he want her to get an abortion?"

"Not that I ever heard. But they were both pretty close-lipped about it, like I said."

"Was there anyone else competing for Amir's attention? Did he… choose Rose over someone else? Or was someone else there to catch him when he fell…?"

"Oh man… well, it was a few years ago." Jenna gave a little laugh. "I'm not old enough to claim Alzheimer's, but that seems like another lifetime, sometimes. Were we ever that young?"

Zachary *mm-hmmed*, hoping she would refocus on the past and answer the question.

"Well, I guess so. I mean, I went out with him a couple of times myself, but I guess we weren't really compatible. It never went anywhere. And there was Nikki. She really liked Amir. She wasn't Muslim or Middle Eastern, but she had dark hair, eyes, and darker skin and figured that she would fit into his circles better than the rest of us. She would make a better wife because she looked more like them...? I don't know. I guess people imprint on a certain 'type' sometimes."

"And they dated?"

"I don't remember if they did, or if she just wanted to. Figured that Rose should leave Amir for her. Kind of like the tall girls hate it when the short girls date tall guys, because then there are no guys left who are tall enough for them to look up to. You know?"

"How resentful was Nikki?"

"I don't know. Do I think that she would still be bitter about it today? No way. I don't think she's the one who took Rose's little girl. No way."

"Have you talked to her recently? Have any idea of what's going on in her life?"

"No. We don't run in the same circles. I stayed in Burlington. I'm not sure where she went or whether she is working, or if she settled down with a family somewhere... we didn't keep in touch."

"What was her last name?"

"It was... Nikki Brown, I think? Or Braun? I think it was Braun with an 'au' but pronounced like Brown."

Zachary wrote it down.

"And how about the other boys? Or *men* in the program. Was there anyone else who liked Rose, or who didn't like Amir? Competed with him?"

"I don't think so. I mean... there were plenty of guys who liked Rose. And those who didn't. Some didn't think women belong in the sciences or can't stand it if they get better grades. Rose was smart, and didn't have any reservations about reporting cheating or inappropriate behavior." She shrugged. "Like I said, there were a lot more men than women, so we all had our coterie of admirers. But there wasn't anyone stalking her or fighting Amir for a chance at her hand. At the end of the program, we all had different directions to go, and no one was following Rose to Roxboro."

17

Keeping an eye on the time, Zachary decided there wasn't enough time for another call before Kenzie arrived home. He wanted to do something for her to make up for forgetting about her family dinner the day before. He couldn't go back in time to change the way that he had acted or guarantee that he wouldn't screw up again the next time despite his best intentions, but he could at least show her that he was thinking about her and not just himself or his case.

He shut the lid on his computer to keep himself from going back to it to check one more thing, which could lead to following a rabbit trail and forgetting all about his plans. He went to the kitchen and looked through the fridge to see what he could do about supper.

He pulled out a package of refrigerated pasta that could be cooked in the microwave, which he found easier than preparing dry pasta. At least if he got distracted from a microwave meal, he didn't have to deal with boiling water bubbling up and all over the stove, or letting the pot boil dry and ending up with burned pasta, a smoky house, and the smoke alarm screaming away, sending him into flashbacks to the fateful Christmas Eve fire.

If he forgot a microwave dinner, it just got cold and had to be rewarmed. They used the microwave often enough that the chances of the meal being left in the microwave for several days until it stank up the kitchen were remote.

He lined up the pasta, a jar of bottled sauce, and precooked strips of chicken breast on the counter. He needed to cut the chicken into cubes but, other than that, he wouldn't warm the dish until Kenzie was home and out of the shower. But before that, he could make a salad. There was a small selection of bagged salads in the fridge because Kenzie was trying to eat more vegetables and Zachary was trying to follow her example, though he wasn't keen on leafy vegetables. Or any vegetables other than carrots or potatoes.

But he could chop some additional fresh vegetables into the bagged salad, which Kenzie always appreciated. He held up the taco salad kit and tried to remember whether it was one of the salads he was supposed to dress ahead of time or just prior to eating. For some, like coleslaw or kale, he was supposed to add the dressing ahead of time for it to soften and absorb the flavor, and for some, he was supposed to wait so that it didn't wilt and get mushy by the time they ate. Then there were salads that were supposed to be wilted, but Zachary couldn't abide the texture and eat it without gagging. On balance, he decided not to dress it before Kenzie got home, just to cut up the additional vegetables.

He was setting the table when Kenzie arrived. He had the plates and glasses set out, but would have to remember to pick up where he had left off and add cutlery and a pitcher of water once he'd had a chance to greet her.

Kenzie started slightly at finding Zachary in the kitchen instead of hunched over his computer on the couch. "Oh, hey. How are you?" Her eyes went to the table, and then she surveyed the rest of the kitchen, taking in the half-prepared food lining the counter. "All right—what did you do?" she accused.

Zachary laughed at her tone. "I wasn't ready when you got home yesterday. So I'm trying to make up for it. I know it doesn't fix anything, but…"

"But it's a nice gesture," Kenzie said. "Well, it looks great. Do I have time for a shower before supper?"

"I'm counting on it."

"Okay." She hung her coat on a peg and gave him a peck on the cheek. "I'll see you in ten minutes."

"Make it fifteen," he told her generously.

"Fifteen, then."

When she returned to the kitchen, refreshed and dressed in her flannel jammies, he had everything arranged on the table and was checking one more time to make sure he hadn't forgotten forks or anything else vital to their dining experience. He wiped his fingers on the towel draped over his shoulder and waited for Kenzie's verdict. She took in everything at a glance and nodded, taking her seat.

"This looks great. How was your day? You must have had a nap."

Zachary thought back over his day but couldn't remember taking a break. He'd forgotten about not getting any sleep the night before, but his body hadn't reminded him that he'd needed it, so he had just kept going.

"Yeah, a good day," he agreed, not addressing the question about sleep. "And I wanted to make sure that yours ended well. Anything interesting at the morgue today?"

"Things were pretty quiet."

"Well, that's probably a good thing. You don't want your patients to be too animated."

"No," she agreed with a chuckle. "We wouldn't want any of that kind of excitement."

"You haven't ever had a body that turned out not to be dead?"

"No. That kind of thing is rare. I know you see it on TV, but I've only heard of it happening a couple of times. And generally, that person dies in the next couple of days anyway. You don't usually get miraculous recoveries from the morgue table." Kenzie dished up her salad. "Though I always check."

"To make sure they're really dead?"

She nodded. "It only takes a few seconds to make sure. Sometimes not even that, if they are already… past their due date." Her eyes danced.

She knew that Zachary didn't mind autopsy talk over dinner like most people did and would not squirm over the words "decomposing" or "putrefying."

"This looks good," Kenzie approved as she dished up the pasta.

"Leave some room for dessert."

"Ice cream?" Kenzie guessed.

"And cake," Zachary advised. He checked to ensure he'd remembered to take the cake out of the freezer to defrost.

"I'd better make sure I eat enough vegetables to make up for it."

But he noticed she didn't add extra salad to her plate after saying this.

18

Zachary drove around Rose's neighborhood for a while before stopping near her house. He looked for places that anyone might have watched her from. Good spots to sit and surveil the house. He also watched for bad surveillance locations. Places where an amateur might be noticed by alert neighbors or stand out as not belonging there. It was not a community where a person had to have a parking pass to park on the street. But there were a lot of people around. Walking dogs, taking kids to school, shoveling walks. There was a fresh layer of fluffy snow over everything, and it sparkled, turning the bare trees into beautiful sculptures.

He took the opportunity to take a few pictures with the camera he carried with him everywhere. Not the trusty old camera that Mr. Peterson had given him for his birthday when he was a kid, which he had carried everywhere he went for years. That had been lost in an apartment fire around the time he'd met Kenzie.

Over the past year, he'd been trying to take more walks and indulge in his photography hobby more, and the results had been positive. His body felt better after walking, calmer and more focused, and photography helped to take his mind off other things and improve his emotional state.

The snow had transformed the little suburban neighborhood into a winter wonderland like the front of a Christmas card. Zachary shook his head abruptly, cutting off this thought. No, like a postcard. Like a travel postcard one might find at a tourist shop. Or in a coffee table book. Mr. Peterson had suggested that he could prepare a book of his own photography through one of the many online vendors that offered this service. Something that he could put on the coffee table at home for people to browse through when they visited or give away as a present. Maybe he would. He didn't usually share his photography with anyone but Lorne, but Kenzie and Tyrrell had encouraged him to. And so had Mindy, who he had discovered was also a photographer with a wonderful eye for composition.

Maybe he would.

He took a few extra shots of Rose's house, neighbors' houses, and the street. Those would be for the file. He might need them later, depending on where the investigation went.

After another quick glance around, Zachary went to the door of one of Rose's immediate neighbors. He didn't even have to knock on the door. The older lady who faced him looked fierce.

"Who are you?" she demanded. "You're out there snooping around, taking pictures of the place. Who do you think you are?"

Zachary smiled reassuringly. "I'm not here to cause any trouble, ma'am. I'm glad to see that you are aware of what is going on around you. It's good to have watchdogs in a neighborhood who keep an eye on things and look out for their neighbors."

She looked surprised at his response. "Well, yes, I always thought so," she agreed bullishly. "But you didn't answer the question. Who are you?"

He handed her one of his business cards. "I am investigating the disappearance of Mrs. Bircher's daughter." He gave her an appropriately grave look. "I assume you heard about that."

"Oh, yes. I asked her where Claire was, and she told me... What a horrible thing," the woman agreed. She studied the business card, then stepped back and invited him in. "I'm Cora Johnson. Mrs. Cora Johnson," she impressed her marital status upon him. "I can't believe something like that could happen to someone I know." She gave him a fierce look. "But it didn't happen at home, so why are you looking around here?"

"I don't think that it was a random stranger. All the evidence points to this being well planned out ahead of time. And with that being the case... I expect he probably had Rose and Claire under surveillance for at least a few days."

Her eyes widened. "You think he was here? Watching them?"

Zachary nodded. "Who have you noticed in the past few weeks that didn't belong? Anyone sitting in their car? Watching the house? Maybe showing up before or after school, without kids of his own?"

Cora nodded slowly, pursing her lips. "I keep an eye on things..."

"I know you do." He had seen her looking through her curtains when he had been outside taking pictures. She hadn't been dissuaded by the fact that he was just taking photos of the beautiful trees, she had still been suspicious of him.

She picked up a coil-bound notebook from a small table near the window. It was clearly well-used, the pages puffed out rather than laying tightly flat.

"You think I'm just a nosy old lady, but you never know when something I see might be important. Someone has to watch out for the neighborhood, to be aware of what is going on. People who are walking their kids to school, dragging along dogs and toddlers and having arguments over homework and permission slips, they have no idea what is happening around them. Commuters so bleary-eyed they don't see a thing walking from their houses to their cars and back again at night."

Zachary nodded encouragingly. "Someone needs to look out for people," he repeated.

Cora nodded again, studying him closely before opening her notebook. "I have your car description here. Couldn't see your license plate because you parked too far away. But I wrote down the time and your description."

"And has there been anyone around that you've been concerned about? Who might have been watching Rose and her daughter? This is the time you are put to the test. This is the time when all your hard work pays off."

She was obviously anxious about how she would be seen. Others had probably criticized her before for being a nosy neighbor. Told her that her concerns were unfounded. That she wasn't helping anyone out, she was just bothering people.

But after a moment of consideration, watching him carefully, Cora decided that Zachary was on the level and really did believe she might have information that might help him. And in a kidnapping case, no less. What she did might actually save a child.

She sat down with her book and started to go through it, considering dates and times and what she had recorded there and offering suspicious vehicles or persons up to Zachary one at a time, tentative.

"I could just take a picture of each page," Zachary suggested. "Then I can process all of them, make sure no one falls through the net."

"No," she shook her head, mouth wrinkled like a prune. "We have to respect people's civil rights. Can't just go accusing people because they drove through the neighborhood or stopped to make a delivery."

"I could weed people out based on the description," Zachary offered, still hoping to get his hands on the full log. But Cora was not going to budge on the matter. She would only share the descriptions of the people she thought suspicious. Even so, there were a surprising number of strangers or visitors to the neighborhood in the span of a couple of weeks.

Zachary carefully noted each one, a laborious process with his writing disability. He could write quickly or clearly, but not both. He needed to be able to look up each person or pass their descriptions on to the police. Some of the descriptions were not detailed enough for him to be able to look anything up, but the police might have traffic cams of nearby streets where they could pick up license plates based on the information in Cora's logbook.

Eventually, Cora Johnson closed her notebook, keeping it balanced on her knees. "Do you think I got him? Do you think it is one of these people?"

"I hope so." He gave her an encouraging smile. "You might just hold the key to breaking this case and saving that little girl."

"Oh, I hope so," Cora's voice wavered as it hadn't previously in the conversation. "I do hope so. That poor little girl. What it must be like for her, being kidnapped by a stranger and then held somewhere in a dark basement or chained in some room... I've heard about these things happening before, you know. People say that it doesn't happen. The kidnappers either let them go or kill them within the first two or three days. But sometimes they keep them for years, in horrific conditions, being tortured daily." Cora licked her lips and shook her head in distress at such a thing.

Zachary's heart thudded. He didn't need to imagine it. He knew what it was like to be at the mercy of some psycho with a blade and evil intentions. He flashed back, paralyzed, unable to move as Archuro whispered in his ear all the terrors he had planned. He had taken years to develop and refine his ritual. He gloried in the dreadfully depraved things he would do.

"Mr. Goldman, are you all right?"

He couldn't catch his breath, caught in the nightmare. He couldn't pull away. He couldn't breathe, he couldn't make a sound.

Zachary struggled to escape the images. He knew in a remote way that it would help if he could anchor to physical sensations around him. He could pull himself back into the room with Cora. But she was so far away, so inconsequential.

"Mr. Goldman." She shook him, her clawlike hands digging into his arm. "You need to come out of it! Listen to me! Listen to my voice. Look at my face."

Her demands started to separate him from the nightmares. Her hand on his arm. Her insistent voice. Her face in front of his. He wanted to see the logbook again, to verify to himself that it was real, that he was firmly entrenched in the present.

Her face swam into view. He drank it in like a dying man, looking at each of the individual parts first.

Her mouth. Her nose. Her chin. Her penetrating eyes.

Then they pulled together, making her a person. A person in the same room as Zachary. Not a nightmare, not that monster from his past or another of the abusers he had faced over the years. Just Cora Johnson, a little old lady who watched the world go by outside her window and carefully recorded everything she saw.

A good woman. A woman who wanted to help find a lost little girl. Who was pulling lost Zachary back from his flashback.

He rubbed his face. Felt it to make sure that he was really there, that he could feel his own familiar features. "Water?" he croaked.

He listened to her moving in the kitchen, opening the cupboard and fridge and filling a glass with water and ice. She brought him the cold glass and pressed it into his hand. Zachary lifted it to his lips, sipped, and then gulped the freezing cold liquid. It helped to clear the cobwebs away, to convince his brain that he was there with Cora and not in some other time. He didn't have to live his life in both places. He could leave that reality behind. It was over. He didn't have to keep reliving it.

But he still did.

Not as often. The nightmares of Archuro came less frequently, fading slowly. One day they would be gone and he wouldn't go back there again.

At least, that was what he hoped and what he worked toward during his therapy sessions with Dr. Boyle.

"Thank you," he whispered to Cora Johnson.

"What happened? Was it a fit? A seizure? I thought I was going to have to call the ambulance."

"I'm sorry. It was... I sometimes have flashbacks, and... it took me by surprise."

"Were you in the war?" Her eyes were big.

His own private war.

"No. Not like that. I've been through some things." He knew he would have to explain it better for her to understand. And he was working hard at not hiding his mental illness but talking about it clearly, to try with others to reduce the stigma. Maybe to eliminate it one day. "I was kidnapped myself." He held the cold-water glass fiercely, trying to keep from sliding into the memories. "It was… it *was* terrible. And almost incomprehensible, even to me. I'm still trying to deal with it. And thinking about Claire being held… I got too close. Lost my professional distance."

Cora nodded slowly. She watched him with curiosity. He felt like a circus sideshow.

"I'm sorry. I didn't mean to scare you," he told her.

"You didn't scare me. I'm fine. And you are, too," she said firmly. "You will be strong, and you will get through this, too."

Zachary breathed out slowly. He sipped the cold water. "I hope so."

"You will do it," she insisted.

He gave her a half-smile. "Okay," he agreed. "I will."

She beamed at him. She settled back into her chair, watching him like a benevolent dog owner. He was now her pet. Her project. Zachary wiped sweat from his forehead.

"Tell me all about what happened," she invited him.

Zachary shook his head. His openness about his mental illness did not extend to telling anyone the details about the things that had happened to him. He had no wish to relive every detail, to horrify anyone with the description or to titillate them. Kenzie and Dr. Boyle had a general idea of what had happened to him there, and in his childhood, but he couldn't tell anyone about the details. Especially not this craggy old crone.

He gulped down the rest of the water and put the glass on a coaster conveniently located on the little table beside him. He wanted to go. He didn't want to sit and discuss himself and his issues, or have the woman sitting there pitying him for what a wreck he was at just the mention of kidnapping and torture.

But he had an opportunity there that he might not get again. He needed this woman to move his case forward. "Tell me about Rose," he told her. "What can you tell me about Rose and Claire?"

"Well, they're my neighbors. It wouldn't be proper for me to talk about them."

"Rose wants me to investigate this. And Claire is depending on us to help her."

If she were still alive.

"I don't feel right about it," Cora objected again.

"Is she a good mom, do you think?" Zachary plowed right into it. She *would* talk to him about the mother and daughter. He needed the insights that only someone who lived close to them and saw them coming and going every day could provide. "She doesn't seem very demonstrative. But not all parents are. Some people mask their emotions, but they still have them."

"Oh, she's a good mom," Cora protested. "Mothers these days have so much that they are required to do. They don't just stay at home with the kids anymore and go to PTA meetings and take care of the house. They are expected to do all those things *and* work full-time outside the home. Things were different in my day. Most women worked from home. Or part-time while the children were at school. Now, there is no way for most families to survive on one income. And I don't think Rose was getting anything from the child's father."

"No. He hadn't been involved in her life at all."

And none of the descriptions that Cora had given him of strangers and visitors who had been in the neighborhood in the last couple of weeks matched Amir. No mention of anyone Middle Eastern, or even just tall and dark-haired. Zachary knew that Amir did not wear traditional Saudi dress, but he wished he did. He would have been much easier to pick out of Cora's descriptions.

"So it's hard, you see? No one can expect her to be able to do everything. You can't be a mom *all* the time and a scientist and the housekeeper and cook."

Zachary nodded. "It's too much to put on one woman, she can't do it all at the same time."

"Yes."

"Did you see her with Claire very much? Did you ever see them… argue? Or have a loud discussion? In the yard or through the windows, maybe?"

"Children are prone to temper tantrums. Claire was still very young."

"Yes. Did she have a lot of tantrums?"

"Well… more than I would have put up with. But parenting these days is different too. You don't want to hurt your children's feelings. You want them to think for themselves. To learn to self-regulate."

Zachary remembered parents or group home leaders trying to teach him self-regulation. It wasn't something that could be forced. It wasn't learned from a few whacks with a cane or being locked in a dark closet.

"Did she have trouble controlling Claire? Getting her to behave?"

"She said that the girl was *spirited*. I think that is code for hyperactive. People have to be so careful these days to describe things in a way that doesn't hurt anyone. Even if you know that she was a brat."

"Was she a brat?"

Cora looked thoughtful. "No, I don't think she was. She might have been hyperactive. I think that is still what they call it these days."

This made All Played Out a good place for Rose to take Claire where she could run and play to her heart's content while Rose could sit and read a book, her email, or catch up on social networking.

"So she probably played in the yard a lot? Made a lot of noise? Or did you hear them inside the house, playing loudly?"

"Playing… or yelling at her that it was time to come in… or that it was time to go to bed. It must be challenging to get a child like that to bed."

Zachary could attest to that fact. Even now, it was almost impossible to settle his brain for sleep at the end of the day. Even when he was physically exhausted. Kenzie was a big proponent of sleep aids, but Zachary didn't like to take a pill to go to sleep unless he really had to—meaning that he had gone several days without enough sleep. He didn't like how dopey the pills made him feel in the morning, all foggy, clumsy, and easily confused.

In foster care, he hadn't had a choice to take the medication or not. He took his day meds when he was given his day meds and his night meds when he was given his night meds. And then he went to bed. And he'd better not get back out of it again.

"Do you think Rose was abusive in any way? Not physically, but maybe verbally? Emotionally?"

"Oh, no," Cora assured him. "No, of course not. I didn't mean to imply that she was doing anything wrong. Just that Claire might sometimes be a difficult child to control. To parent, I mean."

"The yelling wasn't… excessive?"

"No. No, certainly not. All parents raise their voices some of the time."

"Was there ever any investigation by DCF?"

"DCF?"

"Department for Children and Families. Social workers. Into accusations of abuse."

"She never said anything to me about them. And no one ever came to my door to ask if she was… that way."

"And you would have told them no."

"No. I never saw her hit the girl. No. Drag her in and out of the car, sometimes. But she didn't hit her."

"Dragging her out of the car?" Zachary repeated.

"You know. Grabbing her arm, pulling her out of there. Sometimes, kids need physical redirection. You can't just talk them into or out of the car."

Zachary nodded slowly. He wondered what he would have thought when observing Rose and Claire together. Would he have been worried about abuse? Or would he have been able to tell that Claire was just parenting a child who was difficult to control?

"You know, you have been very helpful, Mrs. Johnson," he told Cora finally. "I really appreciate the information from your log, and the water, and the information about Rose and Claire. I needed someone like you today."

Her pale skin turned pink. "Well, I'm just a person who is always trying to do my part," she told him.

"I appreciate your patience today. Especially with my… episode. I'm sorry for frightening you."

"Oh, you didn't scare me. That's quite all right. I'm glad that you came to talk to me today. I'm glad someone is trying to help poor little Claire. I do hope… that you can find her unharmed."

Zachary pressed his lips together and forced them into a smile. "Yes, I hope so too," he agreed.

And he did. But at the same time, he knew that she had been gone for too long. Every day was another nail in the coffin.

19

Zachary sat in the car for a few minutes before attempting to drive home. He was feeling wrung out after the flashback and knew that he was still behind on his sleep. Tonight might be one of those nights when he was forced to take a sleep aid. He needed to get caught back up to operate at his best. And as Kenzie would tell him if she didn't think he was paying enough attention to his health, sleep was needed for good mental health. He would be that much more susceptible to depression if he didn't get the sleep that his body needed.

He should probably call it a day. Even though there was more work to be done and he keenly felt the passage of time, there was only so much he could do in a day. He was one man. He didn't have the resources of the police department or the Department of State.

But he held on to hope that he might still crack the case before it was too late.

The vibration of his phone in his pocket made Zachary jump. He pulled it out and saw *Roxboro Police Department* on the screen. Funny that he should get a call just when he had been thinking of them and wishing he had more resources. He hoped it wasn't about an unpaid parking ticket.

"Zachary Goldman," he answered briskly, trying to sound more awake and alert than he was.

"Zachary. Sergeant Campbell."

"Oh." He and Campbell had helped each other out several times in the past. Sometimes, Zachary was able to pass information on to Campbell about an ongoing investigation to see that the right people were arrested and, sometimes, Campbell was able to smooth something over for Zachary, provide some background that he needed, or open an investigation for him or Kenzie. If there was anyone in the police department who was likely to help him, it was Joshua Campbell. Or Mario Bowman. But this time, it was Joshua Campbell.

"How can I help you?" Zachary asked.

"Well, I am given to understand that you might be working on the Bircher kidnapping."

"Yes."

"What's your interest in the case?"

"The mother hired me. Rose Bircher. She was concerned that… there wasn't any proof that it was Amir who took Claire, and she didn't want the investigation to languish. I think she felt that the police weren't looking at any other possibilities because they were sure that Amir already had Claire in Saudi Arabia."

"Yes, well, there didn't seem to be any reason to look further than that, I'll admit. I don't blame the investigators involved for assuming the guilt of the non-custodial parent who fled the country after the kidnapping with a child who reasonably fit her description."

"No," Zachary agreed. "There was definitely reason to suspect that he had been involved."

"Well… things have been moving here. I have been informed that the Saudis have a possible address for Amir and are moving in with pictures of both girls, in the hopes of identifying which one it was he took with him."

Zachary could only hope that they didn't traumatize the little girl in the process. Separating her from her parents while they tried to establish her identity would frighten her. Strange men in a strange new country where everyone dressed and talked differently from what she was used to. She might be scared she would never see them again as they effectively kidnapped her away from her parents, who may have been totally within their rights in taking her there. Other than the fact that her father had not given his permission, of course.

"That's good. It would really help to know whether we are looking for her in Saudi Arabia or here."

"I wonder if you would be free to meet for a few minutes. Any chance you could come down to the police station?"

"Uh..." That certainly hadn't been in Zachary's plans, but maybe it would help him to get some of the answers he was hoping for. Campbell could find out about things like DFS investigations and running license plates that Cora Johnson had recorded. "I guess I could make it over there. Yeah. Right now?"

"Don't sound so eager."

"Sorry, it's been a long day. I'll come in. Now, if that's what you like. I didn't know if you meant today or that you wanted to set up a time in the future."

"Now would be better."

"Okay. I'm in my car. I'll be there soon."

"See you shortly, then."

Putting aside his fatigue from the interview with Cora and the flashbacks, Zachary started the car. He drove to the police station as if on autopilot, his thoughts and emotions far removed from his actions. It was almost a surprise to find himself outside of the police building, looking for a parking space.

The Medical Examiner's Office was in the basement of the building, and it soothed his spirits to know that Kenzie was not far away, working methodically to unwind the mysteries of life and death. He was glad to be in physical proximity to her, even if he couldn't see her.

After parking, he sat in the car for a few moments to try to ensure that he was focused and ready for the interview with Joshua Campbell. They weren't exactly friends, but they were friendly, and Campbell knew much of Zachary's difficult history and put up with his idiosyncrasies. While his mind didn't work the same way as Zachary's, he respected Zachary's processes and didn't automatically assume that he'd gone off the rails when he proposed a new theory of the crime or connected up a previously orphaned piece of information. Campbell already knew that Zachary wasn't sure of Amir's involvement in the kidnapping and that it was being investigated, so he didn't have to convince him that there might be other directions for the police to investigate.

Zachary looked back at his car a couple of times while he waited for the Duty Officer at the public reception desk. He could see it from where he stood, so he could see that there was no one near it and that it was perfectly safe. But he couldn't shake the feeling that it was vulnerable out there at the curb. But there were people out and about on the street. No one would break into it or wire it with explosives while it was out in the open where they could be observed.

He pushed the feelings away, reminding himself that the compulsion to go back and check again to make sure the security system was armed was just that, a compulsion, and it would go away if he ignored it for long enough. He could ask for an adjustment to his med cocktail, but he didn't want to change anything, especially not so close to Christmas, when the slightest change could have a domino effect and land him in the hospital.

20

"Sir? Can I help you?"

Zachary realized that the man in front of him had been dealt with and the Duty Officer was waiting for Zachary to approach and say what he needed.

"I'm here for a meeting with Sergeant Campbell. He is expecting me."

"If you'll give me just a moment. What's your name, sir?"

"Zachary. Zachary Goldman."

The officer called Campbell to confirm the appointment, and then had a younger cop escort Zachary to Campbell's office.

Zachary immediately saw that they weren't alone. He waited in the doorway, uncertain. Campbell would want to finish with his current visitor before talking with Zachary.

"Uh..."

"Come in, Zachary. Have a seat."

Zachary entered slowly and took a seat in the second visitor's chair. He looked at Campbell, eyebrows raised.

"Zachary, this is Agent Terrence Bartlett."

Bartlett held out a hand in greeting. "FBI. C-A-R-D."

"CARD?" Zachary repeated. Too many letters, already getting mixed into alphabet soup in his head.

"Child Abduction Rapid Deployment. Unfortunately in this case, not so rapid."

"Not your fault."

"No, but it's too bad we didn't get called in earlier. I am also interfacing with IPKU."

"Which is…?"

"The International Parental Kidnapping Unit."

Zachary nodded. "I hope there isn't going to be a test," he said, rubbing his eyes.

The FBI man chuckled. "All you need to remember is Bartlett. Like the pear."

"Don't tell me that, I'll end up calling you Bosch."

"It wouldn't be the first time," Bartlett chuckled.

"Well, as you both know," Campbell took over the discussion. "We are jumping back into this case, rewinding to consider whether it actually *isn't* an international parental abduction. Which means that we're late to the party. Since Zachary has already been working on this for a couple of days and already has more insight into Rose Bircher and Amir Osman and their circumstances, I wonder if he could share some of what he has discovered so far."

Zachary nodded. "Yeah, of course. I went back over the video surveillance at the play place, but it isn't that helpful. There isn't anyone who is obviously suspicious. No sign of Amir or of anyone paying attention to the little girl when she is out in the open. You can't see much of what is happening in the play structures, nothing in the interior, employee-only hallways."

"Our guys are going over the video," Bartlett offered. "We might be able to do a little facial recognition magic, but in the wild… well, let's just say that TV greatly exaggerates our ability to use facial recognition on surveillance video of this low quality."

"I also looked over the sign-in/sign-out log to see if Rose and Claire came in with anyone else or if they met there with friends or a group, but it looks like they just went by themselves. It sounds like Claire is a pretty *active* girl." Zachary was reluctant to say "hyperactive" and pathologize physical activity as being abnormal in a five-year-old. "I suspect Rose would take her there to wear her out and get some quiet time." He grimaced, remembering how loud everything had been at the venue. "That is, some time when she could focus on other things and not have to worry about directly supervising Claire. The place is called 'All Played Out' and that was probably what she was counting on. Giving Claire a positive place to work out all her energy so that she would be able to be calm when it was time to go home and to bed."

Neither man seemed particularly interested in this line of inquiry.

"Rose was not watching Claire while she was there," Zachary explained further. "She might tell you that she was keeping a close watch on Claire the whole time and sounded the alarm immediately when the girl disappeared, but she *wasn't* watching her."

Campbell straightened a little. "So the alarm wasn't raised within five or ten minutes of the abduction."

"No. They were there for several hours. I watched Rose on the tape whenever one of the cameras was pointed in her direction, and she rarely took her eyes off her phone. Claire could have been gone for a couple of hours by the time Rose started looking for her."

Campbell swore. Bartlett scribbled in his notepad. Zachary waited until he was done jotting down his thoughts before continuing.

"If Rose regularly used the play place as sort of a babysitter, then someone who was surveilling her and had learned her patterns and routines might have figured it was a good place to take Claire. At school, Claire was always supervised. After school, she didn't walk home on her own. She walked with other kids, directly supervised, to her after-school daycare. Lots of school kids and responsible adults around. Not a good time to snatch her."

"If the abductor wanted to get away clean, having a couple of hours as a cushion before the police were called would be ideal," Bartlett noted.

"Yeah. Especially if they thought it had *just* happened and that there was still the possibility that she was in the mall. They focus on locking down the play place and the mall rather than putting roadblocks farther away and getting an Amber alert issued."

"By the time that happened, they were probably already holed up at their destination."

"Any idea how he got her out?" Campbell asked. "There's been a lot of questions on how the abductor was able to get her past the guards and locked gates. It isn't supposed to be possible for someone to take a kid out of there that he didn't bring in. No one is allowed to come in without a child."

"Unless it was an inside job," Bartlett said. "But they do run background and criminal record checks on all their employees. They don't have anyone working there who may have been involved in a crime against children in the past."

"I think that the employees *were* involved," Zachary told them, "But not knowingly."

He told them about the propped-open door and the possibility that someone could just walk out the back without swiping a card.

"That would be pretty bold," Campbell said doubtfully. "He would have to avoid being seen by any employees on the way out. And the door would have to be propped open while there wasn't anyone smoking outside."

"Unless the smoking employees didn't want to admit they had seen something. Or didn't know what they had seen." Zachary shrugged. "I haven't seen the route that the abductor would have had to take from the play equipment to the propped door. I don't know how short or long it is or how many people might have seen them along the way. But I know that someone who is confident and appears to belong can walk into and out of a place without being challenged ninety percent of the time. It could be someone in an employee uniform. Water boy. Deliveryman. Carpenter or janitor. Guard's uniform."

Campbell conceded this. Bartlett seemed more skeptical. "But you can't exactly dress the girl up as a security guard. What would a security guard be doing with a little girl? Why would an employee be with her? Why would someone be walking her down the employee-only hallways?"

"Maybe there is a first aid room back there. Or somewhere kids are taken if they can't find Mommy. I don't know. Do they have birthday or event rooms? Bathrooms that could be used if there was a problem with the public toilets?"

Bartlett grunted. "We'll have to look into it more carefully."

Zachary nodded. "I haven't been back there to ask more questions since I discovered the propped door. I just assumed that whoever took her found a way to get through the hallways and out the back door without being stopped. You might want to reinterview the staff to find out if anyone saw an adult and child in the hallway, or an adult they didn't recognize. The abductor could still be an employee, even if they were vetted."

It certainly would not be the first time an employee background review or criminal records check had failed to turn up something that it should have. There could be a juvenile record. A record in another state. Someone using their brother's name and social to get a job because they couldn't get one with their own. There were a hundred ways to foil a background check.

Campbell and Bartlett both nodded, making notes for their investigators.

"Anything else?" Campbell asked.

"That's it from the play place. I haven't interviewed all the employees, so I don't know what else they might know. I didn't think they would know anything about Amir or Claire personally, so I didn't spend much time talking to them. Just the manager to get the lay of the land and copies of whatever I could. You might be able to get something else out of them." Zachary shrugged. "You've got the manpower. I've been moving pretty quickly, trying to gather as much information as possible in a short period of time. Because…"

He trailed off. Both law enforcement officers knew without Zachary having to put it into words. They all knew that Claire might not have much time left, if she were still alive. Zachary had been called in late. The police and FBI were getting up to speed even later. It was a disaster. They should have been looking for the kidnapper the first couple of days when the police had decided Amir had taken her out of the country. Now, all they could do was regret their assumption.

"Do you have anything else you can share with us about it? Are there any areas that we can explore further?" Campbell asked.

"I've talked to Amir's parents. That's where I learned about his girlfriend and her child and the story about her being stalked. I didn't verify anything, but I did pass it on to the guy from the Department of State. Uh, Schultz. Derek, I think. He said they would try to follow up with the Embassy in Saudi, see if they could verify the identity of the girl that Amir brought into the country." Zachary looked at Bartlett, who nodded, obviously up to speed on this already. Of course he was. That was why he was there. They'd suddenly been called in to help when the PD realized they had fallen down on the job and left all kinds of avenues uninvestigated. Bartlett already knew what was being done in Saudi Arabia through his office. He undoubtedly knew more than Zachary already.

"Have they been able to do that?" he asked Bartlett. "Do we have confirmation of whether it was Maeve or Claire?"

"No. Not yet. Amir and his family seem to be very... shy. They haven't left much of a trail or been to any of the places they were expected to be. The people who were supposed to be sponsoring his immigration, the employer that got him a work visa, all the addresses on the file... are either fictional or he's never been there."

Zachary's stomach filled with acid at that revelation. Why so secretive if he had just taken his girlfriend and child out of harm's way? If they had left the stalker behind in the United States, why were they being so careful in Saudi Arabia? Just because they had gotten into the habit of covering their trail? The constant stress of threatened violence could push a person past the bounds of reasonable caution into paranoia and hypervigilance. If anyone could understand that, it was Zachary.

He swore, but moved on. There was nothing he could do about what was going on in Saudi Arabia. He wasn't going to get on a plane and go over there to look for himself. He would have no idea of where to even start.

"I've talked to one of Rose's friends from college, and I am trying to get lined up with a couple of others. People who knew both Rose and Amir when they were in school. I don't know if this kidnapping has anything to do with the past. But I figured I should at least learn as much as I could about Amir's personality and background as I could. Whether it proves or disproves his involvement... I'm not expecting to learn anything concrete there, just to get a better picture of the two of them, both separate and together."

"Anything promising there? Unusual? Concerning?" Bartlett asked.

Zachary worked through each word as he thought of the interview with Jenna. *Promising? Unusual? Concerning?*

"No, I don't think so. They were part of a group of friends. Rose and Amir got serious about each other toward the end of college. No big fights or resentments that I could find out about. But this friend did not think that they were well-suited to each other. They broke it off before graduating."

"Was Amir violent?"

"No. No red flags that I've been able to find yet. But I still need to talk to more friends."

"That's it, then?"

"Saving the best until last," Zachary told them, unable to suppress a smile. Campbell and Bartlett both leaned toward him, eager to hear what else he had to offer.

21

"I visited Rose's neighborhood to get a feel for it and see if I could find anything out about her and Claire, their relationship, and whether anyone had been hanging around or stalking them."

"And I take it you were successful?" Campbell asked dryly.

"Next-door neighbor Cora Johnson. Your stereotypical nosy neighbor."

"She saw someone hanging around?"

Zachary wondered how long he could tease Campbell and Bartlett, dangling the potential clue enticingly in front of them. It was nice to be in the driver's seat, with them looking for information from him rather than his trying to convince them to listen to what he had to say.

But he didn't want to sour his relationship with Campbell by being a jerk. Campbell had helped him out in the past when he had desperately needed it, and Zachary knew he was going to give them the information they wanted eventually. It made more sense for him to give it sooner rather than later.

"And she kept a log of any strangers, walking or driving, with makes and license plate numbers when she could see them."

Campbell's face broke into a grin. "Oh, she did, did she?

Always nice to have the neighborhood kook on your side. I *assume* you got her on your side. That you got a copy of this surveillance log?"

Zachary nodded, then held up his hand to temper the answer. "She didn't give me the whole log. Maybe you can convince her to hand it over or subpoena it. She didn't want innocent people being accused of something so awful, so she wouldn't give me everyone's details. Only the ones that she thought were suspicious."

"Well, it's a start. Maybe it's best to get it in layers. Gives us a priority of who to search first, who she thinks is most likely to be bad."

Zachary nodded. "So I wrote down..." He flipped open his notebook and looked at the details he had written down. "Uh... my handwriting leaves something to be desired. I hope you can read it..."

"Your handwriting, if I remember right, can hardly be called handwriting," Campbell said good-naturedly. "We might need a cryptologist to decode it for us."

"Kenzie says that calling it chicken scratch is an insult to chickens," Zachary offered.

They all had a chuckle over that. "Maybe I should read it to you," Zachary suggested. "That might be faster than trying to figure out what it says."

"Let me run copies," Campbell said. "Then we can go over it together and you can clarify anything particularly cryptic."

He pressed a button on his phone to call in his administrative assistant, who took Zachary's notebook and nodded when Zachary indicated which pages he wanted to copy. He returned a few minutes later with two copies and the original, which he distributed to each of them. He slipped back out the door, leaving them with the information to review.

It was tedious work, but probably a good thing that Zachary had just taken down the information hours before, so it was still fresh in his mind and he could interpret the chicken scratch. The license plate numbers were, at least, painstakingly drawn so that the police could search them. It took a long time to go through.

Zachary pulled his phone out of his pocket, where it had been vibrating for a few minutes with a repeat caller.

"This is just Kenzie," Zachary advised Campbell, motioning to the phone and giving her a call back.

Campbell nodded and filled Bartlett in. "Our assistant medical examiner."

Bartlett paled. "Does that mean...?"

"Oh, no. It doesn't mean anything," Campbell assured him. "If a body had been found, they would be calling me, not Zachary. They're a couple."

Kenzie answered the phone before it went to voicemail. "Zachary. Sorry to interrupt. Can you talk?"

"Briefly. I'm with Campbell."

"Ah. I could see by your shared location that you were somewhere close by. Wondered if you were coming over here or if something was wrong. Or," her voice was teasing, "maybe you were just paying off all of your speeding tickets."

"I don't have any speeding tickets," Zachary protested. His driving always made her nervous, but he never got caught. He couldn't remember the last time he'd had a moving violation. "Parking, on the other hand..."

"Where do you park that you get ticketed? You're usually in front of the house."

"Well, when I'm on surveillance, there isn't always a convenient *legal* place to park."

"Oh, I see." She laughed. "So... should I wait for you? Go home and make dinner? Come up there?"

"We're nearly done, so whichever you want to do is fine. Then we can go home for dinner. Or pick something up."

"Tempting! I'll come up and say hi, if no one minds. And then we can decide."

"I'm sure Campbell would be happy to see you."

Campbell smiled and gave a nod. "Any time Dr. Kirsch chooses to grace us with her presence," he agreed.

Zachary slid the phone back away when Kenzie ended the call, and finished up his business with the two law enforcement officers.

"Well, I appreciate all the work you've done and information you've shared with us," Bartlett told him. "It saves us a little legwork. And then we can focus on the vital areas."

Zachary nodded. It was always nice to have law enforcement interested in his findings instead of telling him that he was poking his nose into something that wasn't any of his business, or that his theories were nonsense. He'd had his share of both in the past.

"How is Kenzie?" Campbell asked Zachary in a confidential tone. "Is she... having any trouble with the time of year?"

Zachary tilted his head, wondering what Campbell was talking about. Zachary was the one who dealt with cyclical depression around Christmas time, not Kenzie. And he didn't see how Campbell could have gotten it wrong. He knew Zachary's history well enough.

"The time of year?"

"Coming up on the anniversary of her kidnapping."

"Oh... yeah, I hadn't thought about that." Zachary had been in the hospital when Kenzie had briefly been kidnapped by Russians trying to coerce Walter into something he was reluctant to do. She had been released within hours and had not elected to tell Zachary about it at the time. He hadn't found out about the incident until months later, so he didn't associate it with Christmas. "I guess... she's been okay so far."

Maybe that was part of the reason she had been so angry about his not being prepared for the dinner with her family. She was already feeling the emotional strain of the upcoming anniversary. And the events that had taken place had centered on her parents. She had been quite concerned about both of them a year ago, and then Zachary forgot about them as if they didn't matter.

"Good to hear," Campbell acknowledged. "Anniversaries can be quite traumatic."

Just look at who he was talking to.

Kenzie poked her head in the doorway a couple of minutes later. She was introduced to Agent Bartlett and greeted Campbell familiarly. She turned her eyes to Zachary and raised her brows.

"You're looking a little worse for wear," she commented. "Did they rough you up?"

Zachary looked at himself, not understanding. He was in a stain-free, wrinkle-free shirt. He hadn't been in a fight; there were no bruises or other marks on his face. He shook his head. "What do you mean?"

"You just look… like you've been through the wringer." She shrugged. "You can tell me about it later." She nodded to Campbell and Zachary. "Good to see you."

They walked out of Campbell's office together to the main lobby, where Kenzie would need to take the elevator to the parking garage to get her car.

"Seriously," she said. "Are you okay?"

He thought about her comment about going through the wringer, which was exactly how he described his feelings after a panic attack or flashback. She must recognize it, even if she wasn't sure why he looked so worn out.

"A bad flashback," he told her. "Earlier this afternoon. I'm okay now, just…"

"You're not caught up on sleep, so you're physically and mentally exhausted."

"Yeah."

"You look it. Are you okay to drive? We can leave your car here and pick it up tomorrow. We'll just tell them to add your parking ticket to all the rest."

Zachary grinned at that. "No, I'm fine driving home." He had at least regenerated a bit since he had left Cora Johnson's house. He'd felt pretty unsteady at that point, but sitting down and reviewing the case with the two law enforcement officers had given him a boost. "It's not far. I'll see you at the house."

"You want me to stop for something on the way home, or do you want to order in?"

"Let's just order in. I don't want you to have to do any extra work."

"Okay." She gave him a quick kiss on the cheek. "I'll see you there."

22

Zachary looked for something to do while they waited for their dinner to arrive. Kenzie opted for a shower and they couldn't both be in the bathroom; someone had to be out to answer the door when their takeout arrived.

He hadn't yet talked to Tyrrell about getting together with the other siblings for a family dinner. And talking to his little brother usually gave him an emotional boost—as long as Tyrrell was doing well emotionally, which, as far as Zachary knew, he was. Tyrrell had been working for a while now with Kenzie's family foundation, helping with administrative work and researching good causes for them to fund. The foundation was focusing a lot more on mental health and addiction issues due to Zachary's addition to the family, and Tyrrell knew a number of those organizations from his life experiences, namely, his own mental health and addiction issues.

Like Zachary, Tyrrell had experienced a lot of trauma as a child and, even though he had been younger when the family dissolved and he was adopted into the same family as Vince and Mindy, he had always been an outsider. More deeply damaged than the youngest children. He hadn't been able to bond with their adoptive parents and had self-medicated with alcohol from early on.

But Tyrrell was good now. He was in a good place. Sober,

employed doing a job he liked, with people who kept an eye on him and were determined to support him through any relapse rather than just letting him go. He was renting Zachary's old apartment and enjoying being independent and mostly self-sufficient.

Zachary checked the time and figured Tyrrell should be home from work, so he dialed Tyrrell's number.

"Zach, my man," Tyrrell greeted cheerfully. "How's it going, bro?"

"It's good," Zachary assured him, deciding against saying anything about his flashback or emotional state. "We haven't talked for a while. And I wanted to ask you about something."

"Sure, whatever I can help you with. What's up?"

"I, uh… I'm trying to plan a family dinner. For all of us. The siblings. Since we've never all gotten together to eat before. Since we were separated, I mean."

"Oh." Zachary expected the silence and gave Tyrrell time to process it and see how he felt about it. "Well… I guess there's no reason *not* to," Tyrrell said, his tone still buoyant, but quieter than it had been. And the awkward pauses told their story, too.

Tyrrell had been in contact with all the other siblings before Zachary, yet he had been slow to introduce them. And he had never introduced Zachary to Mindy and Vince. Zachary had not met them until Tyrrell had disappeared on a binge, and Zachary had gone looking for him, taking it upon himself to call his two youngest siblings, as well as some of the half-siblings that Tyrrell had been in contact with.

So Zachary knew that Tyrrell didn't necessarily want to integrate all those different parts of his family. He had been keeping that part of his life a secret from Zachary and the older sisters.

But now they all knew anyway. Tyrrell's alcoholism was no longer a secret. But that didn't mean there weren't other things he hoped to keep quiet by not encouraging the older and younger siblings to meet.

"I think it would be really good," Zachary said. "I think it would be a good step toward healing our family."

"Yeah. Uh-huh. I guess."

"So you would be okay with that?"

"Uh…" Tyrrell again took time to think this through. "I don't like to be put on the spot. But I guess… yeah, why wouldn't I be okay with it? It's what we've always wanted, isn't it? Isn't it what all of us have wanted since we were split up in the first place?"

"Yeah. I've met everyone. But I think… getting everyone together would be another step."

"Of course."

"Do you want to sleep on it? I wasn't trying to put you on the spot. You don't have to answer right now. If you want some time to think about it or to talk about it, that's okay."

"Talk about it with who, you?"

"If you want to talk about it with me. Or if you want to talk about it with someone else."

"No. No, I don't think I need to talk with anyone about it. I'm okay with getting together for dinner. I mean, it's just dinner, right? It isn't like anyone will get upset over having a meal together. It's what normal families do."

"Heather needed some time to think about it. She said she didn't think it was a good idea to start with. And I've been thinking about it for a long time. So if you need some time, you got it."

"No. I said I'm okay with it."

"Okay." Zachary took a deep breath in and let it out again. He wasn't sure he was convinced that Tyrrell was okay with it, but if that's what he was going to keep saying, that was fine. Maybe Zachary should leave the next step for the next time they talked. After Tyrrell had a chance to adjust to the idea.

"What is it?" Tyrrell asked. "What else?"

"Nothing. I'll just leave it at that."

"If there's something else, just tell me. You don't have to protect me from anything, Zachary."

He could blow off Tyrrell's question. Say that Kenzie had just gotten out of the shower or their dinner had arrived and he had to go. But if Tyrrell didn't want to be protected, sheltered from anything, then Zachary should respect that.

"We wondered if you would talk to Vince and Mindy about it.

You're the one who knows them. We figured you'd be the best one to approach them and see if they were willing to get together, too."

"They might not want to. If Vince says no, then you know Mindy isn't going to agree either."

"But we won't know until we ask."

"No, I guess not."

"Do you mind bringing it up with them? They're still practically strangers to me. I don't want them to feel like I'm forcing them into something."

"Yeah…" Tyrrell's voice was hesitant, even though he was giving the right answer. "I could do that."

"We'd really appreciate it."

"You and Heather? It was your idea?"

"Yeah."

"Who's gonna tell Joss?"

Zachary laughed. "Heather. She seems to think she might be able to talk Joss into it."

"Good luck to her. Joss didn't even want to meet everyone."

Zachary wondered whether Joss had wanted to meet him. They had all surprised him, Tyrrell and Heather and Joss, when he had gone to see the Petersons. Zachary was pretty sure that Tyrrell had said at that time that Joss wanted to meet Zachary. But that might have been a lie. Tyrrell or Heather, or both together, might have talked Joss into the meeting.

"Heather is going to try," Zachary said lamely. "I guess… she'll let us know whether it works out."

"Is it going to be everyone?" Tyrrell asked. When Zachary tried to form an answer, wondering whether he was referring to Berk, their father, Tyrrell continued. "The kids, I mean. Alisha and Mason? Do I bring them too?"

Zachary really enjoyed Tyrrell's children, and didn't want to exclude them from the festivities, if Tyrrell was able to get permission from their mother. "Yeah, that would be nice."

"So what about Heather? Is she going to bring her husband and kids? Will her kids come?"

Zachary hadn't met them. Heather's kids were adults and had

moved out on their own. He didn't know how Heather felt about them meeting her siblings.

"Uh, I don't know. We didn't talk about it. They're welcome to come, but I don't know if they will want to."

Even as he said it, he worried about the number of people now invited to this dinner. All siblings would be a lot for Zachary to handle at once. He had trouble with even just the four of them together. Add spouses or significant others, kids, grown kids, their children if they had any... that was a lot of people to deal with, keeping an even emotional keel throughout the evening. Trying to keep dinner conversation going and no one getting angry or uptight about anything. Mostly Joss. The rest of them tried not to bring up anything from their childhood that might have resulted in hurt feelings or bad memories, but Joss sugar-coated nothing. She didn't mask how she felt about the bratty little brother who had caused the family break-up. She was pretty open about her decades of drug addiction and being trafficked. She didn't suffer fools gladly, or at all.

"Sounds like fun," Tyrrell said cheerily, his mind not following the same pathways as Zachary's. "A little pre-Christmas dinner. We could even do a gift exchange. White elephant or drawing names."

"That might be... a bit much."

And he didn't want to go somewhere there would be Christmas decorations. He didn't want it to turn into a Christmas party, where he wouldn't be able to relax and would probably have to take anti-anxiety meds until he was a zombie. Not the kind of dinner he had planned on.

"Let's not make it a... holiday dinner," Zachary croaked, unable to even use the word Christmas to describe it. "No big do. No presents or expectations. No music or..."

"No music or decorations," Tyrrell finished. "No *Santa Baby* playing over the radio."

Zachary's throat was hot and constricted. He could barely breathe. "No," he agreed.

"Okay, Zach. Don't worry about that. I'll pick another theme.

Maybe Marvel superheroes. Or monster trucks. The bakery makes these great theme cakes."

Zachary tried to force a laugh. "Yeah," he agreed. "That sounds much better. But I don't know if the girls will want a truck theme."

"Well, I'm not doing a Barbie theme," Tyrrell declared.

Zachary laughed again, weakly. "I have to go now. I think I hear the deliveryman," he told Tyrrell. He looked out the living room window, scanning the street for any sign of him.

"Okay. Talk to you later, bro."

"Talk later," Zachary agreed, and ended the call.

23

Zachary just sat watching out the window for their dinner to be delivered. As he watched the street outside, it was surprising how many people got deliveries in the afternoon and evening. Online shopping, food delivery, groceries, the list went on and on. He thought of Cora Johnson sitting in her living room, carefully taking down notes on every vehicle that did not belong on her block. All the deliveries, visitors, and possible stalkers out there. A private investigator's surveillance could end up being scuppered by someone like Cora, who took note of everything that happened on her block.

What about at night? She had to sleep sometime. But if someone had been watching Rose to discover her daily routines, they wouldn't be watching at night. They would watch during the day, like Zachary was watching his neighborhood now. Cora might miss the burglars and night stalkers out there while she was sleeping, but she wouldn't miss anyone who had been watching Rose during the day. The kidnapper hadn't tried to take Claire from her home as she slept. He had taken her while she was away from home, out of her mother's sight.

"It's not here yet?"

Zachary startled at Kenzie's question. He hadn't seen her come into the room. A great detective, very observant. He put his hand over his heart and tried to slow his breathing.

"Sorry," Kenzie apologized, laughing at his reaction. "I thought the food would be here."

"Should be any time."

"What are you watching out there?"

"Nothing. Everything. Just... thinking."

"Well, don't think too hard," she teased. "I see a little bit of smoke coming out of your ears..."

Zachary chuckled. He put his phone back in his pocket.

"I thought I heard you talking when I got out of the shower. Were you talking to someone?"

"Yeah, uh, Tyrrell." Zachary tried to pull his thoughts away from Cora and the investigation and to focus on Kenzie. "We're talking about having a dinner."

"Oh, are we?" Kenzie's eyebrows went up. "This is the first I've heard of it."

"I mean... all of us. I was just checking whether Tyrrell would come and whether he could contact Mindy and Vince to sound them out."

"All of us," Kenzie repeated. "Meaning you and Tyrrell..."

"All of the siblings. I asked Heather first, and she thought it would be okay. After she thought about it for a while. So we're seeing if we can get everyone to agree..."

"Oh, I see. And... where and when were you planning to do this? And would I be invited, or is 'all of us' just you and your siblings?"

"Of course, you would be invited too," Zachary assured her, unsure why she sounded so prickly. "We don't have all the details hammered out yet. It is still in the planning stages. No date or place yet."

"Well, be sure to tell me when you know."

Kenzie went into the kitchen and banged cupboard doors as she got herself a drink. Not just water or a soft drink, but a glass of wine, which was rare for Kenzie. Wine was usually reserved for a special evening between the two of them when everything had been carefully planned out and Zachary would not be taking any medication that contraindicated alcohol consumption.

But she didn't offer him any or get out a glass for him. It occurred to Zachary that he hadn't been very attentive to Kenzie. She had noticed that he was a little the worse for wear, but he hadn't even asked her how her day had been. He stood up and went into the kitchen.

"So… how were things at work today? Any interesting cases?"

"Don't pretend to care about it now. I don't need any fake interest."

Zachary shook his head. "It's not fake. I am interested. I'm always interested in anything you have to share."

"But you're not interested in sharing back? You're just making all these plans without me. At Christmastime. Here I'm going out of my way to make the season pleasant and not trigger you with anything even vaguely connected with Christmas, and you're planning a big party? What happens when you can't follow through and it all comes crashing down? You'll expect me to fix it then."

"I'm not… planning it without you. I just haven't gotten that far yet. There's no point in telling you we're doing anything when I don't even have everyone's agreement to do it."

"And you don't need my agreement."

"I… will. But I know you'll go if we set something up. The others… it's emotional, and I don't know whether they'll all agree to get together. Heather and Tyrrell said okay, but even they were not sure about it. It's going to be harder to get Vince, Mindy, and Joss."

Kenzie took a long sip of her wine. Zachary wondered whether she was even tasting it, or just trying to get it down as quickly as possible to calm herself down.

Was this what Campbell had been asking him about? Was she getting all emotional over nothing because of the anniversary of her kidnapping was coming up, just as the anniversary of the fire and the destruction of his home and family was coming up for Zachary?

Usually, he didn't feel like he could plan anything in the weeks before Christmas. The closer it got, the less he could see the future or plan for it. It felt like the world was truly ending and he would not exist after Christmas Eve.

But he hadn't hit that point yet. It was difficult to plan anything, but not impossible. And maybe with the med cocktail he was on and all the therapy he'd been diligently doing, it wouldn't get that bad this year.

But Kenzie didn't have any experience navigating the anniversary of her kidnapping. She hadn't been through it before and didn't know how it would make her feel and react.

"I'm sorry. I didn't realize it would make you upset."

"I'm not upset by the party—"

"The dinner. It's not a party."

"I'm not upset about your party," she repeated firmly. "I'm upset because you didn't even think to mention it to me. I thought that we did things together and that we were working on communicating better with each other. And then I hear you're making plans without even talking to me."

"Okay. I'm sorry about that. I didn't think it was to the point yet that it was worth bringing up. It's still in the idea phase. There have been other things going on."

"I've been turning down Christmas party invitations in order to be with you because I know you won't want to go to them."

"I…" The best thing would be for Zachary to say that he would go to her Christmas parties since they were important to her. But he couldn't. He couldn't go somewhere where there were going to be Christmas trees and decorations and Christmas music playing in the background. He knew it would throw him into flashbacks and a panic attack. "I'm sorry. You didn't say anything. If you want to go to some of them alone…"

"I don't. That's why I haven't accepted them. But I'm just a little angry that you would go ahead and start planning a party—a dinner—of your own."

"It's not for Christmas. I already told Tyrrell no Christmas music or decorations."

Kenzie shook her head in irritation. "What are we going to do about my family? They will want to do something for Christmas too."

"Okay, sure…" Zachary was starting to feel strangled. He didn't want to be coerced into some family Christmas party. But he couldn't very well tell Kenzie that it was okay for him to have a party—a dinner—with his siblings but not with her parents. "We *did* just have dinner with them. I didn't know they would want to have something again so soon."

"Christmas is time for families. Of course they're going to want to do something. They always ask, but I've had to say no because of you. And then last year…" She choked up and didn't finish.

That was when the doorbell rang. It was an extremely inconvenient time to be turning away from Kenzie to answer the door. But he couldn't ignore the deliveryman. He would just keep ringing. He sighed and went to get the door. Maybe the short interlude would be enough time for her to get her thoughts together and clearly and coherently tell him what she wanted of him.

The deliveryman—delivery woman—looked him over. "You ordered in?" she asked.

"Yes." Zachary waited for her to hand it over, but she didn't. "I already paid online."

"Is everything okay here?" she was looking around Zachary. She couldn't see into the kitchen through the door, but maybe she had seen their animated discussion through the living room window before coming up to the door.

"Yeah. Everything is fine. Thanks." Zachary reached to take the dinner bag from her.

"You having a fight?"

"Look, it isn't any of your business. Just give me the dinner, please. We're tired and hungry. Things will go a lot better when we have something to eat."

Kenzie came around the corner into the front hall. "Is something wrong?"

The delivery woman looked Kenzie over with sharp eyes. "Just making sure everything is okay," she advised. "Are you all right?"

Kenzie looked at the woman uncomprehendingly. Zachary put

his hand over his eyes, embarrassed. "She thinks we're having a fight. She thinks maybe I hit you."

Kenzie's eyes went wide. She laughed shortly. "Of course not! We're having a discussion about which parties to go to. It's not going to come to blows."

"Yeah?" the woman's eyes didn't leave Kenzie's face. "You're sure? You're okay?"

"I'm fine."

The woman finally handed the bag to Zachary. He could smell the sweet, spicy smell of their favorite Thai dishes.

"Thank you," Zachary told her, and he shut the door. He watched through the peephole to make sure that she left. She walked back to her vehicle, got in, and drove away.

He turned back to Kenzie, shaking his head and at a loss for words. They both went back to the kitchen, and Zachary started to unpack the bag without a word.

Kenzie got out plates and cutlery and set the table.

"You know," she said as they sat down to eat, "my parents go out of their way to involve you in things. They want to have dinner with you. They are including mental health organizations in their foundation grants. Dad even said he was going to give a Department of State contact a call about that parental abduction case."

Zachary was surprised. "Oh, is that why they called me! I was wondering how they knew I was involved."

"Yeah. They want you to be a part of their family, Zachary. And… I want to be a part of yours, too."

"You are. I know I do stuff with them alone, too. Having a guys' night with Tyrrell and meeting Joss by myself. But that was your suggestion. You thought that would help things go more smoothly."

"That doesn't mean I want to be totally shut out."

"I won't. I promise. I'll talk to you about dates and other arrangements once we get everyone on board. And I won't leave it all on you to arrange, either. I'll talk to them. Get everyone to help. In case… I can't do very much later in the month. Maybe we'll put it off until January."

But would he still be around in January? Zachary had his first vertigo-inducing glimpse of the dark tunnel that arrived every year, funneling his whole existence into one pinprick of light that terminated on Christmas Eve.

He swore mentally. He had been hoping that it wouldn't come this year. Maybe he would be a little down, a little bit more emotionally raw than the rest of the year, but he'd still be able to function like any normal person.

He ate his first bite of his favorite Thai noodles, not even tasting it, and stared down at his plate, his eyes burning.

24

Nikki Braun seemed hesitant at first to talk to Zachary about Rose Bircher. Still, she eventually relented when he told her about the kidnapping and explained that he only wanted to speak to her about their college days and understood that they might not have kept in touch since then.

She invited him to meet in the morning since she worked mostly in the afternoon and evening. Zachary checked that the address she gave him was the same one as had turned up when he did a background search on her, and headed out once Kenzie had gone to work.

It had been an awkward evening with Kenzie, and he was glad that things seemed to have reset overnight and were back to normal again in the morning. Neither mentioned the discussion the night before about the family dinners, and they just followed the usual morning routine.

Nikki lived in a side-by-side duplex. Alone, as far as Zachary could tell. On her side of the lawn, neatly fenced in, the snow lay clean and pristine other than where she had shoveled the walkway. The other side was trampled with hundreds of small footprints, was bare in some places, and featured a small, thin sculpture that Zachary was certain had once been a snowman. But too much time in the sunny yard had melted it down. There were some sun-bleached plastic riding cars and a small plastic slide. Zachary smiled at the evidence of happy childhood play.

The carpet in her unit was dark brown and old, making the place seem small and dingy. But the furnishings were comfortable and it was tidy. A good starter home for a single young woman. According to her credit report, she had lived there for a few years.

"Thanks for agreeing to meet with me," he told her after she showed him into her living room and supplied him with a cup of coffee.

"I don't know what good you think it will do. I don't know anything about Rose's life or her family." She shrugged. "After we finished school, we all went in our different directions. I didn't keep in touch with Rose. Or anyone else from our graduating class, to tell the truth. I imagine she stayed in touch with Amir…"

"Actually, from what I understand, they broke up before graduation. They never did start a life together."

Nikki's narrow shoulders lifted. "No? Well, that's too bad, isn't it? They got along so well in school, I thought they would stay together. For a few years, anyway. No one stays together *forever* anymore, but if things stay good for a few years…"

Zachary thought about his own failed marriage. He wished he could say things had stayed good for a few years. But they were already starting to break down before he and Bridget got married and, within a couple of years, the marriage was over. He had never achieved that idyllic marriage he had dreamed of. He had imagined wonderful times with Bridget, happy times sitting together at home, watching TV or on the porch watching the sunset. Not the constant public appearances Bridget felt it necessary to put in. That hopeful vision seemed to have stayed just outside of his reach. Always on the horizon. Until things came to a crashing end.

"You aren't with anyone?" Zachary asked, taking a glance around. There was no sign of a man or another woman in the apartment. No pictures of Nikki smiling and laughing with a partner.

"No." Nikki frowned, looking around as if she hoped to find

something different there. "Things didn't work out like we had hoped."

"I hear you," Zachary consoled. Hopes, wishes, and plans weren't enough for a happy, long-lasting marriage or partnership.

"But you're not here to talk about me," Nikki said abruptly. She pushed her dark hair back so that it fell behind her shoulders. "You wanted to know something about Rose. When we went to school. You don't think this has anything to do with school, do you? I can't understand how it could."

"No, I'm not necessarily connecting it to anything at school. Though if she had trouble with anyone while you were going to school together, I'd be interested in hearing about it. You never know when an old relationship might be the impetus behind something like this. I doubt it is, but you never know. If she had an old enemy…"

"Enemies?" Nikki waved this away. "Who has enemies in college? We were just a bunch of kids trying to get our degrees. Make our way in the world."

"Jenna said that there had been some trouble," Zachary remembered. He should have pursued it with her further. "Do you remember that?"

"What kind of trouble?"

"I don't remember what she said. Maybe that Rose had turned someone in for cheating? I don't remember how it went."

"I don't know. I don't remember anything like that happening. Maybe she's remembering something else."

Memories were not the most reliable record of the past. They were changeable and could easily become corrupted over time. Jenna might have been remembering something that had happened in a different class. Or Nikki might have completely forgotten something that Jenna had found memorable.

"Well, tell me what you remember about Rose and Amir, and anyone else in your group. Jenna said it was a small program, so you guys hung out together."

"I guess so. There were always other things to do, too, but it was easy to get together with the people who were on the same schedule. Or to get together to study or work on an assignment. It was kind of nice that we all got along."

"There were a lot more boys in the program than girls?"

"Oh, yeah. There were not many girls at all. And we were all geeks, so it wasn't like the nerdy kids trying to compete with the cheerleaders."

"More of an even playing field."

"Yeah. Though, even then, there was a wide discrepancy in financial and social position. Rose was one of the upper crust. Lots of advantages. People like me—I had to work through the summer to save up for school and then work part-time during the term. Rose didn't have to worry about the money. I guess that was why she was able to have more of a social life."

"Because boys were interested in her money or because she had the time to spend with them?"

"Both, probably," Nikki laughed. "I meant she had more time, but no doubt the boys knew she was much higher class than me. Life's not fair, is it? To those that have, more is given, and from those who have not, it is taken away." She sighed. "People like me always have to fight so hard for everything. If you have to spend money to make money, then you have to have something to spend to start with. It's sort of a losing battle."

"And Rose was rich? Or just better off than you?"

"Those Park Avenue parents of hers gave her everything."

"That must have been frustrating. Did people in the group think that she had an unfair advantage over them? Were people resentful?"

"How could anyone be resentful of Rose? She was always nice to everyone. She didn't flaunt it. If you needed something, she was happy to help. She was sweet. But she had more than her share of the breaks."

Until she got pregnant. And lost her boyfriend. Despite those challenges, she had still gotten a good job, had a nice house, and seemed to be doing well with single motherhood. Until a few days ago.

"This time, she's had a pretty bad break," Zachary pointed out. "Having her daughter kidnapped."

"Do you really think it was Amir that took the little girl? I heard he ran away to Iran or something."

"He went to Saudi Arabia. And they thought he had Claire with him, but now they are not sure. It might have been another little girl."

"Why would he take another little girl?"

"He and his girlfriend had planned to take her daughter on a trip there," Zachary said, deciding Nikki didn't need to know anything about the possible stalker. "But it is taking authorities in Saudi a while to find them and verify that it is his girlfriend's daughter with them."

"Oh." Nikki nodded. "I wondered... I've heard a lot about little girls being trafficked in some of those countries. You know that in some places like that, they marry off little girls? And I'm not talking about fourteen-year-olds. I mean little ones. Six-year-olds. To dirty old men. And it's totally legal. Can you believe it?"

Zachary shook his head. He had dealt with human trafficking in Vermont, but that had been of teens or young adults. Not little children. It was sickening to think that there was a market for such young children but, of course, there was. Even in America, there were child pornography rings and pedophile rings. There was a market for everything.

He had imagined Claire being taken by someone for revenge of some imagined wrong, or maybe even for ransom, though none had been demanded. He doubted the kidnapper was a poor, grieving parent who had just wanted to replace their own child or someone confused or mentally ill, thinking that she was their child. That kind of thing happened on TV, but in real life?

"Where did you hear about this?" Zachary wondered whether Nikki had read a news article about child marriages. Maybe as something that was happening in Vermont or about a pipeline transporting kids from the area to Middle Eastern countries. Maybe it wasn't a coincidence that Nikki had heard about it right before Claire had been snatched.

"It's a growing problem," Nikki told him. "Even here in the United States. Little girls are being kidnapped from their families and sold off to these perverts. And the authorities aren't paying any attention. They don't think it even exists."

At that moment, a child started sobbing on the other side of the duplex, a sound that raised goosebumps along Zachary's arms.

"It's the neighbors," Nikki said, reading Zachary's alarm. "These walls are so thin it sounds like they're right in the same room with you sometimes. The toddler probably just woke up from his nap."

They both listened for a moment. The sobbing petered out and it was again silent. Nikki smiled. "Things won't stay quiet for long," she assured him. "Before long, the rest of them will be home for lunch, and they'll be raising hell. Some days, I swear I can't hear myself think. I play music or turn up the TV all the way when I get tired of it."

"I saw the toys outside."

"Yeah. I like it when they play outside. But I can still hear them in here." She rolled her eyes. "I'll bet you live somewhere nice and quiet."

"Yes… I have to turn the TV on for background noise."

"Must be nice!" she laughed.

"Do you work from home, or are you able to get away?"

"I'm a courier driver. So I get to deal with traffic problems while I work, not noisy kids."

"Unless kids run out into traffic…"

She nodded. "Oh yes. You wouldn't believe the number of balls that bounce out into the street, with kids streaking after them. You think it's just a TV trope, but it's actually true. Happens to me all the time."

"So you can't ever escape them. Kids, I mean. You think you have, but then they jump in front of your truck."

"It's true," Nikki admitted. She looked at her watch. "Well, I have some things I need to do before work today, so if there isn't anything else…"

"Yes, well, thank you for your time. I appreciate you taking the time to talk to me."

147

"Afraid I wasn't very much help."

"Every little bit helps. You never know what little thing will be the key to solving a case. Sometimes, it is very small; you might not even know it when you first see or hear it."

25

Had Zachary been ignoring what was right in front of his face the whole time?

Was he suppressing the possibility that Claire's kidnapping was for the purpose of trafficking because he had dealt with trafficking before and it had been so difficult to face what was happening to adults and teens everywhere? In his own country. In his own state. But the thought of child trafficking was just too painful. Joss had mentioned it to him more than once. The number of children trafficked while they were in foster care. He had chosen to hear "teenagers" when she said children. They were the ones who were easiest to turn. That's where the market was. Girls and boys who were just growing into adult bodies and figuring things out. Troubled, confused, maybe a little naive about how the world worked.

But children? Little children like Claire? Even though he knew it was done, he had kept it out of his mind, looking steadfastly at the other options. Her father in Saudi Arabia. Taken by a kidnapper looking for vengeance. Taken by a random stranger for another reason. Not considering the trafficking of children for sex or slavery.

He tried to lose himself in his driving. Driving was one of the things that could calm him down, even him out. It was a kind of moving meditation for him. Like tai chi, except with his foot on the gas rather than moving in incredibly slow contortions. He didn't need to go out of town, but he hit the highway exit anyway. He didn't want the stop-and-go traffic of the town. He wanted to move fast and lose himself in the flow of highway driving.

At first, he thought he would just take the exit, travel a few miles down the highway, and then turn around and go back home. But he didn't want to turn off the highway once he got onto it. He didn't want to turn around and go back. Highway driving was better than an anti-anxiety pill for him and maybe, if he could do enough, he wouldn't have to take anything. So he kept going.

Eventually, he knew he was going to see Joss. The thought made him grimace. He loved his sister and knew she loved him, but she was sharp and bitter and would have strong words for him. She wouldn't put up with any show of weakness, but would expect him to be strong. She would be blunt.

But that was what he needed. He didn't want to be coddled or told that what he was thinking was nonsense. He didn't want to be told that children didn't get trafficked and that Claire was just fine, because he knew it wasn't true. He knew it happened, and the sooner he accepted it and was able to follow that avenue of investigation, the better the chances were that he would find her.

If she were being trafficked, then at least the chances were good that she was still alive. They would want to keep her generating money for them for as long as possible. Discarding an asset was bad business.

But that was just what he didn't want to think of. He remembered Archuro's hands on him, remembered the other abuse that he had suffered in foster care. Too many grasping men and women.

Zachary blinked his burning eyes, focusing hard on the road and the traffic and reminding himself to concentrate on his driving and push everything else away. It wasn't time to think of his case, his past, or anything else. The idea was to put everything else behind him and just focus on what was in front of him.

He was at Joss's all too soon. He sat in his car in front of her house wondering if he should just turn around and return home. The drive had been good for one thing, and that was to clear his head. He was thinking more clearly now. No longer refusing even to consider all the possibilities. It was important to have his eyes wide open, and now he did.

He tapped the screen on his phone and called Joss. She didn't like him just showing up on her doorstep. He was supposed to call her first, see if it was a good time, make an appointment. She had her own work to do. Not just waitressing at a restaurant, like she had told him the first time they met, but now she was involved in rescuing kids off the street too. Getting them out of the life. Zachary had brought her Luke, and she had started picking up her own strays. Her little house was full of girls and at least one boy who she was helping to build new lives.

The phone rang once or twice before she picked up.

"What do you want?"

"I just wanted to talk."

Maybe he should tell her he was calling about the family dinner. Pretend that was all that he was concerned about. Heather had offered to get Joss onboard but, if the opportunity came up for Zachary to talk to her about it…

"You couldn't get a signal in Roxboro?" Joss asked dryly.

Zachary looked toward the house. Obviously, she had spotted him.

"Well, uh… I needed a drive to clear my head."

"So now it's clear, so you don't need to talk."

"Can we just… Can I ask you about something?"

"That never goes well." Joss gave a heavy sigh. "You might as well come in. Talking to you on the phone while you're sitting in front of the house is ridiculous. I'm not going to do it."

She ended the call abruptly. Zachary put his phone in his pocket and got out of the car. He locked the doors, made sure that the security system engaged, eyeballed the locks to make sure they were actually in the locked position, and pressed the button again. He reached for the door handle, then stopped himself and went around the car to cross the street and walk up to Joss's door. She was waiting, and opened it before he could knock or ring the doorbell.

"What's all this fussing?" Joss demanded, pointing to the key fob still in his hand. "Is it not working?"

Zachary pointed it toward the car, pressing the lock button again. He looked at her. "No," he admitted, "just… compulsions."

"Stop that. Get them to increase your meds."

"It's not bad right now. I don't want to mess with anything."

"What if you have to go somewhere in a hurry? What if someone is chasing you and you have to stop to fiddle with your locks?" Joss demanded. "What then?"

Zachary grinned, picturing the ridiculous situation. Of course it wouldn't happen like that. Not like some Three Stooges sequence. And he didn't usually have to run away from anyone. Though there had been a few times in his career when he'd had to make a quick getaway.

"If I was being chased, I wouldn't stop and fiddle," he assured her.

"Then you can control it."

"To an extent. Like forcing yourself not to scratch an itch. But in a case like that, adrenaline would take over, and I wouldn't be worrying about the itch."

She ushered him into the house. It was quiet. If anyone else were home, they were in the bedrooms pursuing quiet activities, as they were supposed to if anyone came by. Not giving themselves away.

"Don't you have any anxiety-driven behaviors?" Zachary asked. "After everything you went through, I'd figure you to have PTSD and some weird calming behaviors, too."

"Not that I let anyone see."

Zachary nodded. Joss was good at masking. She appeared to be decisive and capable. She had no social graces, but he believed that was deliberate, not pathological. She didn't want people to get too close. She didn't fear what people thought of her. She just wanted to live her own life without other people bothering her.

"Coffee?" Joss offered.

"Yeah, that'd be great."

She was a big coffee drinker. Zachary never had to worry that he was drinking too much caffeine around her. She would just encourage him to have another one. Caffeine was a socially acceptable drug. Not one that was usually recommended for people dealing with anxiety and panic disorders. But caffeine helped Zachary to focus and was a milder stimulant than the commonly prescribed ADHD drugs. And it never kept him from sleeping. He could have coffee right before bed, and it just helped him calm down and relax.

Joss prepared a couple of cups in the kitchen and brought them out, handing one oversized mug to Zachary and sitting down with the other.

"So, what did you want to talk about? How is Rhys?"

Joss knew about Zachary's young Black friend who had been challenged by mutism since his grandfather's murder. They had met when Joss and Luke had visited Zachary at the hospital the previous year, though he hadn't found that out until later. Rhys was attracted to Luke, but Zachary didn't want them spending time together or messaging each other all the time, only too aware that Luke could return to the life at any time, and would be required to bring other young men and women into the fold. Zachary did not want Rhys to be one of Luke's victims.

"Rhys is doing okay," Zachary said slowly. Joss also knew that he'd been through some major challenges with mental illness recently, though Zachary hadn't given her many details, trying to give Rhys his privacy and dignity. "It's tough, but I think he's moving forward."

Joss nodded her approval. Zachary glanced toward the bedrooms. "How about Luke?"

Joss rocked her hand back and forth. "He's up and down. He's trying."

Zachary didn't ask what that meant, trying to afford Luke some privacy, too. Was he backsliding on his drug rehab? Going out to party when he was supposed to be asleep in bed? Making contact with old friends?

"So, what did you want to ask about?" Joss demanded.

"I'm working on a kidnapping case. A little girl this time, not a teenager. At first, the police thought that her father had taken her, so there wasn't much of an investigation. But I don't think it was him. And then we're left with… a lot of unanswered questions. A lot of things to look into."

"What kind of kidnapping?"

"She disappeared from a kids' play place. One of those places in the mall with all the climbing walls and ball pits and slides."

"Great place for a predator to pick up kids."

"Well, they have security in place, but in this case… it wasn't good enough. They have locked gates and cards and no one is allowed in there who doesn't have a kid with them. But there were holes."

"There usually are. It's only the appearance of security."

Zachary nodded slowly. He imagined that it would be hard to get all the employees to follow all the rules. They wouldn't want to go through all the trouble all the time. They would allow people to bypass the rules if they had a good story or if the employee was feeling lazy and didn't want to be bothered. Corporate left broken cameras in place to be fixed sometime in the future, more concerned with people thinking they were being watched than with actually watching them. Doors were propped open. Employee background checks would not be done or not be reviewed. People with a legitimate reason to come and go to the play place would be allowed in without being logged or vetted—custodians, repairmen, delivery drivers, IT guys, and all the other service people needed from time to time.

It wasn't like it was an airport. And from what Zachary understood of airport security, it wasn't as secure as people thought, but was more geared toward making people feel safe and protected. And that was what the play place wanted. They wanted parents to feel comfortable bringing their children there. Actually being secure was secondary. It might be more secure than a playground in an open park space, but that didn't mean children couldn't still be taken from there. As had now been proven.

26

"So why did you want to talk to me about it?" Joss questioned. "What do I know about places like that?"

Something, apparently. She was the one who said it would be a good place to snatch a kid and that they weren't that secure. Something she'd had experience with when she had been involved with trafficking?

"I don't know. I guess it would be a pretty good place for traffickers to pick up kids."

Joss shook her head. "Are you kidding me? Traffickers aren't going to take kids from a place like that. Full of people. Parents, security guards, employees, a ton of other kids. They want to grab kids who are alone. Walking home from school, hanging out at the mall by themselves, stuff like that." Joss took a sip of the coffee, thinking about it. "There are guys who will just snatch a kid off the street and force them into the game. But usually, it's more effective to entice them. Befriend them, sound them out, get them lying to their parents if they are still living at home. Use a Romeo to seduce them. You know all of this."

They had discussed how people like Luke had operated, bringing Madison and other teens into the business. But it wouldn't be the same for little kids. They wouldn't be able to get to little kids like that. They needed a different approach.

"But little kids… you wouldn't be able to get them like that."

"Same principles still apply," Joss disagreed. "You still don't want to go somewhere that's so populated. You talk to kids who are alone. Offer them candy or ask them to help you find their puppy. Say that you saw something weird to make them curious. Ask them for directions. You've seen it all on TV before."

Get them far enough away from their parents that they could be snatched and forced into a vehicle. But didn't the same apply to the kidnapper who had taken Claire from the play place? He had made sure that she was separated from her mother, and had somehow taken her out of there quietly. If he had snatched her and forced her out, people would have noticed. Employees would have stopped him to ask questions. His departure would have been noticed. But it hadn't. Somehow, he'd been able to talk her into going with him and then had led her out through that propped door to avoid detection.

"If traffickers started taking kids from these indoor play-grounds, it would be big news," Joss pointed out. "Everybody would know that kids were being stolen from them. They would start cracking down more on security. Not as many parents would take their kids there. The police would start watching them. It would be all over the internet."

That made sense. But that didn't mean that traffickers *hadn't* taken a child from a play place this one time. But why the exception? That would mean that Claire had been targeted specifically, as Zachary had first been thinking.

"So if traffickers took her from this place, there must have been a reason for that."

"Why do you think it was traffickers? A single pedo, that's more likely. Sneaking in or getting on staff, watching for a kid to go to the bathroom alone or something like that, and then telling her that her mom has been looking for her and she's in trouble for wandering off. He's going to take her to her mom. Maybe drugs her, maybe just has a roll of duct tape on hand."

And then got her out the propped door without anyone seeing. Zachary still hadn't settled on a satisfactory explanation for how he had gotten her through the hallways and door without anyone else seeing. The back halls weren't exactly bustling with activity, but the predator couldn't go into it without a plan of some kind. Unless it had been a spur-of-the-moment impulse, and he had just been lucky. Zachary didn't believe that.

"I heard there's a market for little girls as child brides," he suggested.

"Child brides?" Joss scoffed. "The price tag would have to be high. You can only sell a kid into marriage once."

Whereas other methods of exploitation allowed them to keep earning money on one child every day, potentially for years.

"I'm telling you," Joss said. "Traffickers are not going to take kids from places like that. Not even once. It's bad business."

Zachary had come to Joss for her insights; he knew he should trust her judgment on the matter. But he had a hard time letting go of the thought now that it had lodged in his brain.

"How close have you looked at the mother?" Joss asked. "Tell me she doesn't have a new boyfriend."

Zachary frowned. "A new boyfriend? You think that her own boyfriend would kidnap her child? That doesn't make sense. Or that the boyfriend was just showing an interest in her to get close to the girl?"

Joss shook her head. "No. Look at the mother, I said. If she has a new boyfriend, then she's the one who got rid of the kid, and she's just making up the stuff about her being kidnapped."

"No," Zachary shook his head. "I've already checked the surveillance video and check-in and out logs. She took Claire into the play place. She sat and played on her phone. Then she looked for Claire and raised the alarm when she couldn't find her."

"No one saw the little girl taken out of this place, am I right? Nothing caught on video?"

"Yeah."

"So how sure are you that she was taken out? She could have been killed and the body stashed somewhere. Mom puts on a little display of hysteria. Everyone feels sorry for her. All she needs is five minutes unaccounted for. That time that she was 'looking for' the little girl before she raised the alarm."

Zachary shook his head. Yes, Rose had been out of sight of the video cameras for a few minutes while she had been looking for Claire, but it wasn't long enough to do something to Claire and effectively hide her body. It was ridiculous.

"The whole place was searched by the police and the employees. There wasn't anywhere for her to hide a body."

"They didn't find a body. That's a different thing. Are you telling me that there isn't anywhere they were doing renovations or improvements in this place? No open walls? Fresh concrete? Dumpster half-filled with torn-out old structures? Basements? Sub basements? Storage rooms full of boxes or junk?"

"I don't know. Not that I'm aware of."

"There were," Joss assured him.

"But they would have checked for all those things. Brought in dogs to search. And now… it's almost a week later. If she had left a body in there a week ago, it would be smelling pretty bad by now. Someone would have found her."

"How often do they check their storerooms? Whatever is in the basements? Is there a furnace? Incinerator? If someone smells something foul, are they going to look into it, or just spray some air freshener and think that a rat died in the walls?"

Her suggestions made Zachary feel sick. It was bad enough to think that she had been taken by child traffickers to sell her to an old man. The thought that Rose could have killed her and stashed her body in one of the ways that Joss suggested made him feel ill. He was sure that none of those things had happened.

"Her mother is the one who hired me. The police don't think it is her. They thought it was the girl's biological father. He disappeared to Saudi Arabia. Rose hired me because she didn't believe it was him. If she'd done something herself, then she would have been happy to have them pointing at Amir, unable to do anything to prove whether it was him or not. Why would she come to me?"

"People have compulsions," Joss said wryly. "They can't leave well enough alone. They have to be the center of attention, and if the police were focused on the father, then she's suddenly lost her spotlight. She needs someone to stir things up and put the attention on her again. Media, private eye, family members, whatever. She'll do whatever she has to do to get back in front of the cameras again."

"She hasn't been. She hasn't been on the news or in front of the camera. She's not a media hog."

Joss nodded, a crease between her brows as she thought. "See whether she has a new boyfriend. If she has a new man in her life, she's trying to clean things up. He doesn't want someone else's kid around. So she gets rid of the girl and pretends it was a kidnapping."

If there were a body to back Joss's theory up, he would have accepted it. But without a body, he had to assume it was an abduction.

"Still the same Zachary," Joss sneered, looking down at her coffee before taking another drink. "You come to me asking questions, looking for my expertise, but you don't like the answer, so you decide I'm wrong. Why bother asking me if you're not going to listen to what I say?"

27

Joss was right. What point was there in Zachary going to see her if he wasn't going to listen to her?

He had too many directions to look. What had once seemed like a simple, impulsive stranger abduction had been fractured into so many different possibilities. Her biological father? Child traffickers? Killed by her mother? Or the stranger abduction it had looked like in the first place? He couldn't chase down all the different directions at once. He didn't have that kind of time or manpower. He needed to prioritize.

The police were looking beyond just Amir now; that helped. Zachary could suggest some directions for the local police and the FBI to investigate. But what direction should he pursue himself? He mulled it over as he drove back to Roxboro.

Looking at the dash clock, he could see that he would be back in Roxboro a couple of hours before he could expect Kenzie to be home from work, so he still had time to pursue other avenues of investigation before going home. Or he could go home and do computer work to follow up on leads until Kenzie got home. There were a few other files he was working on that he did not want to lose track of. He had more clients than just Rose, but none of the cases was as urgent as a child abduction.

Using voice instructions, Zachary called Heather as he drove.

"Hi, Zachary. What's up?"

She sounded far away. Zachary turned up the volume. "Hey. Is it a bad time? It's not urgent."

"No, it's fine. What's up?"

"The background that you did on Rose, did it turn up anything interesting?"

"What would be interesting?" she countered. "She makes a good living and has a good credit rating, so she isn't in debt, but also not making enough money to warrant a ransom demand. But there hasn't been a ransom call, has there?"

"No. But there have been other cases where a child was taken for ransom, but then… something happened that prevented the kidnapper from trying to collect on it."

There was a pause from Heather. "Because the child died?" she asked.

"Yes," Zachary admitted. "It does happen sometimes."

"I hope that isn't what happened to your kidnapped girl. But… there hasn't been any sign of her, has there? And it's been what, almost a week?"

"Yeah. The odds that she's alive and well are not good. They weren't good when I took the case on, and they get worse the longer this takes. But…" he tried to inject some hope into his voice, "it's not impossible. Sometimes children are found months or even years later."

"But we don't want that to happen either. If that happened… things won't look good for her mental health, will they?"

"Pretty traumatic to be held by a kidnapper for that long. Best we get to her as soon as we can."

He didn't buy into the TV nonsense about kidnapped children who had been raised by loving kidnappers who had just wanted a child of their own. He hadn't ever heard of that happening in real life. There was always some kind of abuse. Sometimes, multiple kinds.

"Anyway…" Heather broke into his thoughts again. "What else are you looking for? With Rose?"

"I'm not sure." Joss wasn't the first person to suggest that they should take another look at the mother. It was true that a lot of the high-profile kidnappings turned out not to be kidnappings at all but murderous parents. "Does she have a boyfriend or other partner? Someone new in her life?"

"Well, she does, actually. Hang on while I look it up."

When Heather came back on, her voice was clearer. She had perhaps switched from speakerphone to earbuds.

"Okay. Let's see, here. Workplace romance. Another researcher or programmer. Drew O'Dell. They've been friends for a while, popping in and out of each other's social timelines. Making comments here and there. Started getting more cozy a couple of months ago. Shots of them together, out for drinks, watching a movie together, stuff like that. No engagement announcements. They are each marked 'in a relationship' but not with a name attached."

"Why didn't she mention him when we met? Or why wasn't he there with her? If they work together and she was talking to me about her daughter being missing, then wouldn't you expect him to be there with his arm around her, supporting her?"

"Maybe, yes. But different people react differently. She may not feel that he is 'part of the family' yet and that this is just a personal matter."

"They're not keeping their relationship a secret from others at work?"

"They're posting about it on social media."

"Mm-hmm." They could hide their posts from certain people, but that was tedious to maintain. All it took was forgetting to mark one post private from each person, and gossip would spread all over the office in short order.

"I'll ask her about it," Zachary decided. "Anything else that stands out on the background search? No one making threats? No controversial posts or weird ideas? Cyberstalking?"

"No. I looked pretty thoroughly for anyone saying anything about her daughter or posting on pictures of her daughter. It's all just the normal, bland stuff you would put on a friend's post. And no one just liking or commenting on kid pictures or coming out of nowhere."

"And nothing else that stood out to you?"

"Uh... she doesn't have a lot of friends. She's kind of reclusive. Keeps to herself. Nothing wrong with any of that, I was pretty much a hermit for years. Just... of note. Her personality. She takes care of her kid and goes to work, and that's about it."

"Except now she has a boyfriend, too."

"Right. Those posts stood out to me as being unusual. Or something new, anyway."

"Okay. That's it for now."

"Do you want me to run background on Drew O'Dell?"

"Maybe... basics. Criminal record. If he's ever been married. If he's just appeared out of nowhere."

"Will do," Heather agreed cheerfully, and they terminated the call.

28

Zachary decided not to call ahead to warn Rose that he was coming or ask if she were free for an interview. He might get more insight if she were caught off guard. She might be very different from when she had prepared for a meeting.

The receptionist looked at Zachary suspiciously as if he might be a salesperson trying to get past the gatekeeper when he asked for Rose.

"Can I ask what this is about?" She lowered her glasses, looking at him over the rims.

"It's personal. If you'll just give Rose my name and find out if she is free."

"If you don't have an appointment—"

"Please just see if she is available."

She didn't like that, but she eventually called Rose to see if she would see Zachary Goldman.

"She'll be right out."

Rose was out quickly. She ran her fingers through her hair anxiously. "Mr. Goldman...? Is there something wrong?" Then she looked at the receptionist, decided she didn't want to discuss it out in the open, and motioned for him to follow her.

The fact that Rose didn't want to talk to him in front of the receptionist made him wonder if she had even told her workmates about the abduction. He could understand her wanting to lose herself in work, not to want to sit at home in the silence waiting for the phone to ring. But if she hadn't even told her coworkers what was going on… that seemed like more than just wanting to have some privacy. Wouldn't she want their support? Wouldn't she want them to know why she was distracted during meetings or had to leave suddenly in the middle of the day? Or who Zachary was and why he was there?

He followed Rose to a meeting room similar to the one he had met her in the first day. She shut the door and immediately turned to him, asking again whether something was wrong.

"No, nothing wrong," he assured her. "I just had some more questions for you and also wanted to update you on a few things."

"Oh." She looked as if she weren't sure whether to relax. "Okay. Well, let's sit down. I thought you would call me first…"

"I was in the neighborhood, and I thought it was about time we met again."

She nodded.

"Did you want to call Drew in?" Zachary asked. "I thought you would want to have the emotional support."

"Drew?" She looked startled. "Why? You said there isn't any bad news…"

"No, no. We haven't found her one way or the other." Zachary paused, watching her. "Does Drew know Claire is missing?"

"Well, of course he knows. I couldn't very well hide the fact, could I?"

"One wouldn't think so," Zachary agreed.

"Drew is… he has his own projects he is working on right now. We don't need him here for this meeting…"

"No. I thought I would let you know that the police are chasing down other leads now. They aren't solely focused on Amir. The Department of State is in contact with the Embassy in Saudi Arabia and is trying to get in contact with Amir, but he is… elusive."

"Why? That's what I don't understand. Why would he be so hard to find and talk to if he hadn't taken her?"

"Because his girlfriend was being stalked and they are trying to protect her and her daughter."

Rose blinked, thinking about that, and pushed her hair away from her face. Then, she wound a tendril around her finger, pulling it tight.

"He was trying to protect *her* daughter."

"That's the story his parents are giving. We're trying to get confirmation."

"I see."

"Both the police and the FBI are working on it. I've met with them and given them what information I could."

"And what have you found? Anything?"

Zachary told her about the propped door. He didn't tell her about her nosy neighbor, writing down everyone's license plate numbers. He would give her that information later if he needed to. Otherwise, he would protect Cora Johnson's privacy. He suspected that Rose and the rest of the neighborhood already knew how much of a busybody she was, watching people come and go throughout the day.

"Is that all?"

Zachary shrugged, thinking about it. It didn't seem like a lot, but there were a lot of leads still to be followed up on, both by Zachary and the police.

"You didn't tell me you were in a new relationship."

She shook her head, bemused. "Why would I?"

"I would think you might mention it. It's a significant change in your life. Things can happen when you try to mix kids and a new relationship."

"What's that supposed to mean? You think that Drew had something to do with Claire being kidnapped? He wasn't there. That's ridiculous."

"Sometimes, men don't want someone else's kids in their relationship. They want a fresh start. They want to be the center of attention."

"Drew isn't like that. He likes kids. He and Claire get along."

Heather hadn't mentioned seeing any pictures of Drew with Claire on their social media timelines, only with Rose.

"Does he want kids?"

"Kids of his own? I don't know. Our relationship isn't that serious."

"He doesn't mind dating a woman who already has a child?"

"Why would he? I told you, he likes kids."

Zachary raised his brows. She was naive if she thought his liking kids meant he wanted to get into a close relationship with someone who already had a kid. Not everyone who liked kids was happy to raise someone else's. No one could go into a relationship like that, thinking he could just step into place as Claire's parent, and everything would be hunky-dory. Yes, she was only five, which meant it would be easier for her to bond with him, but there was no guarantee she would. And from what Cora Johnson had said, Claire was hyperactive; a kid with ADHD was not easy to parent to begin with and might have other invisible disabilities that would make it that much harder.

Sometimes, as Joss had suggested, people just wanted to start with a clean slate. Take out the problem relationship and it would just be Rose and Drew. Like any other singles.

"I told you Drew had nothing to do with Claire's disappearance. That's ridiculous."

"Do you think he would mind talking to me? We could just chat for a couple of minutes."

"So you can feel him out? See whether I'm telling the truth or not? I know what I'm talking about, Zachary. I know what kind of a guy Drew is, and he didn't have anything to do with Claire's kidnapping."

"I didn't say he did. But I'm surprised he didn't want to be here to support you. Is he... working on an important project and can't take the time out?"

"Yes, he has work... but no, he's not putting it ahead of me. I didn't tell him you were here or that I was meeting with anyone about the kidnapping, or I'm sure he *would* be here, whether I wanted him to be or not." She stopped talking and looked like she'd just swallowed something bitter. She hadn't meant to say that he wouldn't respect her communications and boundaries, just that he would passionately support her.

"I understand what you meant," Zachary assured her. "And I'm not going to drill him and accuse him of being involved. But I *do* want to get a feeling for him and how he sees this whole thing. You *did* tell him about what happened to Claire, didn't you?"

"I couldn't very well keep it a secret. He just *might* notice that I suddenly didn't have a little person attached to me anymore."

A tear running down Rose's cheek surprised her, and she wiped it off with a quick flick, irritated. She was trying to stay in control of her emotions, but her polished veneer wasn't quite perfect.

Zachary nodded. "You need to lean on him," he suggested. "If this is a guy that you trust and want to be in a relationship with, then you need his support at a time like this. He could be with you right now. Even if he has important work to do, he could still spare a few minutes to be with you while we talked."

"You're pretty confident about that, are you?" Rose challenged, wiping the corners of her eyes to corral any other tears before they had a chance to leak out. "You know all about relationships. You're an expert in the matter."

Zachary's cheeks warmed. "Not yet, maybe, but I'm trying. Doing a lot of therapy."

"Yeah, I heard you were a little... unconventional."

Zachary gave a bark of laughter. "That's me. So what about it? Do I get to meet Drew?"

She took in a deep breath and let it out. "Okay. Fine." Rose pulled her phone out and started tapping away. It wasn't long before Drew showed up.

He was a tall man with perpetually hunched shoulders. There probably wasn't a desk set up in the office that was ergonomically correct for him. Or maybe he spent all his spare time gaming and could no longer straighten fully. He pushed up a pair of wire-rim glasses and held out his hand to Zachary.

"Uh, Mr. Goldman? Drew O'Dell."

Zachary had wondered whether he would have an Irish accent,

but he did not. Not that Zachary could detect, anyway. Drew sat down and inched his chair toward Rose.

"Just Zachary."

"Zachary, then. So…" Drew motioned awkwardly to Rose and pushed up his glasses again. "Rosie said that you're looking into… that she hired you to see… about Claire." He gulped. "To see if… you could get any leads since the cops weren't getting anywhere on it."

"Yes. Among other things, I have the cops chasing down some domestic leads, the FBI involved, and the Department of State following up on the situation in Saudi Arabia."

He watched Drew's expression and body language carefully to see how he reacted to these revelations. Drew did not appear to be worried about any of this and nodded along as if pleased with the news. He looked at Rose to make sure that she was happy with it as well.

"Sounds like you're performing miracles," he enthused. "I couldn't believe before that they had just… stopped looking when they found out about Claire's father. It was like… case closed. That's all she wrote. But we weren't   Rose wasn't   sure that he was the one who had taken Claire. You can't just assume and stop looking."

"No, I think she was right to pursue it privately," Zachary agreed. "I realize I'm biased, but I think the case had stalled and needed a good kick to get it going again."

"Yeah," Drew agreed, pushing up his glasses again. "A kick in the rear." He reached tentatively for Rose and gave her hand a squeeze.

"I just thought you would like an update on where we are, too," Zachary said. "Rose said that you're really good with Claire."

That wasn't what Rose had said, but Zachary was testing for Drew's reaction. He lit up at the statement. "Yeah, I like Claire," he said. "She's a really cool kid. She's always getting into something…" He chuckled. "That's the scientist in me. I'm sure that Rose isn't always happy with new messes and out-of-the-box thinking."

Rose and Drew both laughed, able to enjoy a happier memory or two together.

"What do *you* think happened?" Zachary asked, coming back at him with a question to throw him off balance.

"Me? Well, I don't have any idea." But Drew was game to think about it, pulling together all the data he had been given to form a hypothesis. "My guess would be... a stranger kidnapping. I know they are rare, but in this case... I don't think there is anything to indicate that it was targeted. I think that it was impulsive, but with some preplanning and forethought."

"Isn't that contradictory?" Zachary asked.

"It sounds like it, but no. I think he's been watching for an opportunity. Maybe he had several of them lined up. Thinking about the best way to get into and out of the building. What he would need to do to get away with it. Maybe... fantasizing how he would pull it off if the opportunity presented itself. And then it did. Everything came together, so he grabbed her and followed the plan he had dreamed up earlier."

Zachary nodded slowly, thinking it through. There was something to what Drew was saying.

But he didn't think Drew was right. The kidnapping had been too well-planned. It had not just been an impulsive snatch. Nothing had been left up to chance. For someone to get into and out of All Played Out as cleanly as he had, it had to have been planned in detail.

And that pointed to someone that Rose knew.

29

Rose's phone rang. She hurried to turn off the loud ringtone and glanced at the screen.

"Sorry, I have it turned up so loud because I don't want to take any chance of missing it—"

The color drained from her face, and she tapped the screen. She held it up in front of her face so Zachary knew it was a video call.

"Amir!" Rose's voice cracked as she said his name. "What the—"

"Rose, are you okay?" Despite the good WIFI signal in the office, Amir sounded far away. Like he was on the other side of the world. Which he was. "I just heard what happened to Claire. I'm so sorry to hear it!"

"They thought it was you!"

"What?"

"They thought that *you* took her. Because you left the country and jetted off to Saudi Arabia with a little girl!"

"No, no!" Amir protested, almost before she was finished speaking. "No, I wouldn't do anything to hurt you or Claire. Listen to me..."

"They were sure you took her and wouldn't look at anyone else!"

"This is so crazy," Amir muttered. "I'm sorry that anything I did had an impact on your daughter. It's just so crazy."

"What's crazy?" Rose demanded.

"We were just trying to protect our daughter, Maeve."

Our daughter, Zachary noted, while Claire was "your daughter." Amir had taken on the role of co-parent of Maeve's. That confirmed his parents' reaction when Zachary had mentioned his daughter being kidnapped.

"That's what Zachary found out from your parents. I don't know why the police didn't talk to them. They could be a lot further ahead on this investigation than they are now if they had just followed up on all the leads."

"Who is Zachary? Is that who you are with?"

Rose angled the phone to show Drew in the frame. "No, this is Drew. Zachary is a private investigator. He is here…" Rose started to turn the phone toward Zachary, but he waved it away. He didn't need to be on the video feed. "He's here, but I guess he's incognito." She settled into position again, the phone pointing at her and Drew.

"So this is Drew. Your boyfriend."

They both nodded awkwardly.

"Ask him why he left the day he did," Zachary told Rose. "Why did he leave the same day that Claire disappeared?"

Rose repeated the question to Amir.

"That's the crazy thing," Amir said, his voice growing stronger. "It was the threats. We wanted to get as far away from him as possible. Immediately. We were just about ready anyway, and we decided… we had to get out of there. If other things had to be tied up after we left, we would have a lawyer or agent deal with them."

"What threats?" Rose asked, voicing Zachary's own question.

"Michael's communications had always been directed at Orna before. Sometimes threatening her or Maeve harm. Sometimes begging her to be a part of his life again. Swinging back and forth between extremes. He is probably on drugs."

Rose nodded, focused intently on her screen. "Is that why you wanted Claire's picture? Because you knew you were leaving?"

"Yes. I wanted something to remember her by. But we couldn't tell anyone who wasn't directly involved that we were leaving. We didn't want word getting back to Michael about what we were planning, and anything we said might get back to him. We just wanted to make a clean getaway, and if he knew we were planning to leave, he might decide to take action."

"Then what happened?" Drew asked.

Amir didn't respond immediately, but Zachary could hear noises over the speaker. Shuffling, scratching, scraping sounds.

"Then this," Amir said, and it was obvious from the change in tone in his voice that he was reading something. A paper that he had just taken out of his wallet and unfolded, maybe.

"You'd better tell that girlfriend of yours that her time is up. Maybe when her daughter is gone, she'll think twice about the lives she's ruined."

Rose gasped. She was as pale as a ghost. Drew squeezed her hand again, but she pulled away from him.

"He threatened to kidnap Maeve?"

"That's what we thought. We were sure it was a threat to do something to Maeve. We already knew that the police wouldn't do anything to keep him away. They couldn't keep us under guard twenty-four hours a day. Even if they had tried to protect us, he would just wait until they gave up and left us alone again. Nothing we ever did made any difference."

"That's what you *thought*? And now you think…?"

Amir's voice lowered. "He must have meant Claire. He thought that you and I were still together, that you were my girlfriend, and Claire…"

"But why would Orna's ex threaten me and Claire?"

"We assumed it was Michael, even though it wasn't like anything he'd ever done before. But it must have come from someone else. Someone who thought that you and I were still together."

Zachary tried to get the words of the threat down in his notebook before he forgot them or they went too far into the discussion.

Someone had threatened Rose? Michael had threatened Rose? Zachary was pretty sure that it wasn't Michael. Amir and his girlfriend had made an incorrect assumption. And that misunderstanding had sent Amir and his little family fleeing for Saudi Arabia ahead of schedule in an effort to get as far away from the threat as possible. At the same time, Rose remained, completely unaware that her child had been threatened. Just going about her normal life as if it had never occurred, because for her, it had not.

"I can't believe this," Rose said in a strained voice. "Why didn't you tell me this had happened? Why didn't you tell me what was going on?"

"I had no idea it was about you," Amir said helplessly. "I thought I needed to protect my daughter. I had no idea…"

"That your actual biological daughter was in any danger?" Rose snapped.

She was lashing out at the wrong person and, deep down, she probably knew it, but she needed to strike out at someone, and the person she wanted to fight wasn't there. She was swinging at shadows.

"I didn't know," Amir repeated.

"How did you get the threat?" Zachary asked, raising his voice so Amir could hear him. "How did it come to you?"

"Just in a letter. Plain white envelope."

"Mailed to you? Delivered? Left on your doorstep?"

"Delivered to me at work. I don't know how he knew where I worked, because online, I just have a fake company listed in my profile. Someone had to know where I really worked. And he left that threat with the receptionist at the company I work at."

"Who knows where you actually work? How well-known is that?"

"I don't know. The people I deal with daily. People I give my business card to—but I don't give it out very often. I know that anything I give out could end up getting back to Michael somehow. Vermont is such a small state. It's like trying to keep something quiet at a family reunion."

Zachary had to laugh at that. He had also run into unexpected connections and coincidences in Vermont. Everybody knew everybody else—if not directly, then through just one or two connections. Forget six degrees of separation. If you needed an introduction to someone, you rarely needed to make more than one or two phone calls.

Just like Rose, when she had needed someone independent of the police to investigate the kidnapping of her daughter, had placed a call to an acquaintance and they had referred her to Zachary. Zachary wasn't sure who had given her his name, but it was not a rare occurrence.

"You need to get in contact with the police," Zachary told Amir. "They've been trying to reach you, thinking that you were the one who took Claire. That's where they have been spending their time and resources. No one is going to find Claire if they're only looking at you."

"The police have not been any help in the past," Amir disagreed. "In fact, they've probably put Michael back on our trail more than once. The whole 'small world' thing works against you. The whole point in coming here was to leave him behind and he wouldn't know where we had gone."

"They still need to hear from you. Is Maeve there?" Zachary tried to figure out what time it would be in Saudi Arabia. "Can we talk to her?"

"It's almost midnight here," Amir snapped. "She's in bed."

"Can you show her to Rose anyway? So she knows the girl you have with you is not Claire?"

Rose rolled her eyes at this. She was already convinced that Amir was not hiding Claire from her. Of course, he had Maeve with him, not Claire. But Zachary wanted it proven. He wanted there to be no doubt that the girl who had gotten into Saudi Arabia on Maeve's passport was Maeve and not Claire. They needed the police to pursue viable leads, not a red herring.

"I suppose so," Amir said grudgingly. He didn't know Claire, but he must have known what it would feel like if she were taken away. He'd had enough compassion and concern to call Rose when he had heard about Claire's abduction.

There were quiet noises from the phone. Zachary got up from the table and walked around to Rose's side so that he could see what was going on. He wanted to know for himself, too. He wanted to be one hundred percent sure that they were pursuing the right leads and not cutting off the wrong branch of the investigation.

Amir took his phone into a small room that seemed more the size of a closet than a bedroom. There was a child's bed and a dim lamp. The lack of light made the picture grainy, but it was still reasonably clear. Amir panned the camera over the little girl lying asleep on her bed. There were similarities to Claire. Both were about the same age, but their faces were different, and Zachary's business often hinged on being able to recognize faces. He knew almost immediately that it was not Claire. This was Maeve, not Rose's missing child.

Rose began to cry softly.

30

A t least they knew now that Amir was a dead end. He was not the one who had abducted Claire. And he had provided them with another clue. There *had* been a threat to Rose. She just hadn't known it at the time. Someone had not just picked Claire by chance, so they could also let go of the possibility that it had been a random pedophile. The answer was in Rose's past somewhere. Someone that she had harmed. Or multiple people. The *lives* she had ruined. That was what the threat said.

At some point, somehow, Rose had hurt someone. Had thrown his life off the rails. Whether it was something recent or from further in the past, Zachary didn't know. Rose had shaken her head in bewilderment at his questions. She seemed to have no idea who might hold a grudge against her. Especially who she would have hurt enough that they would go to such lengths to retaliate and hurt her. Zachary wondered whether it were something to do with a child, since the kidnapper had felt it appropriate to avenge himself upon a child. Most people wouldn't immediately go to harming a child rather than the person who had actually hurt him.

He got home just ahead of Kenzie. She drove past him on the street as he parked, giving her horn a little toot and waving as she passed him. She turned into the alley and would be parking as he walked to the front door to let himself in as she came in the garage entrance.

"Can't get much better timing than that," Kenzie laughed. "Not even if we tried."

They embraced and kissed briefly. Kenzie pulled back.

"You went to see Joss today?"

She must have checked his location on her phone. As someone who liked to keep track of his partner's location himself and to check on her at random times during the day, Zachary wasn't upset by Kenzie noticing that he had left town to see his older sister. It wasn't like he was sitting in front of Bridget's house as he had in the past. There was nothing wrong with going to see his big sister.

"Yeah. Needed to talk to her."

Kenzie would know there was more to it than that. After all, he could call Joss on the phone whenever he wanted to. And even if she didn't want to be drilled with questions or asked for advice that he then didn't follow, she would still answer the phone. Because, of course, if she didn't, he might end up on her doorstep.

"Everything okay?" Kenzie asked.

"Yeah. Just some thoughts about my case. I had to... clear my head... and ask her about some things."

Kenzie nodded. "Okay. Good. How are you doing now? You look okay."

"Sure. We've made some progress. At least... been able to eliminate some of the possibilities."

Could he eliminate the possibility that it was a random stranger? What were the odds that someone would threaten to kidnap Claire and then she would be kidnapped by someone else? That was beyond belief.

"Do you want me to put something on?" Zachary indicated the microwave. "While you get changed?"

"No, let's just do it together." Kenzie went to the fridge and freezer to check out the options. If she wasn't showering immediately upon getting home, she probably hadn't done any autopsies in the afternoon.

"How was your day at work?"

"Oh, pretty good. Things are quiet right now. It won't last, but I am going to enjoy it for as long as it does. Get caught up on some administrative work."

"How is Dr. Wiltshire doing?"

She glanced at him. "You mean Dr. Cook?"

Dr. Cook was the doctor who had temporarily taken over Dr. Wiltshire's work as the Roxboro Medical Examiner while Dr. Wiltshire's hand healed from a severe break.

"No, I actually did mean Dr. Wiltshire. How he is healing. Have you heard anything?"

"He'll be getting the external fixator removed soon, I know that. Then he'll be doing physio."

"Will he be able to get all of his function back?"

"Don't know yet. He had the best surgeon he could get do the repairs, so hopefully, yes, he'll be able to get back to where he was, or at least to the point where he can competently do basic surgery again. It's not like our patients will complain, but you still can't be a hack."

Zachary grinned. "Well, technically…"

"You can't release a body to the family looking like the local butcher did the postmortem."

He couldn't help but snicker at the image. It was morbid, but part of what drew him and Kenzie together was their morbid sense of humor and interest in forensics. There were not that many people who were happy to discuss postmortem findings over dinner.

"So you've made progress on your… missing child case?"

"We've got confirmation that it wasn't the biological father. The child that he has in Saudi Arabia is not Claire."

"And he couldn't have ended up with both of them?"

"Only one passport. You'd have to do some fancy footwork to get two girls into the country on one passport."

"I suppose so," Kenzie admitted.

"And he hasn't come back here to get Claire from wherever he stashed her, to take her back to Saudi on a second trip. We've got his passport flagged in our system, so we know he hasn't been back for a second girl."

"So he's out. He didn't take her."

"No. And he had some other information that suggests that Claire's abduction wasn't random. So I need to focus on revenge kidnapping."

"Is that a well-known thing?"

"It isn't at the top of the list, but they are known to happen."

"Revenge on whom?" Kenzie asked, opening various packages to start the magic of meal preparation. "It must be something pretty bad for them to take revenge by kidnapping a little girl."

Zachary nodded. "Yeah, I know. Mother claims not to know anything that anyone holds against her. I don't have anything specific about the biological father, but the threat referred to the mother."

"There was a threat?"

"Yeah. Against the mother. Only she didn't get it." Zachary waved this away, not wanting to explain the details. "I'm going to need to do some digging to see if I can find out who her enemies are, because she claims not to know."

"Seems odd that if it was something that life changing for someone else, that she wouldn't know it."

"I think she's got to know. Whether she's lying to me or just not thinking straight, I don't know. Something like this could mess with your brain. And maybe it's obvious, but she's just so stressed out she doesn't see the connection."

"She must be frantic."

"Well… that's the thing. She's not. She's gotten emotional a couple of times, but mostly, she just seems… normal. She's going to work, doesn't seem to have talked to anyone about it other than her boyfriend. Everyone handles emotions differently, but she seems… distant."

"She probably is just less demonstrative… but you're pretty good at reading people, so don't ignore your feelings about it. If you think she might be involved somehow, you need to follow that up too."

"I've had a couple of people tell me that she must be involved. We've seen too many cases where the mother kills the children and then tries to pass it off as an abduction or murder by a stranger."

"Do you think it's possible?"

"If all I was considering was her emotions and personality, then yes, I would definitely dig down deeper. But looking at the other logistics of the case, I just don't see how she could have been involved. She is on camera bringing the girl into the play place. Then she stays on camera occupied with her phone for a couple of hours. Then she looks for the girl and raises the alarm within about fifteen minutes. So she would have to find her, kill her, and dispose of the body in a way that no one would find it, all during the fifteen minutes when she disappears into the play structure before asking for security to help."

Kenzie pursed her lips as she spread some frozen fries on a pan. "That's pretty tight. She would have to know exactly what she was doing. Both in killing the girl without screwing up and disposing of the body."

"And if she hid the body in the building, then where is it now? It's been almost a week. What happens to a body left at room temperature for that length of time."

"It would smell to high heaven. I don't know how anyone could ignore it."

"That's what I was thinking. Unless it is sealed or mummified or incinerated, and how could she do that in fifteen minutes?"

"She couldn't. But I also wonder how someone could get her out of the building. Through that propped open door? I have been thinking about that..."

"Me too. How does she get past the smoking employees? Or any other employees in the back hall? Wouldn't they recognize her as not belonging there? They would know that she wasn't an employee. How could she walk out of there with a little girl without being questioned? Or with a body?"

"How could anyone?"

Zachary sighed. "Even if we assume it was an employee,

someone who had a legitimate reason to be there, how did they get her out of there?"

"Maybe not through the propped door. Maybe through another door that was swiped. The loading dock. An underground passage. A door connecting to an adjoining business."

"You've got a lot of ideas today," Zachary commented, impressed.

"I guess since I'm not solving a medical mystery, my puzzle-solving brain needs something else to chew on. The mother could not have accessed any of the employee-only areas, right? She needs a swipe card to get into them, and she wouldn't have had one."

"She's a computer science graduate. I have to assume she would be able to do something like cloning a swipe card without too much trouble."

"But that doesn't make her invisible. She would still be seen."

"Maybe..." Zachary closed his eyes and tried to imagine how it could work. If Rose had wanted to whisk her daughter out of the building without anyone noticing it, then how would she? "If she has access to the employee areas with a swipe card, then maybe she had access to employee uniforms. Throw on a Play Specialist t-shirt, or a cook's hat and apron, would anyone look at her twice?"

"Dragging a little girl by the hand or carrying a body out?"

"No. She would have to put her *in* something so that people wouldn't see." Zachary sighed and rubbed the space between his eyebrows, trying to massage away a headache. "We need to see if anyone was seen carrying a large box or duffel bag."

"You look like *you* need a break. You want to sneak in a hot shower before dinner? Are you getting enough sleep?"

Zachary shook his head. "I'll be fine." He surveyed the items Kenzie had pulled out and put on the counter. "Are you making burgers?"

She looked pointedly at the hamburger patties on the counter. "What would give you that idea?"

Zachary laughed. He was pleased; they didn't usually have burgers. Usually Kenzie tried to stay away from junk food or meat-heavy meals. Fries and burgers sounded awfully good.

"Great!" He watched Kenzie for a few minutes while she started prepping everything. "You haven't had any unidentified bodies come in during the last week?"

"A little blond girl? No. I think I would have figured that one out. If she was dumped somewhere, she hasn't been discovered yet."

"She *could* still be alive."

"It's possible," Kenzie agreed. But her flat tone of voice told Zachary that she wasn't any more optimistic than he was that Claire would be found alive. They both hoped it. Everyone hoped it. But so late in the game, it was very unlikely.

"Can we change the subject?" Kenzie asked abruptly.

"Uh… sure." Zachary was surprised. Usually Kenzie was happy to talk about anything.

Her back was turned to him, so he couldn't see the expression on her face. But he could hear the stress in her voice and see the tense, hunched position of her shoulders.

Maybe the discussion of a kidnapping was too much for her. The anniversary of Kenzie's abduction was coming up. The first anniversary, which had to be hard. He vaguely remembered dealing with the first anniversary of the fire. He had been so agitated he couldn't focus on anything. Not school, not anything his foster parents said, nothing. He'd had increasingly long and frequent therapy sessions but still couldn't put his grief and pain into words.

He couldn't tell them what was bothering him, not because he didn't have the opportunity, but because he didn't know that was what was bothering him and didn't know what he wanted or how to fix it. He remembered running away and refusing to go back to his foster home, which meant that he was taken back to Bonnie Brown, a residential care center for children, to be housed with delinquents and the more severely disturbed children until he could be sorted out. But it had been a relief for him. Getting away from hazardous Christmas decorations and wood frame houses that could go up like a tinderbox to the concrete walls and starkness of the institution had helped him to get through the first few Christmases.

"What can I do for you?" he asked Kenzie.

"Set the table."

This was his usual chore, so there was a bit of snap in her voice as she told him, like if he didn't know that by now, he was really in trouble.

Zachary started to take the plates, cutlery, and other items he needed out of the cupboards and drawers. "I will. I meant... are you okay? Is there anything else I can do to help?"

She shrugged her tense shoulders, curling further into herself. "I'm fine. I'd just rather talk about something else now."

31

Zachary did his best to connect with the other students who had been in the computer sciences during the time that Rose and Amir had been. He had managed to get a couple of names out of Jenna and Nikki, but it was hard to nail people down to being interviewed. Especially when he wanted to meet with them right away. They wanted to put him off for a while. To think about whether it was something they really wanted to do or whether they wanted to blow him off. They would put him off for a day or two or a week or two to decide whether they had a good reason to talk to him. Or a good excuse to get out of it.

Brent Slocum was a professor at the college, so maybe he felt like he had some duty to answer questions about his college days and how much he had liked the program that he was now in charge of. A sort of a walking, talking advertisement for his time while he had known Rose and Amir.

"It was great," he told Zachary with restrained enthusiasm. "I really loved the program. I enjoyed my student days. I guess you can tell that by the fact that I stayed on to teach." He chuckled at this.

"You must have really taken to it," Zachary agreed. There were so many people who got degrees but couldn't find work in their chosen area of study. It seemed like a waste for a graduate of a computer sciences program to become a short-order cook or courier driver. Brent had at least been able to find work in his chosen area of study. And computer science wasn't like history, where the course of study never really changed. He wouldn't be bored. Computer science changed so frequently that it was amazing that anyone could stay on top of it. The curriculum must change constantly.

"And you were friends with Rose Bircher and Amir Osman while you were a student?"

"They were in my graduating class, yes. We spent time studying together."

"You weren't friends?" Zachary asked.

"Well, I suppose we were, yes. We did things together. Studying, socializing. Taking breaks together. Ordering a pizza. The kinds of things that students do."

"Did you like Rose?"

"She was a nice girl. Sure, I liked her. She was… maybe out of my league. Rich parents. She outclassed me. But she was always nice. She wasn't snobby. And she wanted to be in the program, you know? It wasn't something that she was taking because her parents decided she should. She loved computers and she picked up programming really quickly. If you had a routine that wouldn't work, she was the one you went to. She could sort it out."

"The two of you ever date?"

"No… not really. We hung out together as a group, not individually. Or in pairs, I mean."

"But Rose and Amir were romantic partners by the end of the program."

"By the end of it, I think they were broken up," he countered. "I don't think they were still seeing each other at that point."

"Yes, that's right," Zachary agreed. "You didn't see that as your opportunity to get closer to her?"

"No. By that time, I could see that she was going away and I was staying. So it would have only complicated things to start a relationship."

"Did she already have a job somewhere else?"

"No. But she knew she wasn't staying here. She didn't like the… atmosphere of the school? I don't know how to put it. The politics of the whole thing? It was so competitive, and people cheated and did other things that were not right. It was too easy for Rose to get caught up in it. The things that everyone else should be doing."

"And not paying attention to her own?"

"No. Rose was a rule follower, not a rule breaker. She was very strict with herself as well as others. An enforcer. The kind who was probably accused of being a tattletale or squealer in grade school."

"Not a way to make yourself popular." Zachary pondered whether any of those rules she had enforced had ended up "ruining" someone's life.

"No. On the one hand, everyone agrees to the rules, and it's best for everyone to follow the same set of guidelines. But there is quite a stigma attached to being a tattletale. Doesn't matter if you call them a good citizen, a whistleblower, or a rat. People don't like being reported, even if they know what they did was against the rules."

"Is it still the same today? I mean, how would she fare in today's academic climate?"

"Hard to say. On one hand, you've got the whole 'see something, say something' where you're supposed to report people or things or activities that might be dangerous. But is that just for terrorist threats, or does it also apply to other issues? On the other hand, you've got the opinion that if it isn't hurting you, then mind your own business. I think she'd have a hard time. She wasn't good with nuance."

"So she might have stepped on a lot of toes, left people with a lot of resentments or hurt feelings."

"But she was sweet," Brent objected. "She was always kind and generous with others."

"But that doesn't stop people from being upset if she involved herself in something that wasn't her business."

He shrugged and nodded, conceding the point.

"Do you know of anyone in particular she had a problem with? Toes that she had stepped on? People she had reported?"

"I couldn't say, I really couldn't. It was years ago now, and I've had a lot of kids and their college drama to deal with since then. They all start to blur together. You'd really have to ask her."

Zachary had already asked Rose if she knew of anyone who hated or resented her, but he would have to go back to her with it yet again, with some specific questions that would hopefully jog her memory.

"What about the computers? You guys have computer records going back that far?"

"Records of what?"

"I don't know. What kind of thing was she likely to do? If you input her name into the system, what would pop up? Reports that she made? Or just classes attended and the grades she got?"

"There is no one system that tracks what complaints a person has made. She would go to the individual professors of the class she had a problem with. And they wouldn't all handle things the same way. There are certain things that might be input into the system. But... well, because of privacy concerns, you can't just search random people's names to see what they were up to. And you have to have certain system permissions to do a global search like that. A professor like me, I wouldn't be able to find out what my students were doing in other classes, or if they were up to date on their tuition, or who their emergency contacts were. And I wouldn't be able to search anything for kids who weren't in my classes. That would include Rose."

"But you teach the classes she would have been in, so maybe it would recognize that and let you."

"I don't know. I never tried to search historical records. And I'm not going to do it for you. That wouldn't be right."

Zachary didn't point out that he hadn't asked Brent to do such a search. Of course it had been obvious that was where he was headed.

"Being a computer genius, could you hack the system?" Zachary suggested.

"Who said anything about me being a computer genius?" Brent laughed. "I'm not. I was never at the top of my class for anything. I was a middle-of-the-road student, and no more. And I'm not a hacker. Not even a programmer, to tell the truth, I can't remember the last time I wrote any actual code for a practical application rather than just student assignments."

"So you're really no good to me," Zachary joked.

"No good at all. I wish I could help you—or I wish I could provide some clue to help you find Claire—but I told you from the start that I didn't think I had anything helpful to provide."

"Will you call me if you think of anything?" Zachary asked, putting his business card down on Brent's desk. "Now that it's on your mind, something might surface after a day or two."

Brent picked the card up reluctantly. He nodded and put it back down again.

"Sure. If I can think of anything that might help you find Claire, I'll let you know."

32

Brent had been more resistant to helping than Zachary had expected. But the man hadn't really wanted to provide any details of what had happened when they had all been going to school together.

The stuff about privacy and permissions on the school computer system might be true. It made sense that Brent could not provide confidential information to any private citizen who stepped in off the street. But Brent didn't remember anyone who'd had bad feelings toward Rose? He remembered that she had ratted out her fellow students, but couldn't remember anything specific? They had been together for several years. He couldn't see how he could completely forget whose toes she had stepped on and if she had gotten anyone into serious trouble.

Zachary would have to come at it from another angle, find another friend who was more willing to dish the dirt on who Rose had offended during their time at college.

And if she had been a tattle back then, and probably in the earlier grades too, then what about since? Had she exposed the failings or cheats of anyone in the company she currently worked for? Or anything in between?

Zachary pulled up to the house and parked the car. He saw a

small brown package on the steps, so he cut short his usual car-locking routine, curious to see what had arrived. He saw the familiar swoosh on the side of the cardboard box and tried to remember whether he had anything on order that he was expecting to be delivered today. Usually, he only bought items with next-day delivery, so he didn't lose track of anything, but occasionally, he could only find what he was looking for with a four- or six-week delivery window. It was easy to forget what he was waiting for between ordering and delivering.

Or it might be for Kenzie.

He looked down at the delivery sticker affixed to the top of the box. It was his own name. His heart sped a little with the anticipation of opening the box and seeing what he had ordered and whether it met his expectations. He was like a kid with a toy catalog when he shopped online, and he loved it when his "presents" arrived. It was heavier than he expected when he picked it up. He gave it a little shake, but it was packed well and didn't rattle. What had he ordered? The weight made him think of a heavy book, but he wouldn't have ordered a book.

He unlocked the door and tapped in the code for the burglar alarm as he stepped into the house. He closed the door and took the box into the kitchen. He set it down on the kitchen table and got a pair of scissors out of the drawer to slice open the tape between the top flaps. He folded back the top two flaps and then the two inner flaps. Something pulled and caught on one flap, and when he yanked it—

Zachary's ears were ringing. He lay there on his back, his body feeling like pins and needles, and wondered how long he had been asleep. He had a massive headache. He'd probably taken a sleep aid, which had left him feeling groggy and hung over. He never liked the way they made him feel in the morning.

The floor vibrated under him, pressed down and springing up as someone stomped across the house toward him. Zachary knew he should get up and answer the door, but couldn't remember if he was expecting anyone. There was pressure on his arm, somebody crowding too close to him. Zachary irritably pushed back. He didn't want to be bothered. Didn't want to wake up.

The activity continued around him. The ringing in his ears started to subside. The tingling of his skin didn't go away, but worsened, his skin burning uncomfortably.

"Mr. Goldman. Zachary. Can you hear me?"

Zachary tried to squint through his eyelids, but the room was so bright. He felt like he had big floodlights shining down on him. He cleared his throat, trying to speak, but his mouth was dry and tasted of iron, and he couldn't work out what to say. He wanted to tell them to just go away and leave him alone. They could leave their business cards, and he would call them when he was feeling better.

"Mr. Goldman, we're going to move you. Just stay relaxed."

He didn't move or flail around when they picked him up by his armpits and ankles and transferred him to bed. It was better than the floor, but he still wasn't comfortable. His skin continued to burn. Had he been in a fire?

That thought woke him up more than anything. He moaned and tried to touch the burns, patting his skin and clothing to make sure it wasn't burning anymore. He gasped for breath, suddenly unable to take a full breath and panicking that his throat was closing up. He gagged and tried again to pull in a full lungful of clean, cool air.

"He's having a seizure," someone said.

They rolled him onto his side. Zachary resisted, but there was no point; they moved him firmly into the position they wanted him in. Zachary swallowed dry, hot air and tried to call out to warn the others.

"A fire," he croaked. "Mom! T! Wake up…"

"You're okay," a voice soothed. "There's no fire."

"Get outta the house," Zachary tried again. His voice wouldn't work; it sounded like someone else's. "Please, please!"

The bed moved. Zachary moved with it. There was a babble of

voices and activity. More people. The fresh air on his face was frigid as he had known it would be. "My mom," Zachary protested, "the babies. Get them out!"

"Everything is fine, Mr. Goldman."

"No, no!"

"Let me see him. Let me talk to him." There was a gentle hand on his shoulder. "Zachary. It's okay. There is no fire. Everyone is safe. Focus on my voice."

He drew in another long, strangled breath. "Kenzie."

"Yeah. Kenzie. There's no fire. Tell me five things you hear."

"Voices. You. Who are they all? Sirens? Are the firefighters here?"

He coughed uncontrollably. The fire had burned his throat. Superheated air. It would be sore for a long time.

"Open your eyes and you'll see them. Do you want to see?" Kenzie's fingers brushed tears from the corners of Zachary's eyes. He blinked, trying to open them, but it was still too bright. He had to keep them mostly closed. But he saw figures around him. Firefighters all geared up. He tried to hold onto one of them.

"They're in there!"

"Everybody is out," Kenzie assured him. "Tell him they're all out."

"They're all out," the firefighter responded in a gravelly voice. "Everyone is safe."

"They're out?"

"Everyone is out."

Zachary let his eyes close again and willed his body to relax. He was safe. His family was safe. The fire had destroyed the house. Zachary's actions had destroyed the family. But they had not been killed.

33

Though Zachary was aware of some of what was going on around him and spoke with Kenzie now and then, he wasn't really awake and aware of what had happened until a few hours later at the hospital.

He was aware he was sleeping in a bed. There were voices and activity around him, but none of the voices was addressing him directly. In time, he realized that it was the PA system and nurses coming and going and talking out at the nursing station outside his door. The hospital. He was in the hospital, but what for? It was clear that he was not in the psychiatric ward, the unit where he spent the most time at the hospital. His body was sore and he thought at first that he was burned from the fire, but that didn't seem right. He was sure that didn't fit the timeline.

He reached for the cup of water on the bedside table, relieved that he could move his limbs. He had been afraid he would be paralyzed.

"Hey, how are you doing?" Kenzie inquired from beside him, and took the cup back once he was finished with it.

"I don't know. What happened? Was there… was it a fire?"

"No. No fire," she assured him, which helped to calm the immediate racing of his heart when he put his fear into words. "But

I can understand you being confused. The firefighters were called to the scene and were the first ones to get to you."

"First responders," he discerned. "Was I hurt?" He raised his hand to touch his face, which seemed to be gouged here and there, with cuts, adhesive strips, and stitches rough under his fingertips. It didn't hurt that badly. He held his arms out and looked at them, finding them in similar condition, with fresh cuts in random places.

"Yes. But it is only minor. They are mostly concerned about concussion, but so far you seem to be okay. It's just the shock, and that is wearing off gradually."

She studied him, eyes taking in all the details of his face and expression. "You seem like you're doing better this time."

"Have you told me all of this before?"

"Some of it. In bits and pieces."

"What happened? How did I get hurt?"

"Letter bomb."

"What?" Zachary was taken aback. "I was injured by a letter bomb?" He tried to remember what had happened. He could only vaguely remember getting home. "There was a package on the doorstep. A delivery." After that, things got hazy.

Kenzie nodded her agreement. "We have the door cam video of you picking it up."

"I thought it was an online purchase. It was packaged like one. I never saw anything that made me think…"

"It's so normal for us to have stuff left on the doorstep these days. One of us is always ordering something. There probably wasn't any way you could have known."

"It was heavy."

"It was packed with pennies and nails. Shrapnel. But there wasn't enough explosive for it to do the damage it was supposed to. Most of the shrapnel stayed in the box. Only the top layer was propelled out." Kenzie shook her head, looking at him. "All of this is only superficial. Nothing deep, nothing close to any arteries."

Zachary brushed one hand over his other arm. "I thought I was burned."

"You might have a bit of a burn from the blast. Just like a

sunburn. Nothing that will need any treatment except maybe some moisturizer to keep it from peeling."

Remembering the debriding he'd had to go through after the fire when he was ten, Zachary was glad to hear that.

"So... it wasn't a professional," he suggested. Not if they hadn't put enough explosives in it to spread the shrapnel. That was a rookie mistake. Unless there had been something wrong with the materials he had used. "What kind of explosives?"

"I don't know. You'll have to ask the bomb guy when he comes by. He wants to talk to you when you're up to it."

"Do you have his number?"

"There's no rush. Give yourself time to get acclimated first. I want to make sure that you're up to it before we call anyone in."

"There wasn't anyone else in the house?" Zachary tried to remember. Tyrrell had stayed with them for a while. It was Kenzie's house, so she might have been there. He didn't quite have the time-line nailed down.

"No, you were the only one home. The blast triggered an alert with the alarm company, and they called the fire department."

"There was no fire?" Zachary asked worriedly. If they had called the fire department, there must have been a fire.

"No. No fire. Just a little old bomb."

"What about the car?"

Kenzie's brows drew down and she shook her head. "What about the car? I don't know of any problem with the car."

"I didn't check it... there was a bomb in the car..."

"Not today," Kenzie told him uncertainly. "You had one when you were trying to track down Tyrrell's friend, but that was taken care of."

"No car bomb. Just the one on the doorstep."

"Yes."

"Did they check the car? They should check."

Kenzie nodded slowly. "Okay. When we call the bomb guy back, we'll ask him to check the car as well. Just to be sure. But you were driving it, so I don't think you need to worry."

"He might have made a mistake with the car bomb too. Maybe

it didn't trigger, but it will next time. The one that Robbie put in the car wasn't wired right. Maybe this one…"

"We'll have them check," Kenzie assured him.

Zachary tried to read her voice and expression, even though his head was still a bit fuzzy. She seemed to be sincere. Not just trying to placate him.

"Okay. Don't want anyone else getting hurt."

"No, we don't," she agreed.

There was a tentative knock at the door, and Kenzie and Zachary both turned toward it to see Tyrrell. He and Zachary had similar features. Tyrrell was the younger brother but a bigger man. His growth not as stunted from childhood neglect and meds as Zachary's had been.

Tyrrell looked relieved to see that Zachary was awake.

"Come in, bro," Zachary invited.

Tyrrell entered and bent over the bed to give Zachary a hug. "What's all this?" he demanded. "You thought Robbie was getting too much attention for his scars? Thought you needed to add a few more to the mix?"

Zachary chuckled. "Yeah, you caught me. Just attention seeking. You know how it is."

Tyrrell hugged Kenzie too and sat down in the other visitor's chair.

"So what happened?"

"Just a little letter bomb. Nothing much."

"What are you doing opening letter bombs?"

"Uh…"

"Don't you have an x-ray machine to go with that security system? A bomb-sniffing dog? Something? You can't just open random packages without checking them first."

Zachary nodded. "I think I'll be a little more careful from now on. I didn't think there was anything wrong with it… like I told Kenzie," he nodded to her, "it was just heavy. It wasn't… ticking. Didn't have wires sticking out of it. I wonder how much those wands cost, like they have at the airport. The ones that are supposed to sniff out explosives."

"Maybe you can buy one on Amazon," Kenzie teased.

"But then what would I use to make sure *that* package wasn't a bomb?"

"Send it to my place," Tyrrell suggested. "Since no one is trying to blow me up."

Zachary nodded and pointed to Tyrrell. "Right. Good idea."

"I suppose this means that the family dinner is off?" Tyrrell asked.

"No, I'm fine. I'll be out of here today, right?" Zachary looked at Kenzie. "You said they just wanted to make sure I don't have a concussion."

"They might want to keep you overnight."

"Well, even if they do, it isn't like we had dinner planned for tomorrow. I'll be fine when it comes around."

"You haven't set up a date yet?" Kenzie asked.

"No. We're just seeing if people would come. Did you talk to Vince and Mindy?" Zachary turned his attention to Tyrrell. "Did they say whether they would come?"

"They're lukewarm," Tyrrell said. "I'm sure they'll eventually say yes, but they're not sure yet. It might be hard to schedule everyone in December. There are a lot of... holiday celebrations going on, you know."

"You think I don't know?" Zachary countered.

They all chuckled.

If Vince and Mindy were open to getting together, even just lukewarm, that was good. He would have everyone onside before long. Then they could pick a date, whether it was in December or they had to wait until January when things settled down.

"Just don't get yourself blown up before then," Tyrrell advised. "Be more careful."

"I will."

"Who would do something like this?" Kenzie demanded. "You think this is related to the kidnapping case? Or something else? I can't say I'm thrilled with you taking on cases that result in personal threats or violence."

"I wasn't expecting anything like this. How was I supposed to know?"

"You're obviously getting too close to the truth," Tyrrell observed. "Do you know who did this?"

"No. I'm following up on leads, but…" Zachary shook his head, thinking about his latest activities. It was too fast to have been a response to interviewing Brent Slocum. Brent wouldn't have had time to construct a bomb and get to the house ahead of Zachary. Even if he'd already had something made and standing by, he still had to do the packaging with Zachary's name and address on it. And it would have taken him time to find Zachary's address. At least, it should have. The house was in Kenzie's name, not his, and he directed all his business mail to a PO box.

It was somebody else that he had talked to. Maybe one of the people who had refused to take his call. Someone Rose had gone to school with and didn't even realize she had hurt?

Had someone tailed him home in the last few days? Zachary thought he had been aware of his surroundings and would have noticed if he had picked up a tail. Had he been too wrapped up in the case or his own worries to realize someone was following him?

They couldn't have followed him from his interview with Nikki, since he had gone from there to Joss's, and he would have noticed a tail over that distance. He couldn't see someone following him for two hours there and another two hours back without his noticing.

Maybe someone at the play place. It had been long enough since Zachary had first gone there for someone to have constructed a bomb even if they were starting from scratch. Long enough for them to find his address or follow him within the city to find out where he lived. Then they had addressed it and dropped it off for him.

It was almost certainly someone at the play place. Or someone that they were in contact with.

34

Zachary was still at the hospital waiting for the doctors to clear him and say it was okay for him to go home when the bomb guy and Campbell showed up to talk to him. The FBI investigator, Bartlett, was not in evidence, but Zachary supposed he was absorbed with his investigation of the kidnapping. And if the bombing was related to Zachary's kidnapping investigation, then that was probably the best course of action. A two-pronged approach, with the bomb guy investigating the explosion and the FBI investigating the kidnapping on the other, was perhaps more likely to be successful than bouncing from one investigation to the other.

"Zachary, this is Theodore Rushkin from the Vermont State Police Bomb Squad. He's looking into your little incident."

Rushkin reached out his hand to shake Zachary's, and he obliged.

"Sorry to hear about your trouble," Rushkin told him.

Kenzie, sitting next to the bed, looked awkward. She was sitting in one of the two chairs allotted to the room and couldn't offer both men a seat unless she left. She tensed to stand up, and Zachary motioned for her to stay. "Don't go. If they want to sit, you can sit on the edge of the bed."

He looked at the two law enforcement officers, both of whom shook their heads.

"Stay where you are, Dr. Kirsch," Campbell advised. "I doubt we'll be here for long."

"Doctor?" Rushkin repeated.

"Dr. Kirsch is an Assistant Medical Examiner."

"I think this one has escaped your table this time," Rushkin joked, indicating Zachary. "Unless you foresee him taking a particularly bad turn. Maybe as an Assistant Medical Examiner, you have a special sense about these things."

Kenzie laughed and shook her head. "No, he's not a patient. Not one of my patients, I mean."

"So," Zachary raised his brows at Rushkin. "What did you find?"

"Well, I am still investigating. There will be a few things for me to follow up on. I can assure you that this was not a professional bomb maker, so if you are worried about them coming back and trying again a second time, you probably don't need to be. Chances are, he'll see that it didn't work how he wanted it to and not pursue It. Few go on to develop their skills to become proficient. Those who do usually have a cause or work for an organization. With a retaliation or warning, which seems most likely in this case, from what Sergeant Campbell has told me, they'll probably move on to another method. Something with fewer variables."

Zachary just hoped that wasn't a face-to-face meeting with an unregistered gun.

"Were you able to find out anything about the identity of the bomber?" he asked. "Anything traceable?"

"It was a pretty unsophisticated bomb with run-of-the-mill ingredients. Nothing you can't get at your local hardware or fireworks store. And I suspect it was most likely made with materials he already had in his basement or shed. It did not have as much explosive power as he expected, and there was a good amount of powder. I suspect that it got wet or degraded over time."

"Lucky for you," Kenzie told Zachary.

"Yeah. And nothing was traceable?"

Rushkin shrugged. "We'll keep looking. The pennies may provide more information than the bomber realized. We'll look at the years represented and form some kind of opinion on the bomber's age and how long they were sitting in that basement or garage. We'll see whether there are any traceable fingerprints or DNA. But that will take quite a while. It's not going to provide us with instant answers."

"Did any of the packaging survive?"

"A good amount of it. Some was shredded, but we still have a good amount that we will try to trace."

"Did you get the bar code?"

He nodded. "Enough to run a trace with the retailer, once we get a subpoena. I've got someone working on it."

"What would that tell you?" Kenzie asked.

"The packing looked legitimate at a glance," Zachary remembered. "My name and address. A bar code that the deliveryman would scan for tracking purposes. If the bomber repurposed a bar code from a package he received, it would give us his name and address."

"That makes sense. But he was probably smarter than that," she speculated.

Campbell and Rushkin nodded.

"What about the front door camera?" Zachary asked. "We must have gotten a picture when he dropped it off."

"Seems like the bomber thought of that," Campbell advised. "Not a surprise, since so many people have doorbell cams these days. Hat, puffy coat, face averted. Walked across the yard, staying low, rather than walking up the sidewalk where the camera is aimed. Caught a glimpse of him, but not enough to do anything with. We'll canvass other neighbors for their surveillance footage, but we're not sure we'll find anything helpful. And we don't know what the bomber was driving. He parked somewhere down the street, not in front of the house."

Zachary grunted, racking his brain for any other ways to track the bomber. Rushkin would, of course, already be looking for fingerprints on the packaging and components. He already knew it was an amateur, so they wouldn't be looking for any unique bomber's signature. There were pros and cons to his being an amateur. The biggest positive, of course, was that Zachary was still alive.

Campbell smiled at Zachary in amusement. "We actually came to ask you some questions, rather than being drilled on the bomb maker's skills."

Zachary's cheeks warmed. But he figured anyone in his position would be asking the same questions.

"Uh, sure. Of course."

"Have you received any threats recently? In the course of this investigation? Or any other cases, of course. We need to know if this is about another case, too."

"No, nothing recently. Sometimes, I get threats if people find out that I was the PI who got evidence of their adultery or insurance fraud. But most people never find out my name."

"And you haven't received any threats on this case?"

"No."

"Any pushback? People who were reluctant to answer questions? Didn't want you involved in the case?"

"Yeah, a bit. I'm trying to interview Rose's peers from school, but most of them won't talk to me. Won't even call me back. The ones who answer or say no or say that they can't remember anything about Rose from back then."

"We'll want the names of people you have reached out to. It might be one of them."

"There was…" Zachary trailed off, trying to catch the thought.

"There was what?" Campbell asked after a moment waiting for Zachary to finish.

"There might be something about school. I mean, it's going back a few years, so I can't understand why something that happened years ago would become so important now."

"What are we talking about?"

"I don't know for sure. There have been a couple of mentions about Rose being the type who would turn people in if they were breaking the rules. Or that she *did* turn people in. But I don't have any specifics. Who she turned in over what. I have no idea if we are talking about cheating on exams—who would care about that now?—or drinking or hazing or breaking the school's honor code. It could be anything. But if that is what someone is upset about now, then I assume it was more than unpaid parking tickets."

"I would expect so," Campbell agreed. "What would be relevant now? Does it have anything to do with the little girl?"

Zachary thought about Claire. Was there something in the circumstances around her birth that would have made someone upset? Maybe something that they had just found out recently?

"What if… Claire wasn't really Amir's? I mean, they broke up soon after Rose got pregnant. Did they break up because she was pregnant by another man? Maybe a married man, or someone who was at least 'taken' by someone else? Then they might think about getting even by taking the child that should have belonged to someone else. Or never been born."

"Amir had a paternity test done, didn't he?"

"I'm not sure." Zachary tried to remember what Rose had said about the matter. Had Amir demanded a DNA test to prove that he was the father? He hadn't wanted any rights, so why would he? And Rose hadn't been looking for support, unless she had neglected to tell Zachary that part. "It's possible they did not. They still knew each other casually, but Amir didn't want Claire or Rose in his life. And she didn't sue for back child support."

"We'll have to look into that."

"You might have an easier time asking Rose about it than I would. Asking my own client whether she's lying about the parentage of her child probably won't get me very far."

Campbell snorted. "What? I thought you were the one who could get answers out of anyone."

"Maybe with her child's life on the line, she'll tell you the truth. I don't know why she would keep it from me when I was trying to find her daughter alive and well…"

"People do stupid things, sometimes. They spend so long guarding their secrets that they almost talk themselves into believing them. And they just keep holding them close, no matter what you do to dissuade them."

Zachary nodded. There was no point in expecting people to be logical. More often than not, logic went out the window as soon as emotion came in the door.

"Anyone else suspicious? What about at her workplace now? I understand the place is quite high-tech, lots of industrial secrets and IP. Any chance someone there is selling them out and was hoping to distract Rose from what was going on?"

"Her work relationships do seem a little odd. I don't think she's told anyone other than her boyfriend about her missing daughter."

"Really. Is she on leave?"

"No, she's at work. I've visited her there a couple of times. We haven't met her at home at all, though I went over there to have a look around."

"*In* her house?"

"No, just the neighborhood. Drove around, talked to that neighbor. But at work… I don't know. Maybe she is able to separate herself better from her feelings when she is there. She loses herself in her work. She said she doesn't want to sit at home in the silence thinking about it and waiting for the phone to ring."

"Most people can't actually divorce themselves from their feelings that easily."

"She probably can't either," Zachary said, "but she can try."

Campbell nodded. "Any chance she did it herself? That this whole thing is a ruse?"

"Kenzie and I were talking it over," Zachary looked at her, and she nodded. "We think it would be pretty hard for her or a stranger to get into the back halls at the play place without anyone noticing. Even with the right disguise, it would still be hard to take a child through there, when children are not supposed to be in the back. It would look suspicious. And so would carrying a duffel bag or something large enough to hide a child in. Somebody would notice and at least remember later, even if they didn't stop him to ask questions."

Campbell nodded. "We've questioned everyone there at least

once, and no one can recall seeing anyone suspicious or out of place. No one who didn't belong there or who had a child."

"Then it must have been a staff member. There was no way for anyone to get out the front unless a guard was in on it. And no way for anyone who wasn't staff to get out through the back without being challenged."

"Or something we haven't thought of yet."

Zachary shrugged. He rubbed his forehead, but even just touching his face hurt.

"I think he's probably getting tired, Sergeant," Kenzie said. "Is there anything else?"

Campbell shook his head. He patted Zachary on the shoulder, doing his best to avoid any damage from the bomb. "Take it easy for a few days, Zachary. You're going to need some time to recover. I'll let you know if we get anywhere on the bomber or kidnapper."

35

Zachary fell asleep after Campbell and the bomb guy were gone. He was finding himself very tired as he waited for the doctor to tell him whether it was okay for him to go home or if he would need to spend the night there. He could, of course, sign himself out against medical advice, but he probably wouldn't. If the doctor felt like there were still a need to monitor him, he would stay. It was only one night, weighed against the possibility of serious complications.

Kenzie was probably getting sore and tired of sitting there watching him sleep. But she didn't complain or suggest that it was time for her to go home. Zachary meant to tell her to go to the cafeteria to get herself something to eat and stretch her legs once Campbell left, but he fell asleep before he could.

"He's just resting. He's okay. The doctors don't think there is any permanent damage."

Zachary shifted his position and opened his eyes, the brightness of the room still making him squint. He blinked a few times to focus on who Kenzie was talking to.

"Hi, Feathers."

"Zachy." Heather bent over to kiss him on the forehead. "I didn't mean for you to wake up just for me."

"It's okay." He stretched, testing how much his body protested the movement and confirming that he could still move all his limbs. Having been paralyzed once after a car accident with Kenzie, he kept worrying that when he awoke again, he wouldn't be able to move.

"How are you feeling? What are you doing, blowing up packages in the kitchen?" she teased.

"Just scratched up. Like I got in a fight with a big cat."

Kenzie and Heather laughed at this.

"And a headache," Zachary said. "But I don't think it's anything. Just stress."

"How bad on a scale of one to ten?" Kenzie asked clinically.

"Maybe a five or six. Irritating but manageable."

She nodded and didn't immediately call for a doctor to put him through the CAT scan machine. Apparently, Zachary had given her the right answer.

Heather sat down and pulled her chair closer to the bed. "Are you trying to scare us all to death?" she accused. "The last thing any of us wants to hear is that you blew yourself up."

"It wasn't my plan," Zachary assured her. He looked at Kenzie, worrying about her. Heather could make jokes about it, but he hated to think how she must have felt when she got the news that Zachary had unwittingly exploded a bomb. He remembered his panic-stricken trip to the hospital when he'd heard that she'd been hit by a car. "How did you find out? You were there right away."

"I got a call from the security company that there had been an explosion at the house. I got home as quickly as I could. The fire engines were there ahead of me. They wouldn't let me into the house before they cleared it and got you out. But once they brought you out of the house, I was able to get to you."

Zachary nodded, vaguely remembering it. "You were... there."

"You were having flashbacks to the fire. They didn't know what was wrong."

"Yeah. Thank you... for being there."

"Thank you for not blowing yourself to kingdom come."

He knew her teasing hid her deeper feelings. She didn't want to be vulnerable about how scared she had been when she heard that he had blown up a bomb in the kitchen. Maybe she didn't want to talk to him about it, and maybe it was because Heather was there and she didn't want anyone else in on it.

"Happy to oblige," he told her, matching her levity. Then he turned his attention to Heather. "So, what else have you found out? Anything important?"

"I didn't exactly come here to brief you."

"Well, we might as well save a phone call. Unless you don't have anything. If there isn't anything else, that's fine, of course. You might not have had time or there might not have been anything else to find."

"Well, you asked for anything else on Rose's boyfriend."

Zachary tried to sit up more. Kenzie worked the buttons on the bed to raise the head so that he was sitting up partway.

"Yeah. You found something on him?"

"Well, I wasn't sure exactly what I was looking for. Started with the usual, criminal background, credit check, internet search, social media."

"Uh-huh."

"Credit rating is poor. He's racked up a lot of debt and has not been able to manage his finances very well. Impulsive buys, from what I can tell. You see it playing out on his social networks. Buys a new toy, maybe a motorbike or a kayak or something like that, and for a few weeks, he's 'all in.' He's now a passionate biker or kayaker. But after a few weeks, it tapers off. He isn't getting along with the other bikers. He's not getting the support from his friends, who never were interested in biking or kayaking and don't care to hear about it all the time."

Zachary could understand the pattern. Being impulsive himself, he knew how hard it was not to chase every shiny new thing or experience. If he'd had the money, he could see himself falling into that trap, too. But he'd had to scrape up a living to keep himself off the streets when he aged out of foster care. He'd known how close he was to disaster if he made a wrong move those first few years, and once he was better established, he'd ingrained good habits. He wouldn't charge anything he couldn't pay off immediately, and kept a cushion in his bank account to guard against future troubles.

"Is there anything else? Other than being fiscally irresponsible?"

"Well, I gotta say, I would have problems bringing him into a family with children. This immaturity and irresponsibility... not exactly conducive to trying to co-parent a child."

"You don't think he would be a good dad? But Rose has been a single parent, so she probably isn't looking for someone to take on that role. She's doing it fine on her own. So maybe she's fine with him just being... the entertainment after Claire has gone to bed or occasionally when she hires a babysitter."

"But after digging deeper... you might have a different opinion of him."

Zachary smiled. He loved it when Heather found something interesting. He was proud of his big sister, who hadn't worked until he had taken her on as an assistant. He offered to train her in skip tracing and some of the other PI skills that she could do from her computer, and she had taken on way more, helping him out with accounting, keeping his emails and project lists organized, and doing some of the other things that he was not good at or hated to do. Hearing what she had discovered was just as satisfying as finding it out himself. Maybe even more so.

"What else did you find?"

"He's served time."

He got goosebumps. Was this their guy? "Well, that makes a bit of a difference. For what, fraud? Kiting checks?"

"Nobody even writes checks anymore, Zachary," she told him.

"Okay, what then?"

"All of the details are not clear. I've ordered a few filings to get more information, but... child abuse and neglect."

Zachary was floored. He tried to pick up his jaw from the floor. "You're kidding me."

"Would I joke about something like that?"

Of course he knew she wasn't joking. He just couldn't believe this news. "Wow. Do you know any details at all?"

"He wasn't married, but was living with a woman. Kids were apprehended by DCF. They were in bad shape. All adults in the household were charged. He served the least amount of time, just a few months. So he probably wasn't directly involved in any abuse. But he did at least allow it to go on. Didn't take care of the kids or report the situation himself."

"And this did not show up on his criminal record check? Was it in another state?"

"The conviction was vacated. He kept clean after he was released and applied to have it expunged. He might have testified against the mother; I won't know until I get a look at some of the documents I have ordered copies of."

"How did you find it?"

"A few lines in the news. Most of the articles focused on the mother and the other adults in the house. There were apparently a number of them living together: her sister and her family, maybe a grandparent or two from time to time, or just someone one of them brought home one day. Drew was only a little fish, only tangentially involved, but his name appeared in several articles."

"And even though his record was expunged, you can't expunge those news reports."

Heather nodded her agreement, looking proud of herself.

"Good work, Feathers. That's critical information." He pressed his lips together, thinking about the situation. Had Drew had anything to do with Claire's disappearance? Either himself or by hiring someone to do it? Bribing an employee or two at the play place to look the other way? Alternatively, had he let Rose know that he didn't have any interest in raising a child and she wanted him enough to dispose of Claire? Were they wrong, and Rose's actions at the play place had all been thought out ahead of time and carefully planned? What if she *and* Drew had paired up to pull off the kidnapping? With the two of them working together, could they have done it? Rose to appear on the security camera and establish her alibi, and Drew to grab Claire behind the scenes and…

Again, he stalled, unsure what Drew could have done to get Claire out of the play place without anyone seeing.

They were both tech people. Could they have reprogrammed the surveillance cameras to make it look like Rose had been sitting in the same place the whole time and Drew had not been in any of the employee-only hallways? Even with all their computer skills, they still had to walk by real people who would notice someone taking a child or body out the back way.

"We'll need to get this information to Campbell. He can dig into it further. And I'll need to let Rose know…" He wanted to see her face himself. He didn't want to hear about it second or third-hand from Campbell. He could only trust what he saw with his own eyes.

"But you're going to take a few days off," Kenzie reminded him. "You'll need a few days to recuperate, even if your injuries are only minor."

Zachary felt like he had already spent all day sleeping. He wanted to get up and do something. Talk to Rose. Read through the report that Heather had prepared to get some additional details. He rubbed the bridge of his nose and looked at Kenzie, trying to work out the timeline in his mind.

"Wait… is it today or tomorrow? I mean… It was afternoon when I got home and picked up the package, and now it's…" He looked at the brightly lit window. The sun was high in the sky. He'd slept for hours, much longer than he normally would have overnight. There had been periods of time when he had been unaware of what was going on, tests run, and lots of sleep and fogginess.

Kenzie looked reluctant to answer his question, but she did anyway, not trying to keep it from him. "It's Saturday afternoon."

"It's already been twenty-four hours?"

She nodded.

"And I might have to stay another night?"

"Whether you do or not, you should plan on some downtime. Don't jump right back into things. Give your body some time to recover from this insult."

Zachary buttoned his lip and didn't protest, telling her he had work to do and it couldn't wait.

A little girl's life could hang in the balance. He couldn't afford to take a few days off.

But Kenzie and Heather already knew that. It was clear from their exchanged glances that they already anticipated that Zachary wouldn't wait any longer than he absolutely had to.

36

Kenzie probably knew that once Zachary realized how much time had passed while he'd been at the hospital he wasn't going to stay another night. By the time the doctor made his rounds and talked to Zachary about his symptoms and the tests they had run, Zachary was already halfway out the door.

"I'm not going to insist that you stay," the doctor advised, adjusting his glasses at the end of his nose as he looked down at a tablet computer, "but I want you to take it easy for a few days. You were lucky not to sustain more injuries than you did. Since Dr. Kirsch can monitor you for any increasing concussion symptoms, I'm comfortable with letting you go. But I want to hear back if there are any concerns." He looked at Kenzie to make sure she agreed with this.

Kenzie nodded. She was probably just as eager to get home as Zachary was. He had spent most of his time in bed, either sleeping or unconscious, while she had to endure uncomfortable plastic chairs and rely on vending machine or cafeteria food.

"Well then, I'm ready to go home," Zachary announced.

"I'll get the nurse to prepare the discharge papers," the doctor said with a smile. "We'll get you on your way."

It still took too long for his liking but, eventually, Zachary was walking out of the hospital into the brisk Vermont weather. It felt good to have the cool air on his face after the too-warm atmosphere of the hospital. He felt like he was breathing for the first time since he had arrived there. He took a few deep breaths and smiled at Kenzie, who watched him closely to ensure he was steady on his feet and everything was all right.

"I'm good," he assured her. "All I've got are some cuts and scrapes—nothing broken—and a few stitches that I probably didn't even need. I've dealt with much worse."

"Yes," Kenzie agreed, looking at him with an expression of sadness.

Zachary tried to wave it away. There was no reason to be sad or upset about his minor injuries from the explosion. And anything else that happened in the past was in the past.

Kenzie led the way to where her car was parked and they drove the first little bit in silence.

"It will be nice to get home," Zachary told Kenzie. "Back to our own space. It's just not the same at the hospital, no matter how comfortable they try to make it for you."

And they rarely went out of their way to make him truly comfortable. Maybe they were afraid that if they made his hospital stay too comfortable, he would never leave. But he'd had long-term stays there before, and it wasn't something he wished for.

Kenzie sighed. "Yes," she agreed, though her words seemed restrained. "It's always nice to get back home where you belong and can relax."

"What's wrong?"

"Just that... well, the bomb. It did some damage."

"But it's just..." Zachary started to answer before he realized that she wasn't talking about the damage the bomb had done to him, but to the house. Somehow, the thought hadn't even occurred to him before then. He'd pictured the kitchen looking exactly the same as it had before the bomb had exploded. It had done only minor damage to his body, and he hadn't considered the damage to the room around him.

"How bad is it?"

"Just minor… cosmetic. But…" She sighed. "I just don't want to think about it. To see it. To get someone to come in and fix it up. I know it won't take long and it could be much worse. There could be structural damage. It could be so bad that we couldn't go back there."

"But that doesn't stop you from dreading seeing it."

"Yeah. And knowing that… if the bomber had been more competent, I could have lost you. I can't help thinking about how horrible it would have been. What it would have looked like. Felt like."

Zachary put his hand on her leg, trying to convey his appreciation and how much he cared for her. He worried about catastrophes, too. How many times had he pictured losing Bridget or Kenzie or members of his family to some horrific accident, disease, or violence? He would hate for her to know how much time he spent worrying about catastrophes that would probably never happen.

They drove into the garage without further comment. Zachary climbed out of the car, watching Kenzie, knowing that she was dreading seeing the damage caused by the bomb on the other side of the door. He thought to offer to go in ahead of her, but wasn't sure how that would help anything. She would still see it as soon as she stepped into the house. Even if they went in the front door instead of the door from the garage to the kitchen, she would still see the kitchen sooner or later. She had to walk past the doorway. They had to eat.

Kenzie didn't wait for Zachary to catch up or get in front of her. She just walked determinedly toward the door and opened it without any noticeable hesitation.

Then she stopped.

It must be pretty bad. Zachary had been hoping that she was making it a bigger thing than it was.

He hurried to catch up with her. He stepped up behind her and reached out to give her a comforting hug as he viewed the damage that he had caused by being so oblivious to what was in the package he was opening. He remembered that last tug as he pulled open the flap of cardboard and the world dissolved around him. That last little hitch that had probably been a simple pull-string trigger.

37

The first thing he sensed as he stepped up to Kenzie was the almost overwhelming smell of fresh paint. He looked past Kenzie and saw gleaming white and yellow walls. There were plastic drop sheets on the floor that we speckled with paint. Someone was there in the house. He had thought Kenzie had said she didn't want to call someone, but he must have misunderstood her.

"Are they home?" a familiar voice called out.

Kenzie stepped quickly into the kitchen so that Zachary could enter as well.

"They're here," another man answered.

Kenzie threw her arms around Patrick Parker and clutched him tightly.

"Hey, you're going to get paint all over you," Pat protested, trying to keep Kenzie's body away from the paint that spattered his loosely fitting plaid shirt.

Lorne Peterson entered the kitchen as well and nodded at Zachary. "Welcome home."

"When did you get here?" Zachary went to him for a hug. Mr. Peterson held him gently, mindful of the numerous small cuts.

"Yesterday," the older man laughed. "We saw you at the hospital, but you were pretty tired. I'm not surprised you don't remember."

"You saw me yesterday?"

Of course, it made sense that his old foster father would be the first one Kenzie called and that he and Pat, his partner, would drop everything to drive up to see Zachary and make sure that he was okay.

"You weren't supposed to work," Kenzie chided, laughing. "I told you that you could stay in the guest room, not renovate the house."

Pat shrugged, looking modest. "I needed something to do. We both wanted to do something other than worrying about how this kid was doing," he aimed a fake punch at Zachary's shoulder, lightly skimming the skin.

Zachary looked around the kitchen. Whatever damage the shrapnel had done to the walls had been patched, sanded, and painted over in the day since he'd exploded the package bomb. There was plastic spread over the table and, looking up at the ceiling, he could see that it too had been painted.

"I just need to finish the table," Pat said, lifting the edge of the plastic so that Zachary could look underneath. "You got home a few hours too soon."

Zachary could see that the table's surface had been sanded to bare wood. There was a can of polyurethane with the paint cans on the floor.

"You shouldn't have," Kenzie protested, but she had a big smile on her face. She gave Pat another hug, then stepped over to Lorne and gave him one, too. It was obvious that Lorne had also been painting, presumably under Pat's direction. Specks of paint covered his shirt, as well as his face and head. "You guys are the best."

Lorne patted Kenzie on the back as he hugged her. "We couldn't have you coming home to a disaster area. All it needed was a bit of touching up. We didn't think you would want to make an insurance claim for something so minor. But I did take 'before' pictures if you need them."

"Can I see?" Zachary asked.

Lorne, Pat, and Kenzie exchanged looks in response to the question. But it wasn't an unreasonable request. Maybe they were worried that seeing the damage would traumatize Zachary further, but that was for him to decide.

He needed to see what had happened, to reconcile it with what he remembered. Seeing the freshly painted walls and ceiling and sanded-down table made it seem like that experience had been erased, or maybe like it had never happened.

"Of course," Lorne agreed. "Let's sit down in the living room. Get some weight off these old legs."

Since he rarely complained about the aches and pains of advancing age, Zachary guessed that he wanted to get Zachary off his feet, worried he wasn't up to standing around so soon after leaving the hospital.

But Zachary did not object. It would be easier to sit down and look through the pictures and relax together.

Mr. Peterson had shared his love of photography with Zachary, giving him his first camera for his eleventh birthday during the few weeks that Zachary had been a foster child in the home of Mr. Peterson and his wife, who had long since divorced him.

Lorne picked up a digital camera with all the bells and whistles and handed it to Zachary as they sat down. Zachary opened his laptop so that they could look at the pictures on the larger screen rather than the tiny two-inch LCD screen of the camera. He plugged a cable into the port and waited for it to connect.

A series of pictures displayed on the screen, and Zachary clicked on the first thumbnail, which was obviously the kitchen.

He had not been expecting to be able to see much—a few nicks in the walls and ceiling.

But what he saw was much more dramatic. The black powder had left scorch marks on the table, walls, and ceiling in an outward blast pattern. The shrapnel embedded in the walls was more extensive than he would have guessed and made him consider the cuts that covered his face and body in a very different light. He had thought that the bomber hadn't been very serious about the package bomb, and that was why Zachary had gotten off so lightly.

Maybe the kidnapper had only intended to scare him off the case or to warn him what would happen if he continued to poke his nose where it wasn't wanted. But the pictures made it clear to him that the bomber had intended to get him out of the way permanently.

Zachary hadn't looked at the floor when he had looked around the kitchen at the repairs. The blast had been directed upward and outward and the package had been sitting on the table, so it had not done any damage to the floor. But Mr. Peterson's photographs had also captured the pools and smears of blood on the floor where Zachary had collapsed.

Even a little bit of blood could look like a lot when it was spread thinly over a surface. A paper cut on a finger or toe cut by an ingrown toenail could bleed all over the place before the injured party even knew that they were cut. Zachary had sustained face and scalp wounds in the blast, and the blood vessels were close to the surface so that such wounds always bled dramatically.

It looked as if someone had been slaughtered in the kitchen. There was enough blood for a slasher flick. At least Lorne and Pat had not seen the kitchen until after visiting Zachary at the hospital, so they already knew he was okay. If they had seen the blood first, they would have thought him mortally wounded.

Kenzie, though, had seen Zachary when he had been brought out of the house, flailing like he was having a seizure, yelling about getting everyone out of the house, and covered in blood. She must have been scared to death. But all he remembered was her calm voice and touch, reassuring him that everyone was okay. There had been no sense of panic or worry.

Zachary looked across the living room into the kitchen. In the pristine white and yellow kitchen, Kenzie and Pat were chatting about the work that he had done, and he made suggestions about decorating or making the kitchen more efficient. Pat and Lorne had never been to Kenzie's house before. Zachary always went to them. It was nice having them there. A comfort to come home to someone who would take care of him. He had Kenzie, of course, but she needed a break and needed someone to take care of her needs, too, and Zachary wasn't sure he was up to the task.

"It looked pretty bad," he observed to Lorne. "You guys did a really good job. I don't know how to thank you."

"It looks bad in the pictures, but it is all superficial. A bit of elbow grease to clean up the blood and debris. Then just patching and painting. No special skill required."

"But you completely fixed it in twenty-four hours. All so that we could come home to a nice kitchen." Zachary looked at Kenzie again, calm and relaxed in the kitchen. "She was really dreading coming home to a mess. Having to look at everything and to get someone to do the repairs. This was exactly what she needed."

Mr. Peterson's sunny face was wreathed in smiles, all the wrinkles he had acquired with age curving upward. "Well, we're glad that we could find something to do for you, Zachary. You've been such a support to us over the years. And helping Pat out when Jose disappeared. This was such a little thing for us. I'm glad we could pay something back."

"You give us something every time we come to visit you. We love to come and visit and have Pat's cooking."

"Cooking, yes! I nearly forgot. Pat, don't forget the sandwiches."

"Of course. You guys hungry?" Pat asked Kenzie and Zachary.

"Well, I've had nothing but cafeteria food," Kenzie said. "And Zachary has barely eaten a bite. Just point me in the right direction and I'll serve."

"There are a couple of trays in the fridge. I thought you could just set them out buffet-style in the living room so we don't have to clear everything away in the kitchen."

Kenzie went to the fridge and *oohed* and *ahhed* over the large platters of sandwiches, wraps, and finger food. They had clearly been purchased at a local deli rather than Pat having made them himself. By the looks of the bounty, he had special-ordered platters to be made up rather than just selecting the "assorted sandwiches" option on their catering menu.

"Doesn't this look great?" Kenzie asked Zachary.

"It does. Thank you. It looks delicious."

"Do you want me to make you a plate?"

Zachary shifted to get up and do it himself, but found it harder than expected. His body wanted to just stay in one place for a while, resting and gathering energy. "Uh… yeah, that would be nice. You know what I like."

And then he was probably going to have to go to bed. But the next day, he would get back to work.

38

*Z*achary had seen Rose at her office twice, surprising her there once. He wanted to mix things up again and he wanted to see her in her own comfortable surroundings, see what happened when she let down her guard. So he asked to meet her at her house. It was Sunday, so she wasn't supposed to be at the office anyway.

Rose was reluctant, but she agreed to have Zachary there. He didn't exactly feel like being seen out in public. Not until he'd started to heal. As it was, he looked like a prizefighter who had done very badly in the ring. Bruises had set in around his eyes to complement the numerous cuts from the explosion. Zachary's head was throbbing, but he didn't tell Kenzie that. He just took a couple of painkillers and waited for her to go to work.

Kenzie didn't usually go into the office on a Sunday. But she had left earlier than planned on Friday due to the detonation of the bomb and hadn't been to the office Saturday while Zachary had been in the hospital. She was apologetic about having to go in on their usual day off, but Zachary encouraged her to go so that she would feel better about going in on Monday with everything tidied up and prepped for the new week.

And he had things to do.

Once she was off to the office, under the impression that Zachary was planning to take an easy day and relax at home while doing computer work, Zachary hopped in his car—after checking thoroughly for any sign of a bomb—and headed over to Rose's house.

The neighborhood looked the same as it had during his previous visit, except there were more people outside. The weather wasn't any warmer, but people were going out shopping, building snowmen in the yards, or visiting with friends. A bustle of activity. He never paid much attention to people's Christmas preparations, too triggered by them to care, but he was doing pretty well for a December, especially after having been blown up.

People in Rose's neighborhood seemed to be happy, in festive moods without getting all stressed out about the holiday lights being tangled up or how many people they had left on their presents list.

Or maybe he just perceived them as happy because he was feeling happy to be alive and counting his blessings of his family and friends.

Rose was watching for Zachary and opened the door as he walked up the sidewalk. Her eyes widened when he got close enough for her to see his injuries.

"What happened to you?"

"I had an accident," he told her casually, as if opening a bomb were normal, one of those things like tripping over a crack in the sidewalk or having a fender-bender at a four-way stop. "It looks worse than it is."

"Well, I hope so. It looks like someone put you through a blender. What exactly happened? Was it your airbag?"

Zachary made a noncommittal noise. Rose ushered him inside. The interior of the house was eclectic, with nothing exactly matching, but the furniture and art she had seemed to be well-loved. Some of it self-assembled Swedish pieces. Some of it might have been from a showroom, and some from rummage sales.

Zachary sank into an easy chair and tried to adjust his position so that as few of his injuries as possible were in contact with the chair.

"Have you found anything?" Rose asked plaintively. "You keep coming back to ask me more questions, but it doesn't seem like you are actually bringing anything back or moving anything forward on the case."

"Actually, I think we've had a good amount of progress on the case."

"But you don't know who took Claire or why. Or where she is."

"What do you know about Drew?" Zachary asked, not wanting to get into a discussion about how far he was from finding Claire or if she were still alive. He wasn't sure that solving the case had any possibility of actually bringing her home safe and sound.

Rose opened her mouth, maybe to continue her line of questioning, then she thought better of it, scowling at him.

"What do you mean? We work together. I think I know him pretty well."

"You know about his history, then? Where he was before he started to work at your company? His family situation and background? How he has spent his life?"

"Some of that stuff, yes. I don't mean that I know him that deeply... but I know he's a good guy. I know what kind of person he is."

"Do you? Did he tell you about his conviction?"

She froze. "What?"

"His criminal history. He's told you all about that? You understand what he did? Why he did it?"

"What are you talking about? Drew doesn't have a criminal past."

"Did you do any background on him? Check him out before you started dating him?"

"Well, I wouldn't say we're dating. We... get together occasionally, but it hasn't been that romantic. We're just... friends. Getting to know each other."

"So you don't know if he has a record. He just hasn't mentioned one, so you assume that he doesn't have one."

"Well…" she looked for a way to deny it. But the truth was, few people ran any kind of background checks on their partners or potential dates. They relied on gut instinct, on the reports of friends or family members, and on what they could see online on social networks. They didn't have any idea how to find out about past criminal records or activities.

Zachary shook his head at the thought of dating someone for months or years, even living together or getting married, and then finding out that they had a conviction for child abuse, kidnapping, drug dealing, or murder.

"What is it?" Rose finally asked in a small voice. She didn't want to know. But she had to know.

"Child abuse and neglect."

Her eyes went wide with shock. She shook her head. "But he doesn't have any kids! Does he? That's what he told me."

"He was living with someone who did."

"But that can't be right. Are you really sure? Drew is a gentle guy, and he likes kids. I told you that. He told you that. He's been great with Claire. He never got mad at her or hit her. He encouraged her. Talked to her like she was a real person instead of the babyish way that strangers usually treat kids."

"I'm sure. I don't have any details yet. From what I have found so far, he probably took a plea and testified against the girlfriend. But that doesn't change the fact that he lived with children who were being abused and badly neglected and never helped the kids or reported what was going on. Is that the kind of person you want around your little girl?"

39

Rose dabbed at tears in the corners of her eyes. "No, of course not. But he didn't have anything to do with Claire's kidnapping!"

"How do you know that?"

"Well he was never at the play place. How could he be? You have to have a kid to get in there. I would have seen him. He was never there."

"If he wanted to take Claire, he would have stayed out of your sight. He would have made *sure* that you didn't see him there."

"And how would he get her out? There would be no way for him to get her out."

"That's true of whoever took her from the play place. We still don't know how the kidnapper got her out of there. So he was no more or less likely to be the one to kidnap her."

That was a lie, of course. It *was* easier for an employee to get Claire out of there. But Rose didn't know Drew's background. She didn't know whether he had ever moonlighted at the play place or provided some kind of service to them.

"Has your company ever had a contract with the play place?" Zachary asked, as the thought struck him. "Working on their computers? Some kind of IT support?"

"We're not that kind of computer company, Zachary. We do research and programming, not tech support."

Zachary nodded. "Right. But you would know how to clone a prox card or something like that? You know how their computer system works. The security logs, all that kind of thing?"

"I've never worked there. I have no idea how their system works. I sign in there with pen and ink, not by swiping a card. I don't know a thing about their prox cards, security cameras, or anything else."

"But you would know how to clone a card."

"All you need to do is look it up on the internet. I'm sure you can buy a device that will let you clone cards if you want to. Maybe you already have one. That would be a handy thing for a PI to have. Just clone an employee's card whenever you want to get in a place like that."

Zachary had to admit that it would be tempting to try. Could he get into All Played Out with a cloned card, walk around wherever he pleased, and swipe back out? Would anyone stop him and ask him questions or would they just assume that he was a new employee or had a legitimate reason to be there? He could test just how secure it was.

"How often did you go to the play place? I take it Claire was an active girl? You went there a lot so that she would have somewhere to burn off her energy and you would be able to relax for a while without having to keep track of her?"

"Is there something wrong with that?"

"No." Zachary held up his hands. "That's what it's there for, isn't it? A safe place for kids to play."

She studied him for a moment to discern if he was telling the truth or thought her a negligent parent for taking her child to such a place. After all, Claire had disappeared from there. Rose eventually nodded.

"Yeah, we went there pretty often."

"Did you tend to meet the same people there over and over again? Other parents and kids, the staff, security guards...?"

She tilted her head for a moment, then nodded. "Yeah, sure.

You get to know the people who go there regularly. If it was just someone who dropped in now and then, I have no idea who they were, but if it's someone who is there at the same time every week, or several times a week... then you get to know faces, which kids belong to who, some of the names. We don't walk around with name tags, but sometimes we talk to each other, maybe exchange names."

"Was there anyone who made you uncomfortable? Who paid too much attention to you or Claire?"

"I don't know." She considered the question.

"Someone you didn't like to be around because they were too intrusive? Asked too many questions? Wanted to give Claire presents?"

"Asked too many questions?" Rose repeated. "You mean like you?"

"You hired me to ask questions."

Rose nodded and stared off into the distance. "I don't always read other people's signals well," she offered after a bit. "I would just think that someone was being friendly, and then my brother or a friend would tell me that he was coming on to me, and I was sending out signals. I didn't *mean* to. And I didn't know they were interested in me that way. So... maybe...? I don't know. There were some single dads there, and they would sit with me and chat, unless I told them I had an important job that I had to focus on while Claire was occupied. I don't know if they were paying too much attention to me or were just being friendly. And the same with Claire. If someone was talking to her, I would think that was a good thing. Good that she was making friends, or that she was learning to talk politely with adults, or was polite when she was asking for help."

"No one had tried to convince her to go somewhere else? Taking off without you? Or to keep a secret from you?"

"No. Nothing like that. Not that I was aware of."

"You'd never had any problems at the play place."

"No."

Zachary nodded. He had thought that she would have told him

about that up front, but sometimes he had to ask people questions directly, not assume that they knew what was important and what was not in a case.

"Tell me more about when you and Amir were in college."

Rose blinked a few times. She looked around the room and then back at him.

"That was a long time ago."

"Six years, more or less. Not a lifetime. We're not talking fifty years."

"Well, no."

"So you remember what it was like. It may seem like a different lifetime because that was before you had Claire, before you were working, but you can still remember it."

Rose sighed. "Yes, I remember it. But why would anything that happened that long ago be relevant? How could anything that happened back then have anything to do with Claire being taken? Like you said, that was before Claire. Why would anyone want to take Claire because of something that happened before she even existed?"

"I don't know. Maybe if you tell me about school, I'll be able to figure it out."

She bit her lip and stared off, past Zachary. "Be honest with me, Zachary."

"Okay."

"Is there any chance that she is still alive? Why am I even doing this? If she was taken by a stranger, then there's no way that she is still alive, is there?"

"Until we find her, there's no way to know that."

"But the chances aren't good, are they? I mean, talk statistics to me. What are the odds that she is still alive after a week?"

"Very low."

She swallowed hard and licked her lips. "Thank you for not lying to me about it."

"But not zero. There are kidnappers who have kept kids for months or even years."

She nodded her acceptance of this fact. "So you think it is worthwhile to keep going?"

"I don't think we have found everything there is to find yet. I don't think the police have run down all their leads. Until all of us have checked out everything we can, I think it is still worth pursuing. Unless it is too much for you emotionally. If it's making you suicidal, if you can't hang on anymore, then we can stop. Even though other people might think it is the wrong decision. It is *your* decision. Not anyone else's."

"Suicidal? What makes you think that? I never said anything like that."

"Then my advice is to carry on until we've run down every lead we can find."

Rose nodded. "He was right about you. He said that you would keep going when everybody else stopped. You would keep digging into it until you found out everything there was to find."

"Who said that?"

"Gordon."

Zachary shook his head in confusion. When had Gordon talked to her about him? How did she even know him? Or know that he knew Zachary? But in an instant, he understood. Gordon was the one who had suggested Zachary to her in the first place. Gordon knew that Zachary was relentless. That he could never let a thing go. Maybe he was friends with Rose's parents.

"So, let's talk about school." He brought Rose back around to the subject that she had avoided. "See if that gets us anywhere."

"I don't know how it could help you. No one took Claire because they knew me in school."

"You and Amir were in the same program, so you were in a number of classes together. You worked on assignments together and studied together."

"Along with others in the program. Girls too. Jenna, Nikki, others who had decided to take on a male-dominated field."

"Right. And how did you get along with them?"

"Fine."

"It was you and the other girls against the world."

"Sort of, yeah."

"Were there boys who did not like you being in the program?"

"Were there? I guess so. But it wasn't like an old boys' club, where they thought we didn't belong and were taking spaces from other guys who deserved to be in the program. It was more like… we were weird because we wanted to act like boys. Maybe we were queer or something. Or they didn't like being shown up by a girl. Didn't like it if we got the highest grades in the class and beat out the boys."

"Was there ever any retaliation because of it?"

"No. Nothing like that."

"Did they try to get girls kicked out of the program?"

"No. That wasn't how it worked."

"Did you ever do anything to get a boy kicked out of the program?"

Rose opened her mouth and then closed it again. Zachary could tell that her first instinctive response had been no. Of course, she hadn't done anything to get any boy kicked out of the program. But then she reconsidered.

"You did," Zachary said. "What happened?"

"Well, it wasn't about getting him kicked out of the program. I didn't care if he became a programmer or not. Who cares about that? But… there were other things that I couldn't ignore."

Zachary nodded. Rose couldn't look the other way when she felt that someone was breaking the rules. So who had she blown the whistle on, and for what infraction?

"It was a long time ago," Rose protested again. "If he were going to do something about it, he would have done it back then."

"Let's worry about that second. First, let's talk about how you got him kicked out."

"I didn't get him kicked out. He dropped out or wasn't able to continue."

"Right. Tell me about that."

"He was… his name was Anthony Jacobs. He was in the same computer science program, but a year ahead of me. So I didn't hang out with him, but I knew who he was. Sometimes, we would end up in a study group together because I was taking a class ahead of my age group, or he had picked up another option. It wasn't a problem. He never hit on me, bullied me, or made me feel uncomfortable."

"Uh-huh."

Why had she reported him if he hadn't done anything to her?

"I picked up his computer one day by mistake. We had the same kind. Neither of us had plastered them with stickers like some kids did. You couldn't tell them apart from the outside."

"And what was on his computer?"

"I wouldn't have known… if it had been locked, you know, and I'd needed a password. I would have known as soon as I got his lock screen that it wasn't mine."

"But it wasn't locked."

"He had just closed the lid when he saw me coming, I guess, and it hadn't closed all the way to stop the video. It was still playing, though it was muted, so I guess he didn't realize."

"And what was he watching?" Zachary asked, a lump of dread heavy in his stomach.

"It was pornographic." Rose swallowed. "Child porn."

40

Zachary sat back, thinking about this. Maybe now they were getting somewhere.

"So you reported him."

"Yes. It was horrible. I wanted to wash my brain out after seeing it. He knew right away what had happened when he saw my face. He said it was just some spam email he'd gotten, not something he was watching. He was deleting it or something stupid like that. I didn't believe it. We were computer science majors, and he was trying to tell me some stupid story that he might have told his grandmother. You don't need to view your spam emails to delete them." Her tone was scathing.

"No. He was just trying to cover himself. Like the drug dealer who says that he was holding it for a friend."

Rose gave a laugh. "Do they really say that in real life?"

"How about, 'I didn't know that was there. These aren't my pants.'" Zachary suggested.

Rose gave another bark of laughter at that. "You can't be serious."

"Oh, yeah. I have friends on the police force, and some of the stories they tell... well, most petty criminals aren't really that smart."

"So I reported him to the school. They had an anonymous tip line, so I didn't have to give my name, just the details of what I had seen on Anthony's computer. But it isn't like he didn't know who reported him. He had seen me open his computer and knew that I had seen that horrible video."

"So you got him kicked out of school."

Rose took a quick breath in, then said nothing. Holding something back. Zachary suspected he knew what it was, but he needed it to come from her. She needed to tell him what had happened if he were to have any hope of finding Claire.

"You got him kicked out of school," he repeated.

Rose nodded slowly. "It didn't stop there, though. There were criminal charges. I didn't have to testify; they seized his computer, so they had all the evidence they needed."

Zachary waited for her to say that she felt bad about turning in a fellow student, but she had to do it for the children who were victimized by child pornography. But she didn't express any regret or sympathy toward Anthony Jacobs.

"He was convicted?"

"Yes."

"Did he have to serve time?"

"Yes."

"Did you ever see him or talk to him again?"

"No."

He had been hoping she would say yes; she had seen him just a few weeks ago. But she shook her head definitively.

"No. I've never seen him since then. Since I reported him. Everything happened pretty quickly and he was arrested. I never saw him again."

"He didn't write you, call you, get in touch in any way?"

"No. Why would he? He wouldn't want to have anything to do with me."

"He had a grudge against you. You were the one who had put him there. He might have wanted to rant against you. To threaten you. To say he was sorry for what he did and wanted you to withdraw the complaint."

"Why would I do that? And what good would it do? It wouldn't have gotten him out of trouble. The police already had the evidence they needed to put him away."

"Sometimes people don't understand the way it works."

"Well, I never heard anything from him. Not back then, and not recently." She shrugged. "I haven't even thought of him in years. Until you started asking about school… Anthony Jacobs never even crossed my mind."

Zachary texted Heather as he sat in the car after leaving Rose's house. By the time he got back home, she had already done the preliminary work.

"Anthony Jacobs was convicted of possessing and distributing child pornography."

"What was his sentence?"

"Seven years."

"Ouch. So, he was eligible for parole after a couple of years. Where is he now?"

"I checked the prison system, and he isn't currently incarcerated. So I guess he got out on parole."

"That's got to be it. Thanks, Heather. That's perfect."

He ended the call and tapped through his contacts list to find Joshua Campbell.

"I think we've got him," he announced triumphantly. "Anthony Jacobs. Rose turned him in on child pornography charges and he went to prison. Sentenced to seven years, but he is already out, so he must have made parole."

"Child pornography? And he kidnapped a little girl?"

Zachary's stomach twisted at the thought of what the animal might be doing to Claire at that moment if she were still alive.

"Yeah," he agreed, trying to keep his breathing even. "I've got Heather doing a skip trace to see if we can find an address for him, but you can probably do better from your end. He'll have to be a registered sex offender and his parole officer should have an address.

Whether he's registered his real address with either of those or not..."

"And if I were him, I wouldn't be holding a kidnapped girl at my registered residence," Campbell pointed out. "We'll have to get eyes on the guy, surveil him for a while to see if he will lead us to her. You know how these sickos work... even if he's killed her, he probably still visits the body."

In a flash, Zachary saw Teddy Archuro before him, grinning with delight as he told Zachary all the horrific things he planned to do to him both before and after his death. The feel of Archuro's hands on him and the weight of his body.

The phone slipped from his hands and he couldn't pick it up. He tried to anchor, to push past the images and focus on the room around him. If Kenzie had been there, she would have been able to help him, but alone, he struggled in vain to return to the present and was forced to watch helplessly as the memories played out before him once again.

41

W hen he was finally able to recover himself, he was kneeling on the floor. His clothes were soaked with sweat and he was trembling all over. His phone lay on the floor, dark, no active call. He went to the bathroom and retched until he was exhausted.

Eventually, he crawled into bed and pulled a blanket over his head. He lay there for a long time, cocooned in warmth, until the panicky feelings subsided. Eventually, he turned his phone back on to finish dealing with Campbell. He could see several missed calls from the man. He was probably lucky Campbell hadn't sent a unit around to ring Zachary's doorbell and make sure he was okay.

"Zachary." Campbell cleared his throat uncomfortably. "Sorry. I didn't think. I forget sometimes that I'm not talking to another cop."

"It's okay," Zachary tried to brush it off. Campbell didn't know any details and didn't need to know them. He already knew of Zachary's PTSD and more details of Archuro's assault and his past crimes than the public. "You'll let me know where you get with this guy? If you can have his parole officer pull him in or follow him to where the girl is being held..."

"Not gonna happen," Campbell said heavily.

Zachary sucked in air but didn't seem to be able to get enough oxygen. Maybe because he still had the blanket over his head. "What? Why not? They can't find him?"

"Jacobs was killed in custody. Years ago."

Zachary deflated, putting his arm over his eyes. He had been sure that the kidnapper was Jacobs. Absolutely sure. It just fit. She'd ruined the guy's life, so when he got out on parole, he retaliated by stealing her child. Taking out whatever vengeance he wanted to on the innocent, since that was the way he was bent. Zachary had thought the flashback and resulting exhaustion a small price to pay for discovering the kidnapper's identity. But now, even that was gone.

"Sorry, Zachary," Campbell apologized. "It was a good thought. We'll follow up to see whether there were any other similar incidents. Some people are natural reporters. They'll call in anytime they see something out of line. She may have made a report on someone else for something else, similar or not. You never know."

"Yeah. One of the college friends I spoke to said she was an 'enforcer.' Always making sure that other people followed the rules."

"There you go, then. We'll see where else her name might pop out. I'll send a detective over to drill her on how many other incidents there were. There might be several."

That made Zachary feel a bit better, but not much. He should have checked that himself. He felt miserable, way down in the dark void of his heart. What good was he to Claire, Rose, or anyone else if he couldn't identify the right suspect? All the years he had spent investigating cases, small and large, and he still ran into roadblocks where everything came crashing to a halt.

Zachary couldn't remember saying goodbye to Campbell. Maybe he had just hung up without saying anything else, or maybe he had passed out and Campbell had disconnected himself, and just let him be, knowing that he needed time and space to recover.

"Zachary? Are you home?"

He rubbed his eyes and blinked, but didn't see any reason to crawl out from under his blanket. A few minutes later, there was a quiet tap on the bedroom door, and it opened. He heard Mr. Peterson's voice again.

"Zachary?"

He must have seen the lump in the bed. He approached and sat on the edge of the bed, then peeled the blanket back, allowing the light from the afternoon sun to assault Zachary's eyes.

"Hey. How are you doing, bud?"

"I don't want to get up."

"You don't have to. I just want to know how you're doing. You having a nap? Kenzie said you might be more tired than usual after the... you know."

"No, it's just... I'm just done."

"You were gone when Pat and I got back from the bakery. Were you off investigating?"

Zachary nodded.

"I thought you were supposed to take a few days off."

"The kidnapper isn't taking any time off. That little girl, if she's still alive, isn't getting a break."

"No," Lorne agreed quietly. He ruffled Zachary's short hair like he would have if Zachary were still ten years old. It was a fatherly gesture that did not trigger a panic reaction even with the memories of Archuro's assault so close to the surface. "It's no wonder you're feeling down, if you jumped back into it so soon, when your body is still exhausted and your mind trying to recover from the insult. Right?"

Zachary cleared his throat, which felt hot and constricted. "I know," he agreed.

"I'll leave you to rest. You'll probably feel better after you've had some time to recover. Have you had anything to eat?"

Zachary thought back. He had no idea what time it was. He had a cup of yogurt with Kenzie before she had left for work. He had thrown up since then. Kenzie wasn't back from work, so it was probably still early. She didn't usually work Sundays, and had just needed a couple of hours to catch up on things.

"No. I'm not hungry."

"You will take longer to recover if you don't take care of your body. Nourish it to speed the healing process."

"I don't want anything."

"Pat will put together a tray and bring it in. You can eat it or not. The sight and smell might change your mind."

Zachary grunted. If Pat brought in a tray, Zachary would have to force himself to eat something. He didn't want to insult the man.

"Just rest easy," Lorne advised, patting Zachary's head one final time. "You need a break."

As he left, Zachary pulled the blanket back over his head.

It felt late when Kenzie arrived home. Zachary didn't feel like opening his eyes long enough to check the time on his phone, but the food remaining on the plate Pat had prepared for him was drying out and the smell of cold cuts and sweat hung heavily in the air.

"Hey, are you okay?" Kenzie asked when she came into the room, giving him a nudge through the blanket without pulling it back as Lorne had done. "Phew." She picked up the plate and took it to the kitchen. She returned and gave him another nudge. "Zach? Lorne says you've been sleeping all afternoon. Is your head bothering you?"

"No."

It was hurting, but that wasn't why he had confined himself to bed.

"Are you sure? Do you want to get up and visit for a while? And you should go admire the kitchen table. Pat finished it and it looks fantastic."

He didn't feel like doing anything just to be social. Kenzie could be the social one and make apologizes for him. Everyone could understand that he was still under the weather after being bombed in his own home. No one expected him to be back to normal yet.

"Zachary?"

"No. Just going to stay here."

Kenzie finally did the same thing as Mr. Peterson, sitting down on the bed and pulling back the blanket to get a look at his face. She studied him, checked his pulse, and felt his forehead.

"You're warm. Any of those cuts getting infected? That's one of the concerns about having so many wounds."

"Just warm from the blanket."

"So what's wrong? You're just tired? Tried to do too much?"

"I'm just *done*. I can't do anything else."

"On what? On the missing child case?"

"Yes."

"You don't have any more leads to follow up?"

"Just can't do it anymore. There's no point."

"You sound depressed."

"There's a shock."

Kenzie gave a laugh. "Yeah. How bad is it?"

"I'll live. It'll pass."

"You're sure? You're not having suicidal thoughts?"

Thoughts of not existing anymore. Thoughts of existential death. But not thoughts of ending his life.

"No."

"Do you want to talk to Dr. B?"

"I'm not going to bug her on a Sunday…" Zachary looked out the window. "A Sunday night. She needs time with her family. It can wait until my next session."

"Anything we can do? You want to go for a walk? Get out your photography to show Lorne?"

"Not right now."

"Okay." She sighed. "We'll just give you some time."

Zachary closed his eyes again. "Why were you so long? I thought you were only going to be a couple of hours?"

"Took longer than I expected."

He opened his eyes to study her face. "Everything okay? Did you have autopsies?"

"Just one. I didn't want to have a crazy day tomorrow trying to get caught up, so I thought I would do one today, so tomorrow will be quieter."

"Was it okay? Anything interesting?"

She had been about to stand up, but instead settled back into the bed.

"Just an accident. Nothing unusual."

"You could make something up," Zachary suggested, giving her a weak smile meant to be encouraging. "A novel zombie virus, maybe."

"Just to keep things interesting?" She lay down beside him, face to face, and Zachary backed up a bit to give her more room to get comfortable.

"What fun is a job like that if you can't create panic every now and then?"

"Well, I can't do it very often, or they might be suspicious."

"It's been a while since the last one."

She relaxed, laying her head down. "You're a bad influence, you know that?"

"Gotta do something to live up to my reputation."

42

W hen Zachary woke up next, Kenzie was gone. Listening closely, he could hear her voice and the lower tones of Lorne's and Pat's voices in the living room and kitchen as they had their meal or visited. He went back to sleep.

Maybe everyone was right about his just needing rest so that his body and brain could recover. Maybe he had just done too much too soon. The flashback to Archuro had been so exhausting that he couldn't get over it in a few minutes like he thought he should be able to. He constantly criticized himself for his physical and mental weakness. The life he had been brought up in should have made him tough. Able to easily weather the minor storms of life. But because of what he thought of as his personal failings, he had grown up to have a weak disposition. Easily beset by those little tempests.

But the next day, he awoke feeling better. Refreshed like he'd had a good night's sleep for once. In better spirits, ready to tackle the kidnapping case again. Sure, he could crack it if he just put his mind to it. He felt like he had everything he needed. He could figure it out if he could just pull it together into a coherent narrative.

And Claire, wherever she was... could have peace.

He was up tapping away at his computer as each member of the family got up and started their days. Zachary took his coffee mugs into the kitchen, rinsed them, and put them in the dishwasher, not wanting Kenzie to see how much coffee he'd already consumed. Pat caught him at it and smiled knowingly.

"You're not fooling anyone."

Zachary chuckled. "Who's trying to fool anyone?"

"I'm making eggs for breakfast. Can your stomach handle some eggs with toast?"

Zachary was actually hungry, his body catching up and demanding fuel after fasting most of the previous day.

"Yeah," he agreed. "Scrambled?" He hated eggs that were the least bit runny.

"Sure," Pat agreed. "I'll even put ketchup on the table."

Pat thought it was sacrilege to top perfectly good eggs with ketchup, but he tolerated Zachary's lower tastes. He was probably just happy to see Zachary eating.

The newly finished kitchen table was beautiful, and Zachary admired it aloud, telling Pat what a great job he'd done. All the drop cloths, cans, and paintbrushes were gone, and the room gleamed like a showroom. Zachary frowned, staring at the light over the table—a bright light with a sparkling shade of stained glass.

"Is that new?" he asked.

"Who said you wouldn't notice? A trained observer like you?"

"It *is* new, right?"

Kenzie laughed in the living room as she fluffed the pillows and opened the curtains. "I confess I was the one who said you wouldn't notice," she said. "I didn't think you had any idea what the kitchen light looked like."

"I'm not that oblivious… not all the time." He looked again at the new light over the table. "I like it. Everything looks so bright and fresh."

They had a leisurely breakfast together, even though Kenzie needed to get to the office. Since she'd put in extra hours the day before, she wasn't concerned about rushing in.

"Dr. Cook says I can set my own schedule. He knows I put in more hours than a nine-to-five schedule anyway."

With the kitchen rehab done and Zachary home from the hospital and on the mend, Lorne and Pat were going home. Pat showed Kenzie the food he'd left in the fridge and freezer so they would have plenty to eat with minimum fuss when he was gone. Zachary didn't know how he had accomplished so much in the short time he'd been there. When did he have time to prepare freezer meals? But he had often been amazed at Pat's quiet enthusiasm and efficiency in the past. He was always up to a challenge.

Eventually, Kenzie headed off to work, and the Petersons were hitting the road. Lorne gave Zachary a tight hug. "You let me know if you need anything," he ordered. "We'll come back up. Or video chat. Whatever you need. And don't try to do too much."

"I won't."

Lorne snorted. "Sure, you won't. You know this is a difficult time of year for you. Compounded by nearly being blown up. Don't put so much pressure on yourself."

"I'll try not to."

They both knew it would be a challenge.

Then everyone was gone and the house was quiet. Zachary turned on the TV for background noise and reviewed his notes again, trying to recapture every thought and clue that might lead him to Claire's kidnapper.

He realized that he hadn't passed the information about Drew O'Dell on to Sergeant Campbell. He should know who Rose's boyfriend was and his criminal past. It might be important. Either because he had decided he didn't want a kid around or because Rose knew he didn't want kids or get along well with Claire and chose her boyfriend over her child. They were viable suspects even if Zachary didn't know how Claire had been spirited away from the play place.

Zachary stared out the window, watching a delivery truck make its way down the street, dropping packages at various houses. So many people bought online. The trucks were so common that they were nearly invisible. People didn't even see them. Unless they were eagerly awaiting a delivery.

Thinking of his most recent delivery, Zachary deliberately slowed his breathing and tried to pretend that the thought of receiving another package didn't cause him anxiety. Was he ever going to be able to open a package again? He couldn't make Kenzie do it for him. Maybe he *did* need his own x-ray machine and explosive sniffer.

A wave of goosebumps rushed over Zachary's skin, followed by a warm flush.

The phone was in his hand even before he was aware of it. He looked down at the screen and saw that he had already initiated another call to Sergeant Campbell.

It rang several times and Zachary started to compose a voicemail message in his head. Then, at the last minute, before it went to voicemail, Campbell picked it up.

"Zachary," he greeted. "Can it wait?"

He had to appreciate that Campbell thought enough of him to answer even when it was inconvenient, just to make sure that it wasn't an emergency.

"Uh… yeah. Just a quick question: Have you followed up on any courier trucks that showed up on Cora Johnson's log?"

"No. Not yet. She assumed any couriers were legitimate traffic, and we concurred."

"And the person who dropped off my package, were they driving a delivery vehicle?"

"We already know it was not a legitimate delivery," Campbell reminded him. "The waybill and barcode were fake."

"But that doesn't mean that it *wasn't* dropped off by a courier. In fact, someone who was a courier by profession would have access to those supplies, legitimate bar codes they could copy, my address…"

"Okay," Campbell agreed. "I'll look into it. You never know."

"Great. I'll let you go. Oh, except one more thing—Rose's boyfriend. Did you know he has a criminal record?"

"Didn't know she had a boyfriend."

"A guy she works with, yeah. Name is Drew O'Dell."

"And what is his criminal record for?"

"It's been expunged, but it was for child abuse and neglect."

"Oh, was it?" Campbell's tone told Zachary that he was taking the information seriously. "Well, that puts a different light on things, doesn't it? Why didn't Rose mention him before?"

"Since when do witnesses give you all the information you need? She didn't think it was important. Didn't want us looking into him. She said he was a nice guy, got along fine with her daughter, and didn't believe he would ever have done anything like that."

"She should still have at least mentioned she was seeing someone."

"I think she compartmentalizes. One part of her life isn't allowed to affect the others. What happened in school can't have anything to do with her life now. Nothing that she does at work affects her daughter. Her social life and her daughter's disappearance have nothing to do with each other."

"Well, she may think she can keep them separate, but that's not the way it works."

"No," Zachary agreed. "Anyway, I think I interrupted you, so I'll let you go. Will you let me know what you find out about delivery trucks?"

"Sure. Anything that affects you."

It wasn't quite "anything" when Campbell limited it like that. He could find out all kinds of things about deliveries made on Rose's block and decide that it wasn't anything to do with Zachary.

43

He tried to decide which was better, calling Rose or dropping in on her. Or calling to set up an appointment. He didn't want to wait for her to get back to him, so maybe dropping in on her would be the best thing. It was a weekday, so she would be at work. That was pretty much guaranteed. From what he had seen, she liked work and it gave her an anchor point—something to hold on to and stay focused on when she was worried about other things.

So he drove to her computer lab and asked for her, as he had before. She hadn't really been happy about it the last time, but Zachary didn't want to wait. He felt like he was getting close to solving the kidnapping, and any delay would be excruciating. He didn't know whether Claire was dead or alive, but if she died while he was waiting around for answers, he didn't know how he would live with it.

"Mr. Goldman." Rose frowned. The last time he had visited, she had been comfortable calling him Zachary, but now she had reverted to Mr. Goldman. Was she planning to kick him off the case? Distancing herself to make it easier? "I really do need to work when I'm here. Some of the stuff I'm working on is very important, and it takes a lot of focus and concentration. Long periods of thought without interruption. When you just show up here and expect me to be able to meet with you... Well, it just doesn't work for me."

Zachary waited for her to finish her explanation and accept that they were going to meet, whether she thought it was a good use of her time or not. Or was she going to fire him on the spot? Wouldn't she at least be curious enough about why he was there to talk with him?

Zachary didn't try to argue about why he thought it was best to meet her there or that it was in her best interest to meet him at the earliest possible juncture so that he could actually find out what had happened to her child.

"Have you made some kind of progress on the case?" Rose asked finally when it became clear that he wasn't going to engage with her about interrupting her work to talk to her about her missing child.

"Did you want to discuss it out here?" Zachary indicated the reception area.

"No. No, of course not."

Maybe she had hoped he would quickly tell her what he wanted and leave if she didn't invite him in.

Rose sighed noisily and led Zachary back to the meeting rooms once more.

"What is it? I assume I don't need to get Drew this time."

Zachary sat on the edge of the table when she didn't take one of the chairs, but just stood there waiting for him.

"I need to know some more stuff about school."

"I already told you everything about school. You seemed to think that it had something to do with Anthony Jacobs. But I don't see how it could have been. He had a long sentence. He must still be in prison."

"Actually, he's not."

Rose gave a little gasp. "You mean he was released?"

"That's what I thought at first too. That he must be on parole. But he wasn't. He was killed in custody."

"So he's not a suspect."

"No. He's not."

Rose threw up her hands in exasperation. "This is a waste of time, then. All the time to dig through my past to find a good suspect, and then it turns out that he's dead. What is the point of this exercise?"

"Tell me what else you remember about Anthony Jacobs."

"I don't know. Like I said, he was a year ahead. So for some stuff he was in the more advanced classes. But we still shared a few classes. Studied together. Hung out at the library together. There wasn't any special relationship between us."

"What about between him and any of the other students?"

Rose's forehead wrinkled. "I don't know. I assume he had relationships with other people. He *seemed* like a perfectly normal person. I had no idea he had... such a messed up personal life."

"Did you know what guys he was friends with? What girls? What professors he might have been close to? Were other people upset when you turned him in?"

"I don't know. There was a backlash. People said it was none of my business and I should have stayed out of it. But that would be like condoning the sexual abuse of children. How could I do that? I would never keep quiet about that."

Zachary nodded his agreement. "Who told you that you should have stayed out of it?"

"I don't know." Rose frowned, thinking back over the years. She had obviously not spent the years agonizing over whether she had done the right thing. She had put it behind her, ignoring the arguments against her choice.

"What is the point in this?" Rose demanded.

"Someone might have decided to avenge Anthony's death by kidnapping Claire. He knew who had reported him. Your friends knew that you had reported him. If someone was really upset by what you did, they might come back after you."

"After all these years? When did he die?"

"I don't know. It might have been because of his death or it might have been some other trigger. You don't always know what made someone take action."

"It doesn't seem like something that happened way back in school could have any bearing on the kidnapping."

"If it's not, then we'll go on to the next lead."

She sat back and closed her eyes. "Who was friends with him? Joe Bermot. Kelly Champlain. Suzanne… what was her last name? I'd have to look at a list of everyone's names. And the women might have changed names. Umm… Nikki. She was pretty close to him. I remember her telling me once that I shouldn't have looked at anything private on his computer. Like I had done it on purpose. I promise you it was completely unintentional."

"Nikki Braun?" Zachary asked, trying to keep his voice calm and even and not reveal how important this was.

"Yes. You talked to her, didn't you? So you know what kind of a person she is. Kidnapping Claire? She would never do something like that."

Yes, Zachary had talked to her and, shortly thereafter, had been delivered a package that was supposed to kill him. A coincidence? If Nikki was a friend of Anthony's and had resented Rose turning him in and ultimately getting him killed, then it was more than possible that she had decided to act, retaliating against Rose by taking away someone she loved.

"How close were they? Nikki and Anthony?"

"I don't know. I didn't stick my nose into other people's relationships. Were they boyfriend and girlfriend? I don't know. I suppose they might have been. I didn't see them pairing off, but I wasn't that involved socially with the group. I saw Amir outside of the group, and that was all."

"They might have been a couple?" Zachary pressed.

"Yes… I suppose they probably were, now that you bring it up. Nikki was pretty upset when I reported the child porn on Anthony's computer. But I thought… she must have been upset to find out he had it in his possession. She told me I should have minded my own business, but I don't think she knew he had it before I found out. And that's kind of a deal breaker for most relationships, don't you think?"

Zachary nodded, but he wasn't trying to figure out whether

Nikki had been upset that her boyfriend was watching child porn or upset that Rose had turned him in. He was working out how all the pieces of the puzzle fit together.

44

As soon as Zachary left the computer lab, he called Campbell again.

The sergeant obviously thought Zachary was harassing him when they hadn't had a chance to follow through on all the latest information yet.

"Zachary. I don't have anything for you yet," he growled.

"Have you had a chance to look at any of the delivery vehicles in Rose's neighborhood? Was there a Nikki Braun? B-R-A-U-N?"

"I have to check with my detective to find out whether he has gotten them yet or if we have any plates from nearby traffic cams. Why Nikki? And is this person a male or female?"

"Female. She was Anthony Jacobs's girlfriend. She drives a delivery vehicle, which could drive around Rose's and my neighborhoods without anyone noticing anything amiss. Nikki could have dropped a package on my doorstep and no one would have thought a thing about it. If you are a courier with a delivery van, then people expect you to be dropping off packages. And no one expects you to sign for them anymore. They just drop it on your doorstep and go to the next house."

"I'll check on her in particular. Any indication that she was a part of the kidnapping or the bombing? Or are you just jumping to conclusions based on the fact that she was Jacobs's girlfriend?"

"I talked to her Thursday last week. And Friday the package was dropped on my doorstep. When Rose turned Anthony in, Nikki told her she should have minded her own business and just stayed out of it."

"None of that is proof."

"I know. That's why I'm hoping her vehicle was seen in Rose's neighborhood or mine. Or both."

"I'll look into it. Thanks for the info."

Zachary was on pins and needles, hoping that Campbell would call him back and let him know what was going on. He was unable to focus on any of the other projects he tried to do. If Claire were still alive, then her survival could depend upon Campbell acting quickly and being able to arrest Nikki before she knew she was being investigated.

Eventually, he couldn't just sit at home waiting, and had to go to Nikki's house. Maybe he couldn't do anything there, but he could keep her under surveillance and let Campbell know if he saw anything suspicious or concerning. The police might not yet have enough to arrest her or search her house, but Zachary was free to watch her if he liked.

He drove over to the duplex and looked for a good spot to watch Nikki from. She was probably at work, so he wouldn't see anything until she got home. But by then, he would be comfortably in place, and she would never even guess he was nearby.

He watched the neighborhood for other nosy neighbors like Cora Johnson who might notice his presence. It was a quiet neighborhood with most residents working during the day. The kids were at school. There was an occasional dog walker, but no one paid any attention to Zachary's car parked by the curb.

He became aware of an unusual amount of activity going on around Nikki's house. People walking around, looking into Nikki's car and the windows of the house. Nothing too obvious, but Zachary recognized police activity when he saw it. The various watchers didn't talk to each other or appear to notice each other, but they would all be wearing earbuds to communicate with each other covertly.

He turned on his radio and scanned the most likely frequencies for them to be transmitting on. He heard some staticky chatter and stopped to listen.

"Someone sitting in a white compact on the street," one of the voices commented. "Not moving on."

"It's a man, not a woman."

"She could have an accomplice. Someone she left to watch for trouble while she was gone."

Zachary chuckled to himself. He opened the door and got out, looking around so that they would be able to see him.

"It's the stupid PI," a male voice said in irritation. "Someone get him out of here."

Zachary got back into the car and settled in. He had no intention of moving. He rolled down the window to talk to whatever cop came over.

The police officer who came over to the car was Samsonov, a cop that Zachary had dealt with before. A cop who, unlike Campbell, would not give Zachary or any other PI the time of day, even if he came to them with information about a case. A hardliner.

"Goldman," he blasted Zachary with his baritone. "What do you think you're doing here? You want to screw everything up? Get on your way. Go home."

"This is a legal parking space. I'm not doing anything wrong. I have the right to be here."

"Not interfering with an investigation, you're not. I told you once and I'm not going to tell you again, get out of here."

"You and your guys didn't even notice me for half an hour. I was here long before you were. I'm not getting anywhere near the house. I'm not interfering. I will stay out of the way, in my car, and not do anything to get in your way or impede your investigation. But if my client's daughter is in there, I want to see her brought to safety."

"You'll find out when everybody else does. After the family is called."

Zachary made no further argument or move to leave. Samsonov stood with his feet apart forming a wide, solid base, and his hand on his hip, by his gun, glaring at Zachary.

"I said I'm not going to ask you again."

"Good," Zachary approved.

Did Samsonov really think that his approach would scare Zachary? He'd had to deal with worse reactions from the police department than one cop's angry glare. He'd been arrested and put behind bars to keep him out of the way of an investigation before. But Zachary knew they wouldn't arrest him for sitting in his car well away from the premises being searched. He hadn't done anything to keep them from pursuing their investigation.

"Who do you think you are?" Samsonov demanded. "You think you get special treatment here? You're Campbell's informant, not mine. We're doing everything by the book here, and that means no civilian involvement. You think we want a case like this thrown out in court because of irregular procedures?"

"I'm not involved. You didn't even know I was going to be here. I didn't approach you. I'm not trying to get involved. I'm not telling you what to do."

"You're here."

"That doesn't have any bearing on your investigation."

Samsonov gave him another glare and stomped off. He consulted with his buddies in lowered voices, off radio. Apparently, they convinced him that Zachary wasn't causing any problems and wouldn't be the cause of evidence being excluded from trial, and just going on with their search.

Zachary watched with interest as a single figure approached Nikki's duplex and rang the doorbell. He couldn't see her face but, from the slim figure, he guessed it was a woman.

There was no answer. She knocked sharply, but did not announce that she was with the police. They knew, of course, that Nikki should be at work and lived alone, but they wanted to be sure.

There was still no response from the house. The woman moved in front of the door, obscuring what she was doing, and then opened the front door. Technology made picking most any residential locks a breeze. The cop didn't have to have any skill to use a lock pick gun.

The cop swung open the door, staying back to avoid any gunfire that might erupt from the house. After waiting to make sure it was safe, she ducked inside. Two of the plainclothes policemen who had been watching the house and car entered quickly after her.

Zachary watched anxiously. As promised, he did not get out of the car or approach any of the law enforcement officers. He listened to the radio as the duplex was searched. They went quickly from room to room to start with.

"She's not here," the woman cop who had entered first announced. "No sign of a child."

Zachary hit his steering wheel hard with the heel of his hand. No sign of her? What had Nikki done with her? He had held on to a thread of hope that they would find Claire there, unharmed, and be able to take her safely home to her mother. But she wasn't there. Whatever Nikki had done with her, she had not taken her home and cared for her there until the police showed up.

He sighed. Nikki had probably killed Claire immediately. With a revenge kidnapping, there had been no incentive to keep her alive. Nikki wasn't asking for a ransom or an apology. She just wanted to hurt Rose by taking away something she loved.

He covered his eyes with his palms, trying to soothe away the tiredness and the grit. He had known that this was one possible outcome.

The radio continued to transmit their comments to each other and the rest of the team outside the house, who were still acting like regular walkers, runners, or service people. The law enforcement officers searched the house more thoroughly, giving a running report.

No children's clothes. No surveillance pictures of Rose or Claire tacked haphazardly on a corkboard with red yarn running between them. No weapons.

"There is a child's room," the female cop reported. "But it hasn't been touched. Dust over everything. A nursery. Baby crib, change table, that kind of thing. Not for a five-year-old."

Zachary felt sick. A carefully preserved nursery? For a baby that Nikki had never had?

She hadn't just lost her boyfriend. She must have been carrying his baby when he was arrested. And she had lost it, too. Anthony had been killed, leaving her all alone when she had been prepared to start a family.

Somehow, she had carried on without him, but then something set her off, triggering her to seek revenge on Rose for what she had done.

He sat listening as they finished their search. They had a warrant for the car as well and conducted a very quick search, checking the glove box, under the seats, and the trunk for any evidence of the kidnapping, running over it quickly with an alternative light source to check for any blood or bodily fluids, and pressing lift tape over the carpet of the trunk to gather hair or fibers that might indicate Claire's body had been in the trunk.

And then they were packing everything up and leaving. No one bothered to report to Zachary what they had found—or not found.

45

Zachary continued to sit there in his car, trying to decide whether he should still be there when Nikki returned. He could watch her, tail her if she went anywhere else, as he had planned to. But was there any point? The police had not found anything to indicate that Nikki had taken Claire.

Did that mean she hadn't?

Was it all just a wild goose chase?

Or did it just prove that Nikki had been more careful than expected? The kidnapping had not been a random, spur-of-the-moment thing. She had known what she was doing and planned it out very carefully.

Zachary's phone vibrated. He had placed it in the mounting bracket on his dash so it was visible without fighting to get it out of his pants pocket or one of the various pockets of his coat.

Roxboro Police Department

Zachary already had his earbuds in and tapped to receive the call.

"Zachary here."

"Well, I gather you're already aware that was a bust," Campbell said without preamble.

"I know you didn't find Claire," Zachary amended.

"And nothing to show that she was there. Unless something turns up in the forensics we gathered. But I'm not hopeful."

"Does that mean you don't think it was her or that she covered it up better than you expected?"

Campbell blew out his breath. "That's the question, isn't it? It's not a dead end like it was when we found out that Anthony was dead. But still… it's pretty hard to prove she had any involvement in the kidnapping without some kind of hard evidence. Just saying she was the most motivated to do it doesn't make her guilty."

"They did find one thing at the house."

"What?" Campbell demanded, sounding irritated.

"The untouched nursery."

"Claire wasn't kept there, obviously. Or there would have been some sign."

"I know. But it tells us something else."

Campbell was silent for a moment before offering, "We know that at some point, she was pregnant or expecting to start a family. Presumably with Anthony Jacobs."

"Yeah. But that dream was crushed when Rose Bircher reported Anthony Jacobs and she lost her baby. Rose took her child away."

He could hear Campbell breathing as he considered this possibility. "So she took Claire. Out of revenge. And then… whatever happened to the baby. Did he die? Did she adopt him out because she didn't have the father in her life anymore?"

"I think it's safe to assume that the baby was miscarried, stillborn, or died soon afterward. And I don't think Nikki was trying to replace her own dead child with Claire as a substitute."

"You think she's dead."

"Probably. If this was revenge for her baby dying, she wouldn't be likely to keep Claire alive."

Campbell grunted, neither agreeing nor disagreeing.

"Did you find her delivery truck on Rose's street?" Zachary asked. "Is that why you went ahead with searching her house?"

"Yes. We managed to get the information about delivery trucks from Cora. We had to go back a few weeks to find Nikki's. We had to get in contact with each courier company to find out which she worked for, because the delivery trucks are owned by the company, not the driver. Tedious work. But Nikki Braun did make a delivery to Rose. A legitimate delivery that went through the regular system at her employer, by the way, not something that she was planting."

"Unlike the package she delivered to me."

"They don't have any record of her making deliveries in your neighborhood that day. But they'll pull the GPS trails on the vehicle she was driving to see if she spent any time on your street. It will take some more time. It's a good guess, but we won't know for sure for a while."

Zachary nodded to himself. "So… what's next? Are you dropping the line of inquiry on Nikki since there wasn't any physical evidence at the house?"

"It's not over. She could have killed the kid and dumped her somewhere. Or she could be using a building other than her house to hold her. Or have an accomplice. The boyfriend, maybe. We'll be watching her, investigating her more thoroughly."

"Yeah, good."

"This was not unexpected. Other than familial kidnappers, it's not unusual to hold the victim in a remote location. For exactly this reason. It's much easier to avoid detection if you don't have the victim right there in your house. We asked the judge for a warrant to search the house covertly so that if Claire wasn't there, we wouldn't tip Nikki off that she was under suspicion. So no harm done, as long as she didn't have lookout man in the area and no neighbors ask what was going on today. The boys took a good look around to avoid surveillance." Campbell cleared his throat and waited, saying nothing.

"Which is when they spotted me," Zachary filled in. "Samsonov wasn't too happy about my being there.'"

"So I hear. He had some choice words for you."

Zachary couldn't help grinning at that. He wasn't unhappy to watch Samsonov spinning his wheels and not getting anywhere.

"I didn't see anyone else," Zachary said, "and I was watching for at least an hour before your guys showed up. Maybe two. I'm confident she didn't have a lookout man. Can't guarantee no nosy neighbors, though. Most people seemed to be working today, but there were still a few dog walkers and others in the neighborhood. No one was standing with binoculars at the window, but someone still might have seen something."

"I think we're as safe as we can be. It's still possible that she is our kidnapper, and she will give herself away sooner or later."

"Can you search her delivery truck? If she didn't transport Claire in her car, she might have had her in the delivery truck."

"The judge said we didn't have enough for a warrant for her work vehicle. We're lucky we were able to get as much as we did. He was stretching because it was a child abduction and we hoped that Claire might be at the house and we could still rescue her." Campbell blew out a long stream of air. "Wouldn't it have been nice if it had worked out that way?"

"Yeah."

"Anyway, we are going to have someone tailing Nikki, and we don't want her to get the idea that she is under surveillance. So that brings us to you sitting there on her street."

Zachary knew what that meant. He turned his key in the ignition. "Okay. I'm leaving."

"Can't take the chance that she'll see you there and decide to run," Campbell observed. "If there is any chance that Claire is still alive and Nikki runs, we could be signing her death warrant. If Claire is still alive, we need Nikki to lead us to her. We need her to think she is perfectly safe and has gotten away with it."

Zachary's fingers were crossed, but he didn't think there was much of a chance Claire would still be recovered alive. But if there were any chance at all, he wasn't going to blow it.

46

Zachary hadn't realized how late it was, even though it was starting to get dark by the time he left Nikki's street and headed for home. His mind was so wrapped up in the case that he didn't even think about the time. He arrived to find Kenzie home ahead of him and was immediately worried.

"Oh, Kenzie... I hadn't realized it was so late. I should have called."

She shrugged. "You were working," she said in that flat, clipped way she did when she was upset with him but didn't want to admit it or talk to him about it.

"I was. But I should still have given you an update. Let you know I was okay and would be home... now."

She nodded her agreement. "I appreciate it. But it's a little late to think of it now."

"Yeah, it is. I'm sorry."

"I checked your location. Looked like you were on a residential street. Just sitting there. So... surveillance?"

"Yes." He felt unaccountably guilty, like he had when he had been watching Bridget. Not *stalking*, because he hadn't had any nefarious purpose in mind. He had just felt comforted being able to see her, knowing that she was still home and safe. Even though he couldn't be with her, he'd needed to see her.

But that was over now. He could no longer go to Bridget's street to watch her.

And he had been on Nikki's street not to harm her or even to satisfy his own need to see her, but to try to protect Claire. To find her and recover her, if that were possible. That was his job.

"We have a suspect in the kidnapping case, and I was watching her house."

"You have a suspect? Well, that's good news. And it's a woman. Did you see anything while you were watching her house?"

"Just the police exercising a warrant and searching her house and car. And they didn't find anything," he immediately answered the next question Kenzie would ask. "No physical evidence, anyway. I think… there is strong circumstantial evidence. But there isn't enough to arrest or prosecute her. And arresting her without knowing what happened to the little girl… could endanger her if she's still alive."

"You don't want to do that. So, if you were doing surveillance, I'm surprised you're back already."

She knew that Zachary would want to watch his suspect at least until she went to bed, and here he was, home for supper.

"The police are watching her now. So they wanted me out of there. The more people sitting on the street watching her…"

"The police still think she did it, then?"

"Strong circumstantial evidence," Zachary repeated.

"Do you think they'll be able to get her? And is there any chance…"

"I don't know." He shrugged helplessly. "I wish I could answer that."

Kenzie nodded, understanding. In her line of work, death was a given. When she was trying to solve a particularly difficult case, it was with the knowledge that the victim was already dead. She couldn't stop it from happening. It was the same when Zachary was working on a murder case. They could try to catch the killer to prevent him from killing again, but they couldn't change what had already happened. Claire's kidnapping was different. Though Zachary believed she was already dead, there was still that sliver of hope, and that made waiting excruciating.

"Did you remember that Tyrrell is coming over for supper today?"

Zachary frowned, trying to remember. He didn't think it had been on his calendar. Had he been that buried in the case? He knew he shut things out when he was hyperfocused. It was sometimes embarrassing to come up for air and realize that he'd been completely unaware of anything Kenzie had said or done while he'd been working. He could sit down and have a meal with her and not be able to remember anything about it afterward.

"Did I know that?"

Kenzie shook her head, chuckling. "Who knows what you knew? He'll be here before long. Do you want to change before he gets here?"

Zachary took off his coat and examined himself. He'd had to bundle up in order to sit watching the house without his car engine running, the billowing exhaust attracting attention. But that also meant he'd been overheated defrosting his windows and driving home. He was probably a little ripe for company or for cuddling with Kenzie later.

"Yeah, I'll have a quick shower and change." Zachary checked the time. "Twenty minutes?"

"He might be here before that, but he can keep himself entertained for a few minutes."

Zachary knew that if he rushed, he would forget something important, like drying off before trying to dress or putting on pants. So even though he didn't have long to shower and change before supper, he forced himself to be slow and methodical.

Kenzie and Tyrrell were both well aware of Zachary's challenges, but there was no need to draw attention to them.

When he finished making himself presentable, he could hear Tyrrell's voice as he and Kenzie talked.

"Hey, bro!" Tyrrell greeted when Zachary walked into the kitchen. He gave Zachary a manly hug, slapping him on the back and smiling cheerfully. "How is it going?" He shook his head, studying Zachary's face.

Zachary had decided not to try to shave around all the cuts and nicks that already adorned his face. He would end up cutting himself more and looking like a moth-eaten carpet. So, some of his injuries were hidden under several days' growth of whiskers, but Tyrrell could still see the ones that rose above the level of his cheekbones.

"I'm good," Zachary assured him. He pointed at his face. "This? This is nothing."

"You look better than you did at the hospital."

Zachary tried to remember whether Tyrrell had come to see him at the hospital, but couldn't remember for sure. He'd been in and out of consciousness, and everything was pretty garbled in his brain.

"It's healing. All superficial," Zachary said with a nod.

"Takes more than a little old bomb to put my big brother down."

Zachary's first instinct was to explain that the bomb maker had only been an amateur and had not used enough black powder to properly propel all the shrapnel she had packed it with. Or the powder was old or wet. But saying in front of Kenzie that it just hadn't been a very good bomb would upset her more than she already was. She'd already heard those details but, hopefully, they were no longer fresh in her mind, and he didn't intend to bring them back up.

"That's right," he blustered instead. "It would take a lot more than that to get me off a case."

"Is that what it was about? Getting you off a case?"

"Uh... don't know for sure. There was no message with it. Or if there was, it was blown up. Or the police have it and didn't tell me. So I don't actually know the reason; I can only guess."

Tyrrell nodded. He opened his mouth to ask another question, then apparently caught Zachary's look toward Kenzie and realized that the conversation might be upsetting to her. He cleared his throat.

"Well, glad you're getting better. You look good. I mean, despite the homeless look."

Zachary rubbed his bristles. "I have to maintain my persona. This very sophisticated disguise keeps people from looking at me or engaging with me on the street. No one wants to have to talk to some weird homeless guy, so they look away. They don't even see me."

"You're shaving before the next dinner with my parents," Kenzie warned. "Disguise or not. I'm not taking you to some restaurant looking like that."

"I will," Zachary promised. This time, he wouldn't forget and think that a thirty-second shave was enough to get him by. "And, uh, do we know when the next dinner with your parents is? I just want to make sure it is on my calendar, if you've set a date."

"No, not yet. You know how busy Mom and Dad are. Their next opening might be six months from now."

Kenzie put the last of the food she had prepared out on the table and everyone sat down.

"Speaking of dinners," Tyrrell said, shifting uncomfortably, "I guess… we're all onside with this Goldman family dinner. So we should start talking about timing." He looked at Kenzie. "Like Kenzie says, finding a date that works with everyone can take a long time."

"Vince and Mindy agreed?"

Tyrrell nodded. "Yeah, they said they would be there. I guess they want to get to know the sibs better."

"I haven't heard back from Heather about Joss. Or I didn't ask her what Joss said, anyway. I guess I should give her a call."

"I talked to Joss. She's onside."

Zachary smiled, but was suddenly short of breath. Everyone had agreed to the dinner? All his siblings had agreed to get together as a group for dinner and a visit? He hadn't really believed that it would work out. And now he was anxious about how it would work out. Would it be a disaster? Heather had given all kinds of reasons that it wasn't a good idea, and Kenzie and Tyrrell had added to that with questions about whether spouses or children would be there. And what about Luke? Would Joss bring him? Would Heather want her adult children to attend as well as Grant, her husband? Zachary had never met either of the children, but he felt like he knew them based on how much Heather talked about them.

"So we should start polling dates," Kenzie said, looking at Zachary. "If you want me along, that is."

"Of course I do. I don't know if I could do it without you. But that doesn't mean I want you to do all the work. I'll do as much as I can, and we'll have it at a restaurant, so you don't have to make anything or worry about having company here."

"Is that some kind of slight against my housekeeping?"

Zachary opened his mouth, heat rushing to his cheeks. Then he saw her smile and knew she was just teasing him.

"I got you," Kenzie pointed out with a chuckle.

"Yes, you did. But you don't really want it here, do you? I don't want all that work falling on you."

"No, a restaurant sounds good. I think it is best to be on neutral territory. Not just so I don't get the lion's share of the work, but just because everybody will be more comfortable if they feel like they're all there on an equal footing."

Tyrrell nodded his agreement. "It's going to be awkward at first," he predicted. "No one is going to know how to deal with everyone together. It's been too long since we were all a family, and for the little kids, they don't even remember living together. Vince and Mindy, they don't remember anything before the fire. Not reliably, anyway."

Zachary had seen countless reunions on TV, sometimes of siblings who had been separated for even fifty years, and they always got along together and were happy to be reunited. Sometimes, they had never even met before, but things just clicked when they got together. They picked up as if they had never been apart.

But he suspected that those reunions were cherry-picked. The shows that ran them knew that people only wanted to see happy reunions. They wouldn't show disastrous reunions that had resulted in arguments, fights, and bitter feelings.

"At least we've all met each other individually," he said. "It won't be a big shock."

"Vince and Mindy haven't met Heather or Joss."

"They haven't?"

Tyrrell shook his head. "Heather has talked to Mindy on the phone. But not face-to-face."

Zachary didn't worry about Heather being unable to get along with the younger siblings. Joss, on the other hand, was not the warm and fuzzy type.

"Oh, boy," Kenzie murmured, expressing what they were all feeling.

"Just in time for Christmas," Tyrrell offered, laughing.

"Maybe we should defer it until after Christmas," Kenzie suggested. "I was thinking… everyone is already going to have all kinds of Christmas parties and events to get to. And it's not the best time for you…" She met Zachary's eyes.

They all knew that his mood would likely degrade over the next couple of weeks. He was doing well so far—better than he had been in December in a long time—but things would get worse before they got better. He'd already had a few glimpses of that darkness and knew that worse was waiting in the wings.

But after Christmas Eve, he would start to feel better.

"I'm doing okay," he said firmly. As long as he still felt like he could make plans for the future and had the energy to pursue his cases, he would keep pressing forward. He wouldn't cut off his involvement in any activities because of an anticipated downturn.

Other than Christmas parties, of course. He wouldn't be participating in any Christmas festivities.

"I'll look over our calendar and pick some dates, then," Kenzie suggested. "And you can pass them on to the others and run a poll to see if there is a day that works for everyone."

"Sounds good," Zachary agreed. He took a bite of his potatoes and swallowed strenuously, the potatoes sticking his throat.

47

Zachary always enjoyed spending time with Tyrrell. It was amazing to him to be able to do things with him after decades of separation.

Even though his body was still recovering from the explosion, he found himself unable to sleep for more than a few hours after the dinner. Rather than tossing and turning in bed and keeping Kenzie awake, he moved to the couch where he could open his computer and entertain himself or start working, or he could stretch out on the couch and see if sleep would come more easily away from the bed and his concerns about keeping Kenzie awake.

He decided to try to get another hour or two of sleep. Kenzie and Dr. Boyle and everyone else constantly told him how important getting enough sleep was to his mental health, so he would try to get a little more. Sleep was also an important part of healing. He lay back down with a throw pillow under his head and one of the fuzzy blankets Kenzie liked to wrap around herself in the evening pulled over him.

He closed his eyes and didn't try to sleep, but just let his mind wander randomly from one thing to another. He thought about Tyrrell and the younger kids, and how they didn't remember things the way they had been at home. The younger kids, anyway. Tyrrell remembered some of it.

He could remember playing outside with the other kids. Their parents hadn't really liked them to be around. They were too noisy, too rambunctious, and it was common for them to be kicked out of the house to find something to do outside. They had spent a lot of time playing outside.

Thinking of playing outside with his siblings, he thought about the family that lived next to Nikki. How many children did they have? He remembered Nikki talking about how noisy they had been when they got out of school. She heard everything they were doing over there. She probably also wished she could kick them out to play outside.

They had toys outside. The slide and other things. And they built snowmen and forts and pelted each other with snowballs. There had been evidence of their play in the yard.

But in all the time Zachary had been watching the house, from early afternoon to after sundown, he hadn't seen any activity next door. Where were they? Had they taken time off for an early Christmas vacation?

He sat up, frowning, unable to keep his eyes closed any longer.

Where were Nikki's neighbors?

Where had they been during the search? Where were they after that, when the sun was going down in the sky? No one had come or gone.

He reached for his phone, then stopped himself. It was too early to call Campbell or any of the other cops on the case. He could call 9-1-1, but since when was it an emergency for a family to go on vacation or not be home one night?

Campbell had said he would put a tail on Nikki, but did that mean they would monitor her twenty-four hours a day? Or would her tail go home when she turned out the lights to go to sleep?

Zachary kept a "go bag" containing everything he would need to take if he had to be out of town for a day or two, along with his computer and whatever tech he needed to take with him. It contained a couple of changes of clothes, so he dumped it out and dressed quickly so he didn't have to go back into the bedroom to change and risk waking Kenzie. In the kitchen, he wrote quickly on a sticky note and left it on the fridge for Kenzie to see when she got up in the morning, if he hadn't returned by then.

He had work to do.

He drove down Nikki's street, looking for the cop who should be watching her house and anyone else who might be around. Did Nikki have an accomplice? A new boyfriend or someone in her family? An old friend who had known Anthony? He didn't get the feeling she was working with anyone, but the kidnapping itself would have been easier to effect with two people. Risky with just one. But maybe she had been watching Rose and Claire at the play place for several days and had seen enough to pull it off by herself.

He didn't turn around and drive back down the street a second time. That would be a good way to attract attention to himself, which he didn't want to do. He pulled the car over farther down the street. On days like this, he wished he had a dog. A solitary figure on the street in the dark was threatening. A solitary figure with a little dog was not. It was not unusual for a compassionate dog owner to end up outside in the middle of the night with a restless or elderly dog.

But having a small, yappy dog on surveillance would not do. And if he had to go into a house, he couldn't very well leave the dog on the street to attract attention, or take it into the house where they could contaminate the scene or attract attention. So, he had to find other ways to look innocuous and forgettable.

He walked down the street at a regular walking pace. Not fast enough to look like he was in a hurry or up to no good. Not so slow that he looked like he was snooping or casing the street. Just a resident who happened to be out early or late, on his way home.

He slowed as he walked by the duplex, not stopping to look into Nikki's yard, but into the neighbor's fenced area. He noted the children's toys there as he had the day he had gone to visit Nikki. Had anything been moved? He didn't think so.

The remnants of the snowman and snow fort were old. How old? A week? Two?

There were children's footprints in the yard, not just those of an adult setting a staged scene. But they were old as well. Iced over as there had been some additional snow, melt, and refreezing since they'd been made, the treads no longer clear imprints, but blurred and glazed.

Zachary continued to walk past the house. He didn't see the police surveillance. Maybe they had been deemed unnecessary while Nikki was home asleep in her bed.

At the end of the block, he turned the corner and entered the alley that ran behind the duplex. He walked with care, as the alley had not been paved or cleared, so it was icy and uneven. It was dark, but he did not turn on his phone LED or a flashlight. He let his eyes adjust as much as possible to the low light cast by the moon, the streetlights in front of the houses, and the occasional back door or garage light.

There was nothing significant behind Nikki's duplex. But there was only one vehicle parked on the gravel pad. Nikki's car was parked in front of the house. Her company delivery truck, which she was apparently allowed to bring home, was on the pad behind her side of the duplex. No vehicle on the family's side. So maybe they were on vacation.

"Stop right there," a male voice ordered. "Who are you?"

Zachary didn't move his feet or hands, but swiveled his head to see who had spoken. The plainclothes cop surveilling Nikki's house had stationed himself behind the house in the shadows of the trees.

"Zachary Goldman," he said, raising his hands slightly to his shoulders to show that he was empty-handed. "Private investigator."

"What are you doing here?"

"I was the one who brought Nikki Braun to the attention of the police..."

"I know who you are. But that doesn't explain what you're doing here."

Zachary was happy that the cop at least knew his name and knew of his involvement in the case. He'd be far less likely to be thrown in jail overnight for loitering or trespassing. But they still might like him for impeding an investigation.

"I had to check something out. Have you seen anything of the people who live in the other side of the duplex?" Zachary made a small motion toward the other side of the building.

"No. They're not home."

"Have you seen any lights or movement?"

"Why would I, if they're not home?"

"Were any inquiries made as to where they are? Has anyone tried to talk to them about Nikki?"

"I don't know anything about it. Just keeping an eye on her in case she goes somewhere else. Leads us to a dump site or safe house where she's stashed the kid."

"What if she's in there?" Zachary pointed to the empty side of the duplex.

"She hasn't gone in there. I suppose she might have a spare key. Check on the house while the neighbors are gone, make sure everything is in order. But she hasn't been in there."

"Maybe she can access it from inside."

The cop considered this and nodded. "Possible. There isn't usually any connecting door or anything between sides, but that doesn't mean it's impossible."

"If she's in there right now, Claire could be in imminent danger," Zachary pointed out.

48

"You can turn around."

Zachary turned to face him, which was much easier than trying to look at the man over his shoulder. The shadows of the trees obscured much of the cop's face.

"Thanks." Zachary lowered his hands.

"Even if the child is being held on the other side of the duplex, she's not in any danger right now. Braun is sleeping."

"You don't know that. She could be torturing Claire."

"She went to bed. I saw her go to the bedroom and shut off the light."

"That doesn't mean anything other than that she is keeping up appearances. There's nothing to stop her from walking around in the dark."

"If that little girl is still alive, she'll be fine waiting until morning. Braun is sleeping. I'm not going to rush in and do anything without specific instructions and a warrant."

"Imminent danger is an exception…"

"And I don't see anything that rises to the level of imminent danger. I don't hear any screaming or crying. We don't even know that she's in there."

"There's good reason to suspect it."

"Not yet, there's not. Give the boss a chance to think about it in the morning. Make some inquiries. Until then, we don't know anything."

Zachary itched to find out for himself. He wouldn't have to break any windows or doors; it would be easy enough to pick the standard locks on the back door and let himself in. He could have a look around without touching anything, and then tell the cop whether Claire was in there or not. Or tell Campbell as soon as he was up in the morning so that he could arrange for a warrant and get a team to make entry and rescue her.

But the cop left on surveillance clearly wouldn't let that happen. He wouldn't stand by and watch Zachary break into the house. Any judge worth his salt would rule that Zachary had been acting as an agent for the police and strike down any evidence they collected as a result. That might get Claire back, but they needed to be able to prosecute Nikki too. If she weren't incarcerated, what was to stop her from doing something like this again? Or worse, killing Claire, Rose, or some other victim the next time?

"You're not going to do anything?" he asked.

"I'm going to keep watching the house and the subject like I was assigned to. And if you cause trouble, I'll arrest you, and you can spend a day or two in jail while we sort things out. I don't care if you are a friend of Sergeant Campbell. You're not going to mess up this case."

"I'm the one who is going to solve this case. I'm the one who has provided all the leads so far."

"Maybe so." The cop shrugged. "I don't care."

He stuck to his guns. Zachary had to admire him for that. Most cops, offered a tip during a long night of mind-numbing surveillance, with the possibility of some action and breaking the case wide open, would be eager to jump right into it.

He was probably right about the admissibility of the evidence if they did anything without a proper warrant or acted on information that Zachary provided that hadn't been properly vetted and investigated.

But Zachary could hardly stand there talking with the cop

when he knew that Claire, a frightened little girl, could be in there now, just feet away from them. But he could do nothing. The cop wouldn't let him. If he'd been alone would he have let himself in? Checked it out and then called the police with an anonymous tip? Or would he have had the self-control to wait until morning and tell Campbell about it then?

"Do you think we should call him?"

The cop's head cocked slightly. "Call who?"

"Campbell. If we tell him that she could be in there, he could apply for a warrant. Or decide that she's in too much danger for us to wait…"

"We're not calling Campbell. This is not an emergency and I won't be responsible for waking him up."

"It *could* be an emergency."

"It's not. Braun is sleeping. Trust me on that one."

Zachary gritted his teeth and shook her head.

"Tell you what," the cop said. "Why don't you go back home and go to bed? I'll talk to the sergeant when he's up in the morning, and we'll sort it out from there. You don't need to do anything but wait for our call."

"I'm not going home."

"You'd prefer to be arrested for interfering with this investigation?"

"I'm not going to do anything to interfere. I didn't do anything but walk down the alley. I didn't even enter the property."

"You're still in the way. Attracting attention. Possibly tipping off the subject as to our surveillance. You need to leave. Go home and wait."

Zachary looked back at the house, wanting very badly to charge in and rescue Claire. To act like a cowboy, Kenzie would have said, shaking her head and rolling her eyes. Charging in without thinking about the consequences to himself or the case against Nikki.

"Fine," he told the cop.

Of course, he didn't go back home. He went to his car, but not back to the house. He couldn't see anything happening in Nikki's house from where his vehicle was parked, well away from the scene. Which meant that they couldn't say he had tipped her off or interfered with the police surveillance. But he was close enough to see if other police vehicles started to arrive and something was going down. He wasn't going to miss out on that.

Zachary was zoned out, watching the street as light gradually filled the sky, when his phone rang. He looked at the display, expecting it to be Kenzie. But it was *Roxboro Police Department.* He answered the call.

"Zachary here."

"Are you sitting on my scene again?" Campbell demanded.

"I'm down the street and out of the way. I'm not visible to the house or Nikki's neighbors."

"I thought I sent you home."

"You did, but I had to come back to check something out."

"Maxwell says you have a theory about Claire being held on the other side of the duplex."

"Yeah."

"Tell me about it."

Zachary thought it was pretty self-explanatory, but he obliged. "The other side of the duplex is owned or rented by a family with young children. You can see that kids have been playing over there."

"Sure. I saw that."

"Well, where are they? School let out while the search was being performed, and they didn't come home. When I came around early this morning, they were not home. No vehicle. Your guy—Maxwell —confirmed that it is empty. They haven't come or gone while he's been watching it."

"So they're somewhere else. People are allowed to take vacations, you know. It is even encouraged in some circles."

"Just in time for the search? Or before that? How long have they been away?"

"No idea," Campbell admitted. "It's just a coincidence."

"I looked at the yard this morning as I walked by. There are no fresh footprints in the snow. The snowman is old. It's been a while since the kids have been in the yard."

"That may be, but I'm still not sure I see it as being suspicious."

"It's pretty early in the month for them to be on Christmas vacation yet."

"Maybe they like to avoid the crowds. If the kids are pretty young, there's no worry about them missing anything important during that time. They can make it up."

"So, say they left a couple of weeks ago. Thanksgiving or earlier. Since the footprints that are there are at least that old."

"In your estimation."

"Yes."

"Okay. Let's say they left a couple of weeks ago," Campbell agreed. "As I said, some people like to take their vacations early to avoid crowds and holiday rates."

"Then, who did I hear when I was talking to Nikki?"

Campbell was silent for several long seconds.

"What?"

"When I was interviewing her on Thursday, I heard someone crying next door. She said it was the neighbors and, naturally, I accepted it because I'd seen the kids' stuff in the yard. I knew the family next door had young kids."

"You heard a child crying. How big? How loud?"

"Hard to tell. It was faint. Like a child crying in her sleep, just tired and whiny, not full-on tears. She made a few noises and then was quiet again."

"Like a kid who was drugged."

"Maybe. Or sleeping. Or tied up and gagged."

"Tell me about the footprints."

"They're iced over. The snow has thawed slightly and refrozen since they were made. There are no fresh tracks. Adult or child."

Campbell thought about this. Zachary reviewed the last couple of weeks of weather in his own mind. When the snow had fallen last. Whether it had stuck to the sidewalks. How long it would take old footprints to glaze over.

"There are other possibilities. The kids have been sick and

unable to play outside for a couple of weeks. They just happened not to be there last night. Maybe they left for vacation on the weekend and were still there last week when you saw Nikki and heard the child cry. You may be reading way more into it and it isn't really significant."

"Do you think so?"

"No," Campbell admitted. "Just playing a little devil's advocate. We need to examine this seriously without jumping to any conclusions."

"I can find out who the house is owned by and try to contact them. But your guys would probably be much faster."

"I've already got them looking into it."

Zachary had to laugh. Campbell had thought Zachary's observation credible enough to start the ball rolling before even bothering to call him. Maxwell had undoubtedly confirmed that the family had not been home all night and, if he had been thinking about their absence and whether Claire might be held on the other side of the duplex, he might have had some pretty strong feelings about it himself by the time he called Campbell to report.

"How long will that take?"

"It depends. It won't take long to get an answer of who owns it. But getting ahold of them might be a different story, especially if they are on vacation."

"And in the meantime…?"

"In the meantime, we get a warrant drafted up ready to put in front of a judge. I don't want anything holding us up once we get the information that we need. If the family has been away for two weeks, and you heard a child there last week, then we'll break the door down to get to her."

"No need for that. The locks don't look too troublesome."

"We'll pick it, then," Campbell agreed. "But that's not nearly as much fun as saying we'll break the door down."

"I guess not."

49

Before Campbell called him back to report on his findings,
Zachary saw police vehicles entering the street. Several
police vehicles, both marked and unmarked. He didn't
move his car, but he did get out and walk down the street to watch
from a closer vantage point. It might take a while before he saw
anything happen; it always took way longer than he expected for
the police to actually do anything. They would need time to get set
up, to make sure everyone knew the plan, and then to slowly follow
the procedure they had set up of knocking on the door—or not, if
they had a no-knock warrant— picking the locks and entering, and
then clearing the house one room at a time until they found Claire.
Or didn't.

Zachary didn't want to miss a minute of it. Especially the
moment they opened the door and entered the house. He could be
completely wrong on everything, but he didn't think he was. And if
Campbell was already sending the troops over, he didn't think so
either.

Zachary's phone rang. He pulled it out, expecting it to be
Campbell, but it was Kenzie calling this time.

"Hi, Kenz. Sorry, I wasn't there this morning," Zachary
apologized.

"I was a little surprised. What happened? What came up?"

"Might have figured out where the kidnapped girl is being held."

"Really? That would be really good. When will you know?"

"Police department is assembling now. So within the next hour or two."

She laughed at Zachary's long-suffering tone.

"Well, good luck. I really hope you're right and they find her."

"Thanks. How are you? Your morning was okay? Other than me not being there to serve your every whim, of course."

Kenzie chuckled. "I survived on my own, somehow. I've almost forgotten how to take care of myself, but I remembered just enough to hunt down some breakfast."

"You could always get a donut at work."

"Dr. Cook doesn't bring them nearly as often as Dr. Wiltshire."

"Darn health nut."

"Well, if anyone knows that eating a healthy diet won't keep you from dying of something else, it's a medical examiner. You may as well live a little, because nobody gets out of this life alive."

If they found Claire, Zachary was going to celebrate. He would take Kenzie out to eat—at a fancy restaurant, no ordering in. He would really treat her to a night out on the town.

"I'll let you know as soon as anything happens over here," he told her, and hoped that he would have news soon.

"I see you're staying well out of the way."

Zachary nodded to Campbell, whom he had seen approaching.

"You know I don't interfere with police investigations."

He couldn't quite say it with a straight face, and both he and Campbell laughed.

"Well, I try not to," Zachary affirmed. "Not too much."

"Only when you're being 'helpful,'" Campbell provided.

"Well, by definition, being helpful to you means I'm not interfering with the investigation."

"Only in your eyes."

"Everything looks ready to go," Zachary said, looking at the various law enforcement officers positioned around the house and farther down the street. Though they were visible to him, they would not be visible to someone looking out from the house. At least, that was the plan. They wanted to keep their approach a secret until they were ready.

"Just waiting for the warrant," Campbell agreed.

"Soon?"

"Any minute."

Zachary's heart was pounding hard with adrenaline. It was going to happen. It was going to happen in just a few minutes. He would find out whether he had been right about Nikki being the kidnapper and holding Claire in the vacant half of the duplex.

"What did you find out about her neighbors?"

"They're gone. No longer living there. They left the toys in the yard, some furniture in the house, stuff they didn't want to bother to move. They were gone by December first."

Zachary felt like his heart would beat right out of his chest. "Then it was Claire I heard." And a second realization. "And she's alive. Or was on Thursday."

Campbell breathed out heavily. "Your lips to God's ear," he said fervently.

"It would be very nice to see a reunion today."

"It would," Campbell agreed.

They both waited, watching the cops who were also waiting. Zachary didn't know how they could wait for the warrant to be issued when they knew that Claire could be just on the other side of that wall. The situation certainly qualified as exigent circumstances in Zachary's mind.

A nondescript white car drove down the street. Not that different from Zachary's own. The man who opened the door and got out was a plainclothes cop. He held up a piece of paper folded in half lengthwise.

"We got it." He handed it to Campbell with a flourish. Campbell nodded and took a deep breath. He keyed the shoulder mike he was wearing. "It's a go."

Although they had a good vantage point, they couldn't see much of what was happening. The law enforcement officers at the front and back doors of Nikki's duplex stayed in place, as well as a couple of other officers that were farther back, but still close at hand in case she jumped out a window or something else foolish like that.

Meanwhile, a couple of uniformed officers knocked politely on the door of the other side of the duplex, standing to the side so that they wouldn't be in the line of fire if the resident took exception to their approach.

Even though they knew that the house should be unoccupied, other than by a little girl who had been kept away from her mother for way too long.

There was no answer. They knocked again, rang the doorbell, and called out, "Police, open up!" But there was still no response.

With the lock pick gun, they had the door open in a few seconds. No need to break the door down and make the landlord pay for it. The officers disappeared into the house, followed by several more. Still more stepped into the yard as backup in case there was any trouble.

There was no noise of gunfire or anything else alarming. Campbell listened closely to all the reports over his radio. Zachary couldn't make them all out, but he heard as they cleared each room on the main floor and then went up the stairs to the bedrooms. He held his breath in anticipation.

50

"**W**e've got her!"

The shout was unmistakable. A cheer went up amongst all the law enforcement officers there. Whoops and hollers and congratulations all around.

Campbell slapped Zachary on the back. "You called it," he told him with enthusiasm. "You called it, Zachary."

Zachary was grinning fit to burst. He wasn't the one who had found her, who had been able to go into the house and pick Claire up in his arms and bring her to safety, but he was the one who had brought the police there. He had never been confident that they would be able to find Claire alive, but he had hoped to at least be able to tell Rose what had happened to her. Now, they would be taking Claire home. Rose would have her child back, safe and sound, and Claire, however damaged she was from her ordeal, would be safe with her mommy once more.

Zachary picked up the camera that hung around his neck. He always had a camera wherever he went, either in his pocket or on a strap around his neck. Or both. He started snapping pictures of the jubilant cops first. Then, one of the cops who had entered the house came to the door with Claire in his arms, and Zachary zoomed in to get every detail he could. The cop's expression. The little girl's tear-streaked, grimy face. Her precious arms wrapped around the policeman's neck as he cradled her in his big, beefy arms.

Zachary was totally lost in the pictures, capturing the moment they rescued the little girl. There was a rumble of talk among the law enforcement officers and reports over the radio again as an officer knocked on the door of the other side of the duplex. He and his partner had grim expressions and stood well to the sides of the door, extra careful. Nikki was bound to know by now what had happened. She would have heard the knocks on the other side of the duplex, heard them open the door and enter the house. And she had known what they would find when they got into the house.

There was no answer at the door. The police shouted and knocked and rang the doorbell a few times, but when Nikki did not open it, they used the lock pick gun again and let themselves into her house. Zachary watched in silence and listened to the radio chatter. There was a tightness in his chest as he waited for the report that they had Nikki. Not the same kind of anticipation he'd had about them going into the house looking for Claire. How would Nikki respond? Would she fire on the police? Try to escape? Had she already killed herself when she heard them go into the other side of the duplex and knew that there was no way to escape?

Even though he knew she was the perpetrator of this crime, that she had snatched that girl violently from her mother and held her captive for over a week, he couldn't help feeling some empathy for her as well. She had lost her boyfriend and her baby, and those things had to be excruciating for her. Zachary knew the loss of losing loved ones. The siblings he had not known if he would ever see again. Bridget when she decided that their marriage was over and kicked him out. The child that he had thought that he would have with Bridget, that hope evaporated when it turned out that her positive pregnancy test had been the result of cancer, not an embryo. And the knowledge that he would never get to fulfill that fantasy of having a child with her.

"Nikki Braun arrested without incident," came the report over the radio, and there was another cheer, though nowhere near as enthusiastic as the one for Claire's safe recovery. Zachary watched the door through his viewfinder and started snapping pictures again as soon as they brought Nikki Braun to the door.

Her affect was completely blank. There was no anger or tears over her arrest. No protests that they had the wrong person and she had been set up or vitriolic raving against Rose and what she had done to Nikki or to Anthony. She might have been talking to the cops about dinner plans. Or not even know that they were there.

"Ice water," Campbell said. "That one's got ice water in her veins."

Zachary wondered. Was she so cool because she was a psychopath? Because she felt nothing for what she had done? Or was she so overwhelmed with emotion that she had retreated into herself and her own reality and was barely even aware of what was happening around her?

Either way, she had been very deliberate in wreaking vengeance on her enemy. What she had done had not been done in a moment of rage.

Zachary snapped a few more pictures of her and the police around her and then looked around the scene again, an overview this time, evaluating where everyone was and what they were doing.

An ambulance had been called to the scene before they had gone into the vacant side of the duplex. The police officer who had removed Claire from the house had taken her straight to the ambulance, where she was now being examined by a couple of paramedics. Zachary took a few steps closer to her and took pictures of her sitting on the gurney, looking uncertainly at the man and woman examining her. Her face, dirty and tear-streaked, was also blank. She didn't smile at her rescuers, nor cry at being poked and prodded by strangers.

There was no sign that she had been tied or chained up, so she had probably been sedated. The emotion would come in time, but not yet.

Without asking permission, Zachary stuck to Sergeant Campbell's side as he approached the paramedics to inquire about the little girl's condition and see whether she needed to be transported to the hospital.

"She's not in bad shape," the woman paramedic said. "Dirty and dehydrated, but she's been cared for while she's been here. I think she'll be fine once she's recovered from whatever they drugged her with. But she should go to the hospital to be monitored just in case. We can't perform a full examination here, and she should be examined for any less-obvious abuse or molestation."

"She's been fed?" Campbell asked, looking the little girl over.

The paramedic shrugged. "The doctors at the hospital will be able to answer more questions."

Zachary was pretty sure Campbell had kids. Did he see his own kids when he looked at Claire? Feel fatherly fury rising up in him over what Nikki had put that little girl through? Zachary felt it, even though he had never been a father. He had still struggled to take care of his younger brothers and sister. He had done the best that he could, as a child himself, to ensure that they had enough to eat, a safe place to sleep, and that they were kept out of the way of his abusive parents. He hated anyone who neglected or abused little children, and that included Nikki, no matter what she had suffered with the loss of her boyfriend and child.

Zachary followed the ambulance to the hospital. He wanted to be there when Rose arrived to be reunited with her little girl. As he sat in the waiting room, waiting for her to be brought by a police unit, he selected several pictures and sent them off to Kenzie so she could see what they had been able to do. His phone rang in his hand a few seconds later and he knew it would be her.

"You got her!" Kenzie exclaimed. "Alive and unharmed! That's fantastic news, Zachary. I didn't dare hope that it was possible."

"We got her," Zachary agreed, not waffling that it was the police who had saved her, not him. Without him, would they have eventually realized that she was being held right under their noses? How much longer would Nikki have kept her alive? There was a risk in doing so, as well as a risk in sedating her for such a long period. At any point, she could slip away, and then Nikki would be guilty of murder. So he had saved Nikki too, saved her from becoming a murderer and having to face what she had done to an innocent child.

"That's wonderful. Has her mother seen her yet?"

"No, not yet. She should be here any minute."

"Well, I'll let you go then. You don't want to miss that. Thank you for sending me the pictures. Did anyone else get any film of the rescue? Was there any media there?"

"No. Just me. I imagine some of the police got pictures, too."

"I guess the media will be calling you looking for it."

"They probably will," Zachary agreed. He had already seen them starting to assemble outside the hospital. Someone had passed the happy news on to them. They were eagerly awaiting Rose's arrival and any pictures or words they could get from her.

Kenzie said goodbye and ended the call.

A few minutes later, there was an increase in the volume of the crowds gathering around the doors. Zachary looked up, waiting for Rose's arrival. A couple of police officers escorted her in, wedged between them as they pushed their way through the crowd of aggressive reporters trying to get quotes. Rose looked relieved as they got through the doors. The reporters didn't follow her in, knowing that they would get kicked back out by the nurses who were sternly standing guard.

Rose saw Zachary. She reached her arms out toward him as if to take him in a hug, but then dropped them and took his hand in both of hers, squeezing it. "You did it?" she demanded. "*You* found her?"

Zachary nodded. "It was Nikki, Rose. Nikki Braun."

She blinked, shaking her head. "Why?"

"Because you sent her boyfriend to prison and he died there, and she lost her baby. She delivered a package to your house a few weeks ago?"

Rose frowned. "No, I don't think so."

"According to her company, she did. You didn't recognize her?"

"No, I guess not. I don't remember seeing any courier."

It had probably made Nikki that much more furious that the woman who had ruined her life didn't even look at her or have a clue who she was.

"I'm not very good with faces," Rose explained, looking down. "And I haven't seen her in six years."

"Well." Zachary squeezed her hand. "You'd better go see your baby."

Rose didn't let go of him. "You should come too."

"Do you want me there?"

She nodded. "I don't have anyone else."

Her parents, Zachary remembered, were in New York. Had she even told them about her missing child? Had they said they couldn't make the trip out? They were wealthy, so they couldn't give the excuse that they couldn't afford airfare. But maybe they were too important and powerful to leave their lives in New York to visit her, even in a time of such distress.

Not everyone had the loving, concerned parents that they were always showing on TV. Sometimes, even when parents were not outright abusive, they were still unconcerned with their children's affairs and all caught up in their own lives. Not everyone was cut out for parenthood.

As Rose pulled him to follow her, the two cops in the lead to show them the way, Zachary wondered whether he would ever be a father. He loved children. If it were his choice, he would always choose fatherhood. And he would be engaged and concerned and give his children the emotional support they needed, not just the physical nourishment and protection.

At least, that was how he imagined it. Sometimes, things didn't work out as he imagined. Sometimes, they turned out way, way worse.

But it wasn't up to him. It was a choice to be made with Kenzie, and she wasn't at the point in her life when she wanted to have children. She had a career she really enjoyed and was invested in. Even if Zachary took primary care of the children, Kenzie would still have to deal with pregnancy and all its complications, nursing, and people's expectations.

But she wasn't ready. So *they* weren't ready.

"Come on," Rose directed, even though he was keeping up with her and not lagging behind. "I have to see her. Oh, my baby girl. I can't believe you found her and she is okay."

51

The police escort led them to a hospital bed in a curtained area. Rose released her hold on Zachary, heading for the bed. The occupant was blocked from their view by the various doctors, nurses, and law enforcement officers clustered around her. Zachary was sure that not even half of them were actually needed. Rose slipped between bodies and pushed through all the attendees to get to her daughter.

"Claire! Oh, my baby. Mommy's here!" Rose bent over the small form in the bed, clutching her close. "Oh, I never thought I would ever hold you in my arms again. Mommy has been so sad, Claire." She drew back slightly to look Claire in the eye and to smother her with kisses. Someone had cleaned her face, and she looked small and vulnerable in the large hospital bed. She seemed confused and uncertain, but clutched her mother's arms tightly.

Rose smoothed Claire's freshly brushed hair and pressed her nose into it, inhaling her scent deeply.

"Oh... oh..." She couldn't seem to find the words to express what she was feeling.

Zachary's heart felt full. A deep feeling of satisfaction. He could only imagine how deeply Rose felt being reunited with her lost child. He had some inkling of it, remembering the first sight of

Tyrrell that Christmas Eve a couple of years before. The first sibling he had reunited with after decades of being separated from them. He'd once felt so alone and isolated in the world, and now he had more family than he had ever hoped for—Kenzie at his side, all his siblings, and Lorne and Pat.

He waited for Rose to look back over her shoulder at him, but she didn't. She was too wrapped up in her daughter. She didn't look like she would ever let go of her again.

One of the nurses decided that there were too many unnecessary people gathered around the bed.

"Let's give Mom some privacy now," she told the group sternly. "They need some time together more than anything else. Come on, now…"

A few people protested that they had reasons to be there, but she shooed them all away, accepting only Rose and one doctor to stay. Campbell smiled at Zachary and twitched his head to the side, an invitation to join him. They drifted along the corridor toward the nearest coffee vending machine.

"Nothing like the feeling you get from something like that."

"No," Zachary agreed. "It's pretty special."

"You can pat yourself on the back for facilitating that. I don't know how long it would have taken us to realize that the next-door neighbor's duplex was vacant."

"And how much longer Nikki would have kept Claire alive."

Campbell nodded seriously.

"How was she accessing the neighbor's? Did she have a key? I didn't see any footprints on the sidewalk."

"Hole through the back of her closet into the closet of the neighbor's bedroom. Looks like it had been there for a while. Who knows if she was even the one who made it? But she discovered the access panel and opened it up. It was a fair size, easy for a person of her size to crawl through. Though not big enough for the box."

Zachary was studying the coffee machine. He frowned, wondering what he had missed.

"What box?"

"The large box that she apparently transported Claire in."

They each made their selections from the coffee machine. Zachary sipped his, nodding thoughtfully.

"I wondered how she had gotten a child out of the play place without being seen. But she was a courier. It wouldn't be at all concerning or memorable to see her wheel out a box on a hand truck."

"We'll have to look into her usual routes, but I wouldn't be surprised to find she regularly does deliveries and pick-ups for All Played Out. Roxboro isn't the big city. All Played Out does rentals, 'party in a box' sort of thing, so it would be normal for her to take large boxes out."

"So she just needed to be able to get into the play area to get Claire."

"She had a prox card. We'll follow up and see whether she had one legitimately so that she could pick up deliveries or whether it was cloned."

"Probably cloned. She was a computer science major. She would know all about that kind of thing."

"We know she transported Claire in the box because some of her long blond hairs were in it. Who knows whether she was drugged before being put into the box or whether it was part of a game? 'Let's surprise Mommy, you hide in here and we'll surprise her...'"

"I take it Nikki isn't talking."

"Not a word. And Claire," Campbell looked back toward the little girl's bed. "She's still feeling the effects of the sedation. And that kind of thing can cause havoc with memory. Who knows if she'll remember or be able to tell us exactly what happened. What kind of line Nikki used to get her out of there without making a scene."

"Even if she did protest... that place is full of screaming kids. Those who are having a good time, and those who don't want to go home and Mom or Dad has to carry them out in full tantrum. It wouldn't have been alarming to see a child protesting that she didn't want to go."

Campbell nodded. "It's a pretty chaotic place. Not somewhere I'd want to spend much of my time."

"I guess Rose will be looking for a new place to take her daughter when she needs a break."

"I don't think they'll be separated very much over the next little while."

"How about the bombing?" Zachary asked. "Any evidence that she was the one who built the package bomb?"

"We have to do a deep dive searching the house, the garbage receptacles, her browser history, and so on. I expect we'll find fireworks wrappers and internet instructions, if nothing else."

Zachary nodded.

"The court will not go easy on her for attempting murder to cover up a kidnapping."

Zachary shrugged uncomfortably. Despite what she had done, he didn't take pleasure in the idea of Nikki going to prison for the rest of her life.

52

Zachary had decided he would take Kenzie out for dinner at a nice restaurant if they were able to find Claire. He called and told her firmly that they were going out to dinner. She accepted his declaration without argument, which brought a smile to his face. She didn't have to stay late at the morgue to finish an autopsy, so she promised she would be home to change in time to make it for their reservation.

And she was. They made it to the restaurant in plenty of time. They sat down, enjoying each other's company and Zachary's high from being able to provide the final clue necessary to find Claire and reunite her with her mother.

"Tell me all about it," Kenzie said, and Zachary tried to remember every detail and not miss anything.

As he spoke, he noticed that Kenzie's demeanor had changed. She had been stressed recently. Irritable or angry about things that he didn't understand. He accepted that she had moods just like he did. Hers were nowhere near as bad as Bridget's had been. She could hold on to a grudge, but she wasn't deliberately hurtful like Bridget.

He had thought that it was work. Even though she said things were fine and that the big crunch would come in the weeks following Christmas and New Year's Day. She missed Dr. Wiltshire and maybe Dr. Cook was getting on her nerves with new rules and procedures.

He trailed off. Kenzie had a bite of her potatoes and looked at him questioningly.

"What?"

"This case. How much has it been bothering you?"

She grimaced. "I'm glad it's over and that you were able to get her back to her mom."

"Me too. But… I didn't know it was affecting you."

"Well, with a kidna—an abdu—with a child being taken like that, then yeah… it was hard for me. It wasn't something that we could just mention one time and then go on. It was something you were working on—lost inside of—for days."

Zachary felt guilty for his level of focus on the case. But that was why he was a private investigator. Or why he was *still* a private investigator. If all it had involved was skip traces and surveillance of unfaithful spouses, he would probably have found something else to do years ago. But he had some success in solving the more complicated cases. In gaining purchase even when the police had given up. He was good at it, even with his disabilities and weaknesses that sometimes seemed overwhelming.

"It's okay," Kenzie said, putting a hand over his. "I don't expect you to give up investigating kidnappings because I get anxious about them. It isn't like you have a lot of them. I can deal with one every now and then. It's probably good for me, especially when it has a happy ending."

"Like yours," he pointed out. Kenzie's abduction had been terrifying for her, but she had been rescued within hours. She seemed much more traumatized by it than he would have expected, and he still hadn't quite worked out why.

Kenzie nodded. She reddened a little and lifted her glass to take a drink.

"You would think I had been through a terrible ordeal, wouldn't you?" she said. "Rather than just a few hours when I had to sit in a room and eat a bowl of soup before my dad got there to negotiate my release."

"But that's not how it felt to you."

"No," she agreed. She remained silent for a while, cutting her meat and giving her meal her full attention. Then, she glanced around. "This is a nice place. Are you thinking of coming here for your family dinner?"

Zachary had to suppress a shudder of horror at the thought. He could manage such a high-end restaurant only once in a while, with only Kenzie. Add more people, more distractions, tensions, more danger of Christmas music being played in the middle of the whole ordeal, and there was no way he would be able to get through it without a meltdown.

"No. You think Joss would be happy here? And if Tyrrell wants to bring his kids…"

"Oh, no!" Kenzie shook her head adamantly. "You don't want to bring Mason here."

Zachary nodded his agreement, glad he could blame his answer on Joss and Mason rather than admit that he couldn't handle it.

As if Kenzie didn't already know that. She gave him a fleeting glance that told him she had known even before asking that he would say no.

"Yeah, we'd better get somewhere more casual for the family thing," Kenzie told him with a nod.

EPILOGUE

Zachary was sweating in anticipation of everyone's arrival. Worried that they wouldn't be there, and worried that they would. Although everyone had agreed to come, and they had managed to work out a day that worked reasonably well for everyone, he'd still hardly been able to sleep with the anticipation, worrying over everything that could go wrong.

Everyone could decide not to show up. Or just one person could fail to show up and feel like they were alienated from the family. Or everyone could be there but there could be a big fight. The older kids against the younger, or the marrieds against the siblings who didn't have kids or other family to bring to the dinner. Or Joss against everyone.

Or everyone against Zachary.

Since he knew that the separation of the family had been his fault in the first place, he couldn't ignore the possibility that they could all gang up on him and tell him how he had ruined their lives.

Because he had.

He hadn't meant to. It had been devastating to lose his family that way. But whether he had intended the consequences or not, he was the one who had set the fire that fateful day.

Heather was one of the first to arrive, which didn't surprise Zachary at all. He was surprised to see a young man with Heather and Grant that he hadn't seen before.

"This must be your son," he guessed. The boy looked older than he had expected.

Heather smiled. "This is Michael!"

It took a second for it to compute. Not the son Heather had raised, but the baby she had been forced to give up for adoption. The one Zachary had helped to reunite her with when she had reached out to him to help her with a long-cold case from her past.

"Michael! Wow. Welcome. I hope… that you have a great time getting to know everyone." Zachary looked at Heather, uncertain. "How much does he know…?"

"He knows about the family history and dynamics," Heather told Zachary. "He's been warned."

Zachary laughed awkwardly. "Okay. Because… I'm not sure how this will turn out," Zachary warned Michael.

The younger man nodded seriously. "It's okay. I know that families aren't all perfect. And mine has a history."

Zachary felt warm when Michael referred to it as "mine" instead of yours. Michael seemed prepared to take them as they were, warts and all.

And there were a lot of warts.

Tyrrell brought Alisha and Mason, so Zachary was doubly glad they hadn't picked somewhere fancy. A private dining room at a serve-yourself buffet. They could be walled off from the rest of the restaurant and talk as loudly as they liked and not be worried about Mason's ADHD restlessness. Everyone could eat what they liked in whatever amounts and in whatever order they liked it.

Joss was not the last to arrive. Vince and Mindy were, coming together, completing the group. The only two who had grown up in just one family and stayed close over the years. They took in the large group anxiously, looking the way Zachary felt. It was overwhelming, but at the same time, they were all his family. And he had been able to bring them together. Fitting, when he was the one who had separated them in the first place.

He was in pretty good spirits, especially considering the time of year. The previous year, he had been hospitalized and under suicide watch. This year, he looked as normal as any of them. And before long, the crisis point would be past, and he could make plans for the future. He could never get past December 24 on the calendar until he was past it in real life.

"I guess I should say something," Zachary said, standing. Everyone around the table quieted and turned to him. "I figure I'll say it at the beginning since… I don't know if we'll all still be speaking to each other at the end."

There were chuckles around the group.

"This is… This is the fulfillment of a dream I've had for a long time. Back when… it all happened… I wanted to get us all back together. I begged my social worker to let me see you all again." He looked around at the group. "But she kept putting me off, and I knew it would never happen. She was never going to let me see you again. But now, here we are. Even more Goldmans than before. And we're still family." He started to sit down again, then stopped. "No matter what happens. We'll always be family."

Did you enjoy this book? Reviews and recommendations are vital to making a book successful.

Please leave a review at your favorite book store or review site and share it with your friends.

Don't miss the following bonus material:
Sign up for mailing list to get a free ebook
Read a sneak preview chapter
Other books by P.D. Workman
Learn more about the author

UNLOCK ACCESS TO
ZACHARY GOLDMAN'S CASE FILES!

Get a peek inside Zachary's case
files and see what other
intriguing tales are in store!

SCAN TO UNLOCK OFFER

books.pdworkman.com/sign-up-zg

PREVIEW OF HE WAS DECEIVED

PREVIEW CHAPTER 1

Zachary gazed out the front window at a delivery truck moving slowly down the street. He couldn't help but feel anxious when he saw a courier. The last package that had been delivered to him had not been what he had expected. It would be a while before he could feel the same excitement and anticipation opening a box or envelope left on his doorstep.

"You okay?" Kenzie asked.

Zachary swallowed. He nodded and forced a smile. "Yeah, sure. I'm good."

She evaluated him, her dark eyes serious and her bright red lips pursed. She nodded slowly, her dark curls bouncing a little, a movement that always made him want to touch it and wind the curls around his fingers. But he refrained, turning his attention to the breakfast preparations.

"Coffee is on," he told her, though he wasn't sure whether he had turned on the machine or she had. "I'll pop some toast in for you..." He noticed the smell of the toasting bread mixing with that of the coffee. Obviously one of them had already done that job too. He got out plates and cutlery and found her marmalade in the fridge.

"Where are you going this morning?" Kenzie asked.

He hadn't told her he was going out anywhere, but she could tell from his shirt—a button-up shirt rather than just a t-shirt or polo—that he was planning to meet with someone today. He didn't dress up for computer work, going for a walk, or running errands. Or for a surveillance job, unless he was positioning himself in an office building or somewhere such an outfit would blend better than his usual work "uniform."

"Meeting with a potential client. Not sure yet what kind of a case it is," he anticipated her next question. "He didn't want to discuss anything over the phone. And I like to meet with possible clients face-to-face in the beginning. Remote work and communicating electronically are fine, a convenient way to run a case, but I like to get a read on a person before I accept the job."

"You never know what you might be getting into otherwise," Kenzie suggested.

"Yeah. Surveilling a possibly adulterous spouse is one thing, if the guy is just looking for information. But if he's lying and is really an abuser trying to find an ex who is hiding from him..."

Kenzie nodded, understanding, as she poured each of them a cup of fresh coffee.

"Can you always tell, though?"

"I'm pretty good at reading people. That doesn't mean that I don't ever make mistakes... but if I'm not sure, I'll turn them down, say I'm too busy to give their case the attention it needs right now."

"So someone else gets the job?"

"Well..." Zachary didn't like to think that he was only delaying the abusive husband finding his runaway wife. Still, it wasn't like he could do anything to keep the man from hiring a private investigator who didn't have the same scruples or intuition as Zachary. If he was determined to find his wife, there wasn't much Zachary could do other than refuse the work himself.

"Hopefully, he's so disappointed by my refusal that he can't bring himself to approach another PI," he told Kenzie. "You can see how crushing that would be."

Kenzie chuckled. She took a sip of her coffee. The toast popped and Zachary buttered it before putting it on Kenzie's plate and grabbing a yogurt cup for himself.

"Yes, that would definitely be a consideration," Kenzie agreed. "I can't imagine what it would be like to be turned down by you."

Zachary tried to figure out whether there was any secondary meaning to her statement, but decided just to take it at face value. He sat down across from Kenzie and opened his yogurt cup. He usually had a yogurt cup or a granola bar for his breakfast with Kenzie. He was more in the mood for a granola bar today but didn't want to unwrap one with Kenzie watching him. The noise of the crinkling wrapper was like fingernails on the blackboard, and he wouldn't be able to hide his grimace from her. She was already watching him closely enough without him giving her something else to worry about.

"Do you think it's wise?" Kenzie asked.

Zachary looked at her, uncertain. He had probably missed something else she had said and lost the thread of the conversation.

"Taking on a new client right now," Kenzie said slowly. "I mean… this time of year…"

So close to Christmas. She tried to avoid saying it, but they both knew what she meant. At this time of year, when he might shut down completely and not be able to do any work.

"No… I'll check him out and see whether it is a case I want to take on. And I'll warn him I might need to take a few days off around the holiday. People are usually pretty good about it if you let them know… set expectations."

He was doing really well this year on the new med protocol. At this time last year, he had been in the hospital psych ward, unable to deal with the depression and control the thoughts of self-harm without professional help.

But that was last year. He was much better this year. The anniversary of the fire, that Christmas Eve disaster, was quickly approaching. It was a struggle to keep his spirits up and function at the same level as he did the rest of the year and he dreaded slipping further into the abyss. But he was functional. The work, especially the novelty of a new case, would help him to stay focused on something other than traumatic memories.

If he had to take a few days off, he could do that. It wasn't unusual for someone to take a few days off work for family around Christmas. His client would think nothing of it.

"I just don't want you to be overwhelmed," Kenzie said. "It might be better if you didn't take too much on until after... maybe in the new year."

"It isn't too much," he assured her. "I mean... depending on what it is. If it's too big and he needs answers in two days, that's another story, but most people are not in a big hurry."

"You'll be careful?"

"Of course. Yes, I will."

Kenzie nibbled her marmalade toast and studied him a little too closely. Zachary's face warmed.

"Did I miss a spot shaving?" he asked, brushing his hand over his face to break the eye contact and allow him to look away. "Or are you just admiring my manly scars?"

The numerous small cuts from the explosion were healing, but it would be a while before they were all gone. One or two of the deeper ones that had needed stitches might leave scars. Nothing that bad. They would blend in with his other scars. And when he let his whiskers grow for a few days, as he usually did, they would be camouflaged.

Kenzie smiled and shook her head. "It must be the manly scars," she said lightly. "I just can't seem to tear my eyes away."

He blushed further, even knowing she was teasing him. His ears burned and were probably bright red.

She dropped the conversation thread and didn't insist that she knew better than he did about managing his business at this difficult time of year.

She was having her own difficulties this year, and Zachary wondered whether that was one reason she was so concerned about his state of mind and traumatic memories. Either empathizing with him because of her own feelings or trying to distract herself by focusing on someone else's problems.

Zachary needed to pay attention to Kenzie's mood and stress levels, not just his own. She needed his support just as much as he needed hers.

PREVIEW CHAPTER 2

Zachary had agreed to meet Oliver Dwayne at a coffee shop. Neutral ground. They were past the morning rush, so the venue was not too busy. But it wasn't empty, either. People came and went, both individually and in pairs or small groups. Zachary and Oliver would not stand out.

Zachary ordered a pot of coffee, and the waitress placed a couple of mugs on the table for him. He kept an eye on the door, watching for the man he was to be meeting.

Most people who walked into the coffee shop went directly to the counter or a table and ordered what they wanted. They either settled in to work on a computer or tablet or left with a "to go" cup as soon as they were served. They didn't look around to try to find the person they were to be meeting with.

Then, a man walked in, stopped, and looked at the other customers. Tall and distinguished, dark hair with streaks of grey at the temples. A short, carefully shaped mustache and beard. His cheeks were prominent, face narrow. He looked like someone who had been through a lot, but he was strong and confident. Well-dressed, but a little weather-worn and vulnerable, too.

Zachary stood partway up from his seat, and the man's eyes met his. He walked over. He put out a hand and raised his brows. "Mr. Goldman?"

"Zachary, please. Mr. Dwayne?"

"Oliver."

"Have a seat," Zachary motioned to the table, and Oliver sat down. He poured himself a full mug of coffee and drank it immediately, no cream or sugar. He gulped it so fast it must have burned his throat.

"This is difficult," Oliver said. He put his cup down and dabbed his lips with a napkin. "I suppose we do all of the usual small talk first."

"Sometimes it puts people at ease," Zachary told him, smiling slightly. "But we don't have to. Whatever you're most comfortable with. If you want to jump straight into the case, you can."

"I just want to get on with it. It's hard enough without having to deal with social conventions. I have no idea what the usual protocol is for something like this."

"There really isn't one. Everyone approaches it differently."

Some people wanted to get to know Zachary and build that relationship first. Some of them beat around the bush, hoping Zachary would guess what they were there about. Some blurted it out and then cowered back, waiting for the fallout of having spilled their guts and made themselves so vulnerable.

Oliver seemed to need some questions to get closer to the issue. Zachary evaluated him. Not married, he didn't think. He didn't wear a ring. Didn't have that "cared for" look, the confidence that he was going back to someone who was waiting faithfully for him. So there was probably not an unfaithful spouse to tail. That was a relief because he really didn't like those jobs.

A business deal gone bad? Industrial espionage? It didn't feel like it.

Maybe a missing person? Maybe someone he had lost touch with long ago and wanted to reconnect with?

"This is a personal matter?" Zachary guessed.

Oliver nodded. "Yes. It's personal."

"Family? Someone you've lost touch with?"

An expression of sadness settled over Oliver's face. An expression that was clearly natural for him. Profound sadness. But not a sadness that he shared with others. He put on a different face to deal with Zachary—his public face.

Not a missing person. A loss, yes, but not someone he had lost touch with or fallen out with.

"Someone you lost?" he amended.

Oliver nodded. "Yes... I don't even know why I am here. I dealt with this a long time ago. I put it behind me."

Cold cases were difficult. Evidence disappeared. Witnesses forgot what they had seen and heard. Alibis were almost impossible to establish. And the longer ago it was, the harder it was to get any traction.

"How long ago?"

"Ten years."

Zachary nodded. Better than twenty or fifty, but still difficult.

"Who? What happened?"

Oliver gave a long sigh. He turned his coffee cup in place on the table, rotating it in a circle once, twice, and a third time before he could get anything out.

"My wife."

So he had been married. But ten years ago. Long enough to lose the look of a married man.

Oliver didn't answer the "what happened" immediately. He swallowed, considering how to tell Zachary about it.

"She was shot," he said finally.

Zachary nodded and waited.

"The police said that it was accidental. Just a freak thing. I accepted that and moved on. It was... so tragic. I couldn't spend time wallowing, mourning her, questioning their findings. I had children. They needed me. I had to be the strong one, the one to move everyone forward. We couldn't stay focused on the past, the 'why' of it all. It was an accident... so we went on."

"How old were your kids?"

"Nine, thirteen, and fifteen."

Zachary had been ten when he lost his family. He knew what it was like to lose a mother at that age. Though his mother had not been shot. And she had not been the loving, caring parent he had craved.

"Tough time to lose your mother," he sympathized, staying focused on Oliver's situation and not his own.

"I think any age is a difficult time to lose your mother. Especially so suddenly and violently. But yes, it was terrible for them. We had to draw closer together, help each other through it."

"They were lucky to have you. It sounds like you were there for them."

"I thought I was. Now… I wonder if I was or if I just went through the motions. I had work to do. I still had to support them financially as well as emotionally, and I wonder how well I did. I want to say that I didn't bury myself in my work. But I did to a certain extent."

"It's natural," Zachary said. "Trying to distract yourself. To focus on what you can do rather than… spinning your wheels. The police told you it was an accident, so what else could you do?"

Oliver spread his hands apart. "What I'm doing now. Hiring someone. Digging down deeper into it. Not just taking things at face value."

"Well… you are now. Maybe this will bring you some peace."

Certainly, Oliver didn't look like he was at peace now. More like he was haunted. Zachary didn't know if he could help him find that peace, but he liked Oliver and what he had seen of him so far. He wanted to do what he could, though he didn't know how much that would be after the passing of ten years.

"How did it happen?"

He hoped that it hadn't had anything to do with the children. He could only imagine what _that_ would do to the family.

"She was in her car. Out for a drive. The bullet went through the window and struck her. She was found hours later. There was nothing that could be done by then. The police said it was probably a hunter, kids playing with a gun, or someone doing target practice. Something like that. Just a freak accident that couldn't have been predicted. Out in the country… people think they can fire off their guns whenever they like. They think they're alone, so... why not?"

"Did they talk to anyone who had heard the shots? Had anyone been out target shooting?"

"They never found anyone who had been out that way with a gun. Maybe kids. Kids who never even knew that they had ended up killing a woman with their carelessness."

"How hard did the police try?"

It wasn't a very tactful question. But Zachary would need to know. If there had been an extensive search and investigation, there might be nothing more for Zachary to do. Was there a chance that he might find something ten years later that the police had overlooked?

"I don't think... I don't think they did much investigating at all. I think they just assumed they knew the story. We weren't looking for someone to blame. If it was an accident, I certainly didn't want some kid to go to jail for it. Ruin another life for no reason."

Zachary could understand that. He sipped his coffee. In ten years, Oliver's kids had all grown to adulthood. One or two of them might still be at home with him. They might know other kids in the neighborhood who had been old enough back then to find some witnesses. Or to identify any borderline "bad apples" who might have been experimenting then.

"So... if you didn't want any kid being sent to jail for it back then, what has changed your mind?"

"It's the blasted phone calls."

He Was Deceived, Book #18 of the *Zachary Goldman Mysteries*
series by P.D. Workman
can be purchased at pdworkman.com